D0274518

50P

Also by Stefan Hertmans in English translation

War and Turpentine

Stefan Hertmans

THE CONVERT

Translated from the Dutch by David McKay

Harvill *Secker*
LONDON

1 3 5 7 9 10 8 6 4 2

Harvill Secker, an imprint of Vintage,
20 Vauxhall Bridge Road,
London SW1V 2SA

Harvill Secker is part of the Penguin Random House group of companies
whose addresses can be found at global.penguinrandomhouse.com

Penguin
Random House
UK

Copyright © Stefan Hertmans 2016
English translation copyright © David McKay 2019

Stefan Hertmans has asserted his right to be identified as the author of this
Work in accordance with the Copyright, Designs and Patents Act 1988

First published by Harvill Secker in 2019
First published with the title *De hekeerlinge* in the Netherlands by De Bezige Bij in 2016

A CIP catalogue record for this book is available from the British Library

penguin.co.uk/vintage

ISBN 9781787300125

Co-funded by the
Creative Europe Programme
of the European Union

**FLANDERS
LITERATURE**

This book was published with the support of Flanders Literature (www.flandersliterature.be)

The European Commission support for the production of this publication
does not constitute an endorsement of the contents which reflects the views
only of the authors, and the Commission cannot be held responsible for
any use which may be made of the information contained therein.

Typeset in 10.8/17 pts Minion Pro
by Integra Software Services Pvt. Ltd, Pondicherry

Printed and bound in Great Britain by Clays Ltd, Elcograf S.p.A.

Manuscript T-S 16.100 reproduced by kind permission
of the Syndics of Cambridge University Library.

Excerpt from *Joseph and His Brothers* by Thomas Mann, translated by John E. Woods,
published by Everyman's Library. The English text of manuscript T-S 16.100 is a slightly
adapted version of Professor Norman Golb's translation from the Hebrew in his article
'Monieux', *Proceedings of the American Philosophical Society*, vol. 113, 1, Philadelphia, 1969.

Penguin Random House is committed to a sustainable future for our business, our readers
and our planet. This book is made from Forest Stewardship Council® certified paper.

MIX
Paper from
responsible sources
FSC
www.fsc.org
FSC® C018179

DUNDEE CITY
COUNCIL

LOCATION
COLDSIDE

ACCESSION NUMBER
CO1 012 6570

SUPPLIER | PRICE
ASKEWS | £14.99

CLASS | DATE
823.91 | 18.6.19

מניו

For the woman who kissed a house

The form of timelessness is the now and the here.

– Thomas Mann, *Joseph and His Brothers*

This novel is inspired by a true story. It is the product of both extensive research and creative imagination.

The Convert

I

Mount Jupiter

1

It's early in the morning. The first rays of sun are just coming over the hilltops.

From the window where I look out over the valley, I see two people approaching in the distance. I suppose they've come down from the heights of Saint-Hubert, from which you can see both the peak of Mont Ventoux and the valley of Monieux. It must have taken them some time to cross the sparse oak forest on the high plateau, where wolves roam free.

The famous Rocher du Cire – a steep, majestic cliff where bees swarm up beyond reach and, in the summer sun, the stone sometimes glistens with the honey that drips from the rock face – is desolate and indomitable at this hour, its great mass sunk in the morning mist. All this the two travellers have seen and passed in silence.

The morning light catches the outlines of their still-tiny forms. They descend with difficulty to the spot where nowadays the farmhouse of La Plane watches over the valley like a guard dog. From there, the winding road leads them down to the left bank of the river – the right side, for them, since they're headed upstream. They slip in and out of view, now concealed by trees, now re-emerging. Then they come to a large sloping expanse of grass, and their pace quickens slightly. From there, they can see the half-finished turret rising from the high stone wall like a reassuring beacon. Now the sun is a little higher, its rays reach the low valley and set the village aglow. In their time, all the houses are made of stone, so it's hard to tell in the half-light where one ends and another begins, as if the village has sprung from the cliff by some miracle, carved by sunlight – as if someone has pulled aside a great curtain to reveal a sleeping landscape.

The blue of dawn fades fast, giving way to yellows and greys. The warmth of the morning swells the last clouds into slow, vast boulders in a purple sky; over the length of the river the white veil evaporates before my eyes. A swarm of bee-eaters is already swooping over the rooftops.

Once the pair have come a few hundred metres closer, I see that the man is using a branch as a crude cane. The woman limps, as if walking is hard for her. They both look drained. Did the woman sprain her ankle on one of the stony highland paths? Or do her shoes chafe her feet during their long, exhausting daily treks? I adjust my binoculars; there's no mistaking now that she is pregnant. The man is wearing a loose smock and has a homespun hat on his head. Sometimes he takes the woman's arm to help her over an obstacle. A second man, with a large sack, comes into sight behind them. He follows in their footsteps, leading a mule.

What time did they get up this morning? Were they roused by the cold at the foot of a tree? Or did they wake at an inn? In the quiet panorama of this spring morning, nightingales sing in the bushes by the river. You can hear them from here, letting out their wild, melodious calls. As the sun lifts off the crest of the hill, an owl sails silently over the twisted oaks, not to be seen again until nightfall. Timeless peace; the distant howl of a wolf-dog; the cuckoo's monotone call as it flutters over the lonely woods near Saint-Jean. The landscape smells sublime in these early hours; it breathes an ethereal beauty. On this spring morning all the irises are open, the wild cherry tree is in blossom, the rosemary is dense with bright little flowers, and the scent of thyme rises with the warmth of the dew. Warmth of the dew – Hamoutal. This

Jewish name pops into my head, the man's affectionate name for the woman.

I know who they are. I know who they're running from.

I wish I could welcome them into this house, offer them a hot drink they wouldn't recognise – a cup of coffee, for instance. Where are they to live, now that their house has been gone a thousand years and the medieval section of the village is lost under grass and shrubs? At any moment, today's first passing car may give them the shock of their lives, sending the young woman into premature labour.

The couple are now straggling into my village.

I wake with a start from my daydream, close the window, light a fire for the cool morning hours, make coffee. Now and then I feel the foolish urge to look out of the window. Patches of sun slide across the old tiled floor; the day is still and empty.

*

This village was once known as Mount Jupiter – Mons Jovis. The Neolithic cave-dwellers not far from here were followed, long before the Christian era, by builders of crude stone houses. Though their appearance is lost in the night of time, you can sense their presence in the earliest houses of the ruined upper village. In the old chapel at the edge of the ravine, a stone with Latin inscriptions was once found, dedicated to Mars Nabelcus, a deity worshipped by the Romans in the region.

In the Middle Ages, the primitive houses were scattered among rocks that formed natural obstacles and small oaks that shot up in unexpected places. The village was sheltered by the steep, rocky slope, a natural wall almost a hundred metres high. Sometimes you stumble across forgotten cellars amid the dry grass, undergrowth and thyme-covered rocks. The shadowy recesses smell of mould and soil, even on hot days. Here in this brushland of brambles and withered vetch where I often sit and dream away the day, there was once a room, a place of birth and death.

Around the tenth century, feuds broke out over the deep wells under some of the cellars. During heat waves – the infamous *canicules* – the water turned brackish and poisoned the villagers. Vagrants were accused and tortured, perhaps a vestige of the tradition of ritual sacrifice. The tumbledown houses up on the heights – battered by gales, the mistral and the tramontane – stood with their windowless backs to the wind, so that they could hold out for centuries. They were not fundamentally different from the *bories*, crude stone huts built by herdsmen on the dry plateau or in the oak woods. The villagers had already learned how to make a simple spyhole in the stone, which could be covered in the winter with a wolf or fox skin, or sometimes with a pig's stretched bladder.

On the small plots where the medieval houses were built, the ground was unstable. The walls, several metres thick, were erected in haste and propped up against each other. The buildings grew taller over the centuries, but not because of any technical advances. That explains why, from the late eighteenth century onwards, quite a few houses simply collapsed. The remains decayed into picturesque heaps of stone, overgrown with wild grapevines that turn blood-red in October. The surviving structures have, for ages now, leaned against their narrow, heavy fronts like greybeards resting on their canes. Improvised patch-ups have seen them through the centuries. The crumbled clay-and-sand mortar has been replaced with cement; the old oak struts and crude buttresses have been reinforced with concrete; and the houses are now held together by steel rods thrust straight through the walls, screwed firmly in place and kept there by a clever system of metal clamps, which sometimes resemble a scorpion's pincers.

*

It's easy to see why the two lovers have come here. The village has been a safe haven for passers-by and refugees before: Jews in the eleventh century, Huguenots in the seventeenth. Places with a reputation for tolerance became well known among wanderers. By the eighteenth century, when the village was referred to in the annals as Monilis, it had almost a thousand inhabitants jammed into its narrow streets. Seven hundred metres up, it was dark and dreary in the harsh winters, but cool in the long, hot summers. Filth festered in the gullies, breeding rats, which bred fleas, which bred plague. The first cases of bubonic plague in the region were recorded in the fourteenth century. Four hundred years later, during the great epidemic imported through Marseilles, plague walls were erected: heavily guarded stacks of thick, rough slate. Refugees were beaten to death if they tried to steal past the watchmen. Corpse-robbers made the rounds to strip the fallen bodies of their last possessions, after rubbing themselves with a mixture of thyme, rosemary, lavender and sage. Superstition took care of the rest; the treatment seems to have shielded them from infection. I once heard an elderly woman call this now-traditional herbal sachet *les quatre bandits*. The plague wall is only a few kilometres away, overrun with grass and weeds.

For centuries this rugged region proudly defied the central authority of Paris, and its population grew ever more diverse. Spaniards, Moroccans, Italians and the occasional sailor from Marseilles came and conceived children with local beauties from the dry, desolate hills. The paupers sat in the spring wind, their eyes watering, among the wild irises, poppies and thinly sown spelt. Their children had arched thick-soled feet, a fierce look in their eyes and damaged skin. Sometimes a band of plunderers would pass by, cracking a couple of herdsmen's skulls against a wall, raping a few women and, once the village was paralysed with shock, taking what they pleased. Then they would vanish over the hilltops, leaving a void that filled with wind, sun, silence, fear and prayer.

In this way, like an ancient vagabond, the village drifted into the twenty-first century. Almost nothing has changed; on early-autumn mornings, the shepherds still drive their steaming flocks through the main street. The click of their dainty hooves and the many soft tones of their jingling bells have remained more or less the same since Virgil wrote his *Eclogues*; the animals leave behind trails of droppings and bits of wool on the asphalt as they press forward, the lambs making wild leaps. The patient postman waits in his small delivery van, smoking a cigarette, while the flock passes through the village. In the old Romanesque church, you can still go to Sunday Mass. The congregation sings slightly off-key, a time-honoured mark of sincere religious faith.

In the winter, the village is sometimes snowed-in for days. Then its inhabitants live on the supplies they've squirrelled away in their cellars and freezers. In the long hot summer, the climate is harsh and overpowering; drought exhausts the soil, the lavender is harvested, and the smell of fire spreads over the plateau as the precious oil is extracted from the plants. The loveliest times of year are between these two seasons, when the land can breathe again and wild bees buzz among the creepers. Once there was some fuss about building a railway line straight through the primeval gorge, in the meandering riverbed, to make the village easier to reach from the plain below. This plan was soon abandoned, when it proved impossible to lead so much as a horse through the gorge. Motor vehicles first gained quick access to the highlands in the 1990s, along a highway over the thousand-metre-high ridge of Les Abeilles.

The days have no hours. You can pass the late afternoon staring at a patch of sunlight as it slides across the rough floor, a white light that seems to tremble and scale the wall before disappearing. Nothing happens – that's the big event you can't look away from. Time does its own thing.

2

In truth, it's the village rabbi, Joshuah Obadiah, standing by the synagogue early one morning, who watches the refugees come down the hill, there in the spring of the year 1091. A mounted messenger must have told him a few days earlier that they were coming. He is worried about these young people – not only because they need protection, as a mixed couple, but also because he knows the woman will give birth to her child in a matter of days, and it'll be weeks before he can find a suitable house for them. Until then, they'll have to be his guests. Why aren't they arriving on horseback? He can only guess. Maybe they were waylaid by bandits or horse thieves. Maybe they disguised themselves as commoners to escape notice by their pursuers. He waits impatiently until they're inside the walls and sends his wife to welcome them at the southern gate, still known today as the Portail Meunier. They wind a faltering path to his house – close to the spot where a thousand years later I will spend summer after summer blithely reading, as happy as I've ever been anywhere in this mundane world.

Hamoutal has a nasty scrape on her right foot, and she twisted her ankle so severely that the ligaments have torn. The foot is swollen and red, blood has gathered in black patches under the skin, and her ankle is at risk of infection. The rabbi's wife cleans the wound with a mixture of lavender oil, nettles and lukewarm water. Hamoutal's husband, David Todros of Narbonne, informs Joshuah Obadiah of the latest developments.

The rabbi nods pensively and tugs at his beard; his wife dabs the young woman's delicate, injured foot.

What's your real name? the rabbi says.

She hesitates; is he asking for her old Christian name?

David breaks in. Sarah, he says. My wife's name is Sarah. Hamoutal is a pet name.

He lays his hand on hers.

The four of them sit together in silence.

*

The times are troubled. The religious peace once established by Charlemagne has been eroded over the years by political instability. Feudal warlords have seized control everywhere and rule their territories autonomously; the central authorities are losing their grip; there are tales of misrule; the law is often no more than an instrument of power. After centuries in which Jews and Christians lived side by side in relative calm, there is ever more frequent news of savage attacks on Jewish communities. In recent months, many Spanish Jews have fled to the south of Provence. Most have gone to Narbonne, the town near the coast now thronged with vagrants seeking their fortune or searching for refuge. David's father, the great Rabbi of Narbonne – known far and wide as the King of the Jews, because he's said to descend directly from King David – is getting old. He can hardly take care of his duties any more; exhausted, he passes sleepless nights worrying about his eldest son and his daughter-in-law.

He sent the two refugees to that far-off corner of the Vaucluse region to keep them out the grasp of the Christian knights dispatched from Rouen by the girl's Norman father to bring her home. Heading towards Spain would have been too dangerous; the road to Santiago de Compostela is teeming with Christian pilgrims. The area around Toulouse and Albi was roiled by the struggle against the Manichees and the rise of heretical movements, with constant violent clashes and executions. Nor could they flee to a city; press gangs were rounding up men left and right for expeditions to the Middle East, and bands of irregular soldiers made the roads unsafe, picking fights with passing travellers.

Rabbi Todros sent the young couple by a route that would never occur to Hamoutal's enraged father: past Arles, along the Rhône, beyond the small garrison town of Avignon – which didn't even have its famous bridge yet – on towards Carpentras, and from there into the largely uninhabited Alpine foothills, further onwards in the direction of Sisteron, to the south-east side of Mons Ventosus, where he knew of a small Jewish community in the remote mountain village of Moniou – a corruption of Mons Jovis. The village rabbi, Obadiah, would offer the young couple protection and a roof over their heads. Joshuah Obadiah, from Burgos, Spain, had been friends with Rabbi Todros back when they were young Torah students in Narbonne's Jewish school. The deserted mountain region around Moniou had been part of the Holy Roman Empire since 1032; in other words, it was a foreign land to the Gallic knights who were searching for the woman. Besides, the region had a record of peaceful coexistence between Jews and Christians. Obadiah gave the young Todros an approving nod and told him his father had made a wise choice.

*

Most afternoons I wander around the ruins of the medieval village. The present mayor recently dubbed these remains Le Jardin de Saint-André, after the ruined chapel high above the village at the very edge of the ravine. Here and there, half a Romanesque arch protrudes from the wild grass. I walk up the steep road. Efforts are being made to restore old walls, romantic attempts at reconstruction; most of the stacking is done by a small group of young volunteers who come here for days at a time to drag around stones and pickaxes before returning to their summer camp. They erect little structures that look deceptively ancient, and, without any system, they level and weed patches of land where ruins lie buried, with young elms and oaks growing on them. No one shows the least concern about the fragility of this historical site. It looks like a green oasis these days, a terraced slope of wild flowers, a garden with successive rows of low walls made of medieval rubble. Everything seems to have been here for ages. But this peaceful garden was once the most crowded part of the village, with narrow streets and rows of tall, gloomy houses packed together, full of the noise, stench and riotous colour of everyday medieval life with its tight social control and teeming energy. People lived and died here, slept, worked and cursed here, made love here and brought children into the world under the most rudimentary conditions. Now a brightly coloured snake winds its way under a heap of dry branches, fleeing my footstep. A few goats have broken free of their rickety enclosure and now occupy a crag above me, bounding and chewing, staring out of their demonic yellow eyes as if in ecstasy, and disappearing up over the ridge. Above the tall cliff, a buzzard slowly circles. The silence seems ominous, as if deep in the earth I can hear time rumbling.

*

The synagogue and the home of David Todros must have been close together, at most two hundred metres from the site of the old house where I am writing this. They couldn't have been any further away, because that would have placed them outside the ramparts. The houses on the south side were on such small plots of land that it seems likely that was the Jewish quarter. Jews were always allotted small parcels for building their homes, a way of limiting their wealth and influence. Because those tapering plots, one of which I live on myself, can be found on Napoleonic copies of the medieval maps, I know the village already had buildings like these back then. The two refugees must have passed through this narrow street often. I can still sense their nearness in the vast silence over the land. I make my way back down to the modern village – as if it were nothing at all to step out of a long-lost age, back into the present.

I sit down at my desk and start browsing again through a historical article sent to me some ten summers ago by a retired neighbour from southern Germany who has lived in an idyllic old house here for decades. You should read this when you have the time, he told me. I made a copy and placed it in the drawer of my grandfather's writing desk, next to the notebooks he once gave me. The article, as I later saw, is simply called 'Monieux'. It was published in 1969 by Norman Golb, a renowned expert on Jewish history.

3

Only now, as the young woman soaks her sprained foot in a basin of warm water with lavender oil, does her husband realise how exhausted she is. The swelling won't subside, and her foot is covered with ugly yellow and black bruises. The child tosses and turns in her womb; the rabbi fears she's about to go into labour. She is shown to a short oak bed where she can rest. Because she can't stop shaking, they build a fire. As soon as the warmth reaches her, she falls asleep. Patches of sun slide across the old tiles.

The day is mild and peaceful. A buzzard hovers over the cliff, near the towers under construction at the top; the vague clink of hammers on stone comes drifting down. The rabbi wonders how he will explain to the distrustful priest at the small church of Saint-Pierre, on the other side of Moniou, that this new arrival, a golden-haired woman with blue eyes, is a Sephardic Jew.

Around six o'clock, the sun sinks below the high cliff. From one moment to the next, the light turns thin and bluish; the woods across the valley glimmer a deepening red. A gust of wind passes over the plain; for a few breaths, the trees and bushes by the riverbank make a loud rustle. Then the never-ending silence returns to this deserted highland.

The young woman wakes with a start to find darkness has fallen. She has no idea where she is – a brief surge of panic, and then bit by bit she can make out the contours of a wardrobe, a dark chest, a chair. A sharp pain shoots through her lower back, taking her breath away. She lets out a muffled cry. Right away, the door opens; the faint glow of a flickering flame lights up the walls. It's an old woman, bringing a basin of water and a stack of towels. She sits down in silence to keep watch, head bowed and hands folded, beside the sweating, thrashing woman in the bed. She murmurs ancient, indistinct prayers. After an hour in which the contractions grow stronger, the young woman falls back into deep sleep. In the middle of the night, she shoots awake with a pounding heart, gagging with pain. The woman is no longer watching over her. An improbably large moon is rising over the hill to the east. The light glints and shimmers its way inside through the small glassless window like a living creature. Feeling an urgent need to urinate, she stumbles out of bed half asleep, gropes for the travel-worn shoes by the bedside and staggers outside. A contraction spears through her body. Now panting and savage, she stares down the unfamiliar alley, staggers on, and finds herself ringed by rocks and low bushes. There she squats, dizzy with pain. She thinks she's passing urine, but it's her waters breaking. Her squatting brings on labour, sudden and strong. In a haze of pain, she feels herself tearing open down below. She groans like a dying animal, howls and sobs, and falls backwards between two stones, hurting her lower back. From under her belly, a little head emerges. Panting like a woman possessed, she pushes and moans, digs her fingers into the dry earth, presses her loins helplessly, reaches between her legs, feels the blood running, and shivers with fear and pain. The moon seems to shine still brighter; the night air chills the wet skin of her legs and hips. As the thing glides motionless through her legs into the dust and gravel, she blacks out for an instant. Then all at once the narrow alley fills with cries, footfalls, slamming doors. She is borne up; the afterbirth gushes out of her, along with a thick stream of blood. The ruthless moon glares into her eyes. She weeps, lets out shrill cries, calls her mother's name. The old woman severs the umbilical cord with a dull knife, splashes water over the delirious woman's lower body, grabs the pallid newborn by the feet, shakes him back and forth, and smacks him till she can hear the faint start of his cry, a sob that turns into bawling and howling. As the young woman is carried unconscious into the house by three women, the baker points to something that was lying next to the newborn child: a large snake, almost too sluggish to move in the cold night air, creeping away between the rocks, as slow as a serpent in a dream. By the childbed at the first hint of dawn, young David mumbles the old words: *Baruch atah Adonai Eloheinu melech ha'olam ...*

*

For the first few days after the birth, their fear runs deep. They remember the shadows of men on horseback in an alley in Narbonne and still feel the threat every day. Yet because nothing happens, because the unchanging hills offer rest and the day-to-day life of this remote village seems to shield them, they gradually find a new calm. David Todros spends the evenings beside his wife's bed. In the daylight hours, he assists Rabbi Obadiah in the little synagogue school.

On the eighth day after the boy's birth, he is circumcised. As the historical record tells us, he is named Yaakov. Hamoutal stays in bed but can hear, through the rumble of prayer, the shrieks and sobs of the child below. Then conversations, laughter, drinking. She falls asleep with an ache in her swollen young breasts.

The firstborn son is ransomed, as tradition demands. The baby is brought in on a platter ringed by cloves of garlic. The men in the room each nibble at a clove to drive off evil demons. David gives his son to Rabbi Obadiah, who is acting as kohen. After handing over the ritual payment, he takes his son back into his arms. They sit down to a simple meal. It's a hot day; the sun blazes high over the valley, and the riverbed is almost dry. Lizards dart through the ivy and grapevines across the old stones of the house. Wild spelt and poppies sway in the warm wind. In the cool depths of the gorge a kilometre away, at a little church beneath an overhang, a hermit in prayer to the Lord of the Christians is attacked by a bear, which breaks his neck with a casual flick of its left paw.

That evening, a group of knights rides across the grassy plain by the river, led by the notorious Raymond of Toulouse, an ambitious nobleman of almost fifty, whose gaze is drawn to the village. He turns on his caparisoned steed and calls out to one of the men, What's the name of that eyrie over there, up against the mountainside? The knight shrugs. They are headed east on a year-long pilgrimage, from which Raymond of Toulouse, the fearsome warrior celebrated in later years as a heroic crusader, will return with one eye gouged out. He is aware of the search for the high-born fugitive and even knows how much her father has promised the finder; Norman knights on the way to their captured territories in Sicily often pass through Provence, staying with prominent country gentlemen. The thought of looking for her in this village never enters his mind. The new mother, now twenty years old, has no idea how close danger has come. But David sees the knights down on the plain. His heart races; a dark premonition seizes him. He goes inside, consumed with anxiety, to find his wife kneeling by her bed. What are you doing? he asks in dismay. You promised never to say Christian prayers again, remember? She rises, stiff-jointed, to her feet with a guilty look, one hand on her side. I'm not sure any more, she says.

She lies down again and shuts her eyes. In her memory, she sees incense swirling up past a window in a church by the sea.

4

Now the lime trees and elms are turning yellow and red; the mornings are cold and clear. The young mother sees the men bringing home boar, deer and hares to the village. The charred boar hide gives off an acrid smoke that makes her queasy. Oakwood smoke circles over the low roofs. Rainy days are ahead. The fertile plateau is changing into a dreary grey bowl through which the west wind scours a path.

It's hard for her to adjust to the simple, hard life of the village, unlike anything she's known. The drab cliffs and slopes sometimes seem unreal, as if it's all a dream. One rainy night, she is struck by the quiet presence of the many snails and toads. The toads chirp – like an owl's hoot, but thinner and finer. The lethargic creatures leap up against the house fronts as she passes. Helpless, almost human, they stand there with their front legs outstretched against the wall, as if praying to heaven for aid. Once her footsteps have died away, they sink back into apathy.

The snails are different. They come out after every evening shower, without any sense of danger, onto the small, rounded cobbles of the old streets, creeping together to mate. They often die under the feet of late passers-by, their fine shells cracked and the slime oozing out. Beings that had form and substance become mere matter again, dead and denuded of their delicate structure. Some villagers snatch up the snails from the stones in the middle of their lovemaking, and toss them into a brass pot to be cooked alive and eaten right away.

These things trouble Hamoutal.

She grew up with stories of a natural world ruled by God. The Jewish God, whose name she must not utter, is not very different, but she still isn't always sure where the differences lie. The mere sight of a wasp in a honey jar, stuck fast and dying in loud, buzzing alarm, or of a small, black scorpion crushed underfoot, is enough to make her turn away her eyes, tormenting herself with the question of which God is answerable for this. When she takes little Yaakov, not yet one year old, to her breast, she is sometimes overwhelmed by a tightness in her chest and a formless fear. Is nothing left, then, of her sheltered childhood in that grand house in the north? What is the point of this raw life all around her, absorbed in an anguishing cycle of life and death? The theologians spare no thought for questions like these, as if everything they see around them has a purpose. She sometimes feels that by renouncing her parents' religion, she has flung herself into a vacuum. No matter how much David teaches her about the Torah and the ancient history of the Jewish people, an abyss has opened under her old certainties, and there's no one she can speak to about that. Christians would brand her a witch for burning, and Jews would point out that her doubts are unworthy of a proselyte and refuse to accept her into their community. So she does what well-bred women had to do back then, in all places and at all times: she keeps her mouth shut, bows her head and prays in silence. Sometimes she doesn't know who she's praying to – perhaps to that voice inside her, a lost angel that sometimes seems to land on her shoulder, sending her into violent trembling until she pulls herself together with mumbled incantations.

Although she does her best to find a place for herself in the small community, greeting everyone she passes in the streets, most villagers walk on without responding, indifferent. She is unaccustomed to such treatment, whether as a respected Norman woman or as the privileged proselyte she was in Narbonne.

As it becomes clear to her that she will never fully belong here, she gives up her attempts to be sociable. From that moment on, she is granted a kind of tacit acceptance, because she has resigned herself to the role of outsider. After a while, the Christian worthies give her a gracious nod in passing. The inquisitive gleam in their eyes is not quite friendly, but close enough – given that she's safe here and her husband is a close friend of Rabbi Obadiah. What business brought her here? No one asks. But the silence around her, when she joins the other villagers in the small square, says more than enough. A blonde Jew with ice-blue eyes – there's something wrong here, you can see them think it, though no one moves a muscle. One day a few children throw stones at her, chanting *Mouri, Jusiou, mouri* – die, Jew, die.

She ponders all this as she limps back home in the dusk on her sore, swollen foot that won't heal properly, along the rough, uneven stones of the Grande Rue, no more than a wide alley – which today is part of a walking path. She tries not to crush any snails, or in any case, not the spectacular clumps of intertwined snail flesh, those squishy, mobile masses of undisguised instinct, bulging out of their shells, obscene and overwhelming, in slow, dreamlike intercourse.

5

Winter comes, unexpectedly harsh. For weeks the village lies beneath a thick layer of frozen snow. On clear days, an ice-cold mistral blows through the valley. Life comes to a standstill in the dazzle of white and blue. In the gloomy houses, people sit close to the fireplace, coughing, and burning the oak logs and branches they piled carefully against a low wall in late summer. Blue smoke rises from the ramshackle chimneys and gathers in the rooms. The villagers subsist on whatever remains in their damp cellars and attics: root vegetables and hard spelt, ground with effort into sticky flour, and hunks of salted meat boiled in water or roasted in ash. Famine is near. Dead dogs, frozen stiff in the snow with spots of blood on their noses, are skinned, cut open, and boiled with herbs into a weak, nasty stew. Bunches of dry thyme, brewed in hot water with a little leftover honey, help to soothe inflamed lungs. The straw in the beds goes soggy; the children tremble and grow thin. Rats squeak in the cellars. Day after day, it's deathly white and bright. Nothing moves. Or the stealthy wind sends a rough gust ramming into the walls in the early afternoon, as warm and cold air masses change places in the valley. *Woooovvv*, it howls, *woooovvv*, and through a crack comes a sudden sharp whistle, before the lasting silence returns. David reads aloud in synagogue; the drone of voices consoles him. Icicles hang from low eaves; snow blows into drifts by the doors of the few larger houses. Curses, entreaties, tribulations; praying, waiting, sleeping. Footsteps crunching down a bluish lane. The creak of old hinges. It is the month of Tevet in the Jewish year of 4852. For Christians, it is January 1092, and yet again it's snowing, darkness falls before half past three, a few crows whirl among the snowflakes, which, when you look up, seem black instead of white. They swoop up along the rocky slope, like a horde of tiny scouts combing every crevice; they blanket the mouths of the caves where bears hibernate; they cling to watchtowers and eyelashes. Nothing to do but pray and shiver. A preacher tramps through the snow, shaking his rattle and calling for repentance, announcing the end of days.

In Fontaine-lès-Dijon, a boy Yaakov's age is wrapped in woollens and coddled by his mother Aleth. His name is Bernard. Decades later, when he is full-grown and Hamoutal's skeleton already bleached with age, he will be named after the bright valley where he founded a Cistercian abbey – Clairvaux.

On the rocky slope over the village, a huge mass of stone suddenly splits, a hundred tons of rock prised loose from the mountainside by the bitter cold. A crack forms, metres long and only a hundred metres above the synagogue. If the colossus falls, it is large enough to crush half the village on its way down to the valley. The probable route of its fall passes straight through the Jewish quarter. But it will remain stubbornly suspended where it is, sinking into the gravel and bearing down on the topmost stones of the old rampart. There it stands a thousand years later; I can see it when I open the back door of my house. The mistral still whistles around it. The villagers make the sign of the cross and pray to God to spare them. The young woman dreams of her father's hand striking out, and awakes with a start, trembling, the night the thaw sets in.

6

A few years later. Time slips past. Little has changed in their lives, except that their skin is rougher, their faces are tanned, and their past life is fading.

Most of the time, little Yaakov plays by himself in the street. He sometimes ventures as far as the Place des Boeufs, downhill near the lowest village gate, where the oxen are slaughtered, the watchtower stands, doing double duty as a jail, and all day long the children shout and play. He always returns alone.

David has been teaching Hamoutal the old Provençal language, the *langue d'oc*, but she still has trouble with the local variety, especially when spoken fast. Jokes in dialect go over her head, and the villagers look on in amusement as she stumbles and stutters her way through an explanation in the language of the north. While David debates with Obadiah in the synagogue or sits bent over his Torah scrolls, she wanders the valley with her boy on her back, ranging further and further from home, in the company of a few other Jewish women. They pick herbs, collect edible roots, make nosegays, and sit looking out over the landscape. The Western world is booming with controversy and conflict, with political tensions rising by the day; Christians are at odds with Christians, the pope in Rome is embroiled in a perpetual power struggle with the German emperor, but here, sheep roam the pastures in timeless peace. City people are growing rebellious. There are tales of heresy, robbery, murder, retaliation, rioting and false prophets, and frequent whispers that the Antichrist has come to earth. The monster of the final, millennial age, prophesied in the Apocalypse, has arrived after all this time, they say, but nobody recognises him – beware the Devil and his many masks. Could that misshapen man there, with the gouged eye, be the Antichrist? What if that limping beggar with the clubfoot is the Old Serpent in a crafty disguise?

Any trouble or infectious disease could be blamed on anyone. There is danger at every turn. Fear rules the imagination. Maybe the Jews are to blame for it all; you hear so many stories. Life is getting harder for Jews, day by day, in the narrow streets of provincial towns and villages.

All this news comes to her in bits and pieces. She and her husband pass their lives in exile on this remote plateau, and sometimes, during prayers in the women's section of the synagogue, she reminisces about the rich life she left in such haste four years earlier for love of this man – the man she has now forced into exile with her, though that was never her intent. But above all, in the final hours of dark nights, the image rises before her of her parents in Rouen – her mother, who will grieve for the rest of her days, sitting in the large front room of the house far to the north; her father, whose darling she once was, the man who sent knights after her in anger, whose hand she fears – and she jolts awake, covered with sweat, in the deep silence of the sleeping village under the cliff.

She knows she is carrying another child in her tired body.

II
Rouen

1

In the Norman port of Rouen on a bright autumn day in the year 1070, a girl is born. That day the streets echo with the wails of soldiers mortifying their flesh, with monotonous prayers and incantations, with the slap of scourges on bare backs, the echoing of psalms, the cries of women's voices, the clank and rattle of chains over paving stones, the solemn boom of the big drum, and the plaintive moan of rumbling-pots as the penitents hobble on. The men in this dismal and piteous procession were once merciless warriors in William the Conqueror's army, ruthless descendants of the Vikings. The bishops have ordered them to do penance for the barbaric atrocities they committed four years earlier at the Battle of Hastings. The girl's father is also a descendant of one of the Norsemen who captured this region some 150 years ago, looting, plundering and torching their way ahead until at last they reached the banks of the Seine and settled in the dense woods along the meandering river.

Although they seized land and houses, they tended to respect the Peace of God, at least after those first horrific years. The newcomers brought a more hygienic lifestyle and, over the next few generations, adapted to their host culture. Meanwhile, they made a strong impression on the locals; the men of the first generation shaved off their eyebrows, decorated their eyes with kohl, and wore their hair in a tight ponytail. This seemed hard to reconcile with their belligerence and brutality. Their power inspired fear and, in most cases, a resigned submission. Many Norsemen kidnapped and raped the native women. But they also formed emotional ties, and the material interests of entire families became intertwined. Some people searched for a way to restore the peace that had prevailed for centuries. When the unstoppable conquerors were found willing to convert to Christianity, they were granted rights of inheritance to their possessions and dubbed Normans. Just a century after the first Norsemen arrived, some of their great-grandsons have become prominent citizens, integrated into the life of the fast-growing city. One such Norman is Gudbrandr, the girl's father. Her mother comes from a wealthy family in Arras, distant relatives of the Counts of Flanders who then ruled that city.

The child who comes into the world in their aristocratic household that autumn day is called Vigdis, an Old Norse name meaning 'war goddess'. Since this heathen name is not on the Christian calendar of saints, the priest asks before her baptism if the name cannot be changed. Her father says no; even a converted Norseman has his pride. As a compromise, she receives a second given name during the baptismal ceremony in the local church, the name of her Flemish maternal grandmother: Adelaïs. Her mother's father was of Frankish origin. Vigdis Adelaïs will have a guardian angel of mixed blood. In Normandy, Frankish and Norse birds of prey swoop past each other through the menacing skies, almost colliding, each with a blood-stained wing, as a monk from that time witnessed in a nightmare.

*

Vigdis Adelaïs, with her blonde hair and blue eyes, slightly crossed, grows up in the sheltered environment of this prosperous city, where commerce thrives, and large merchant ships bearing textiles, spices, wood and copper wares lie moored beside foul-smelling fishing boats. By the banks of the Seine, where she plays with other children, the waters are churned by the Norsemen's slender snekkjas. Even the heavier ships that come from England sometimes have a dragon's head on the prow.

The first half of the eleventh century has brought welcome changes for farmers. The climate has improved, and the harvests are more abundant. These days, their animals are fatter and healthier, chronic famine is a thing of the past, and the food supply is more varied. After decades of millennial anxiety and invasions, the looting has dwindled to an end, and society seems to have found a new balance. In the space of a century, the women have grown a few centimetres taller on average. There are far fewer cases of rickets, and average life expectancy has risen from just above thirty to thirty-six years. Vigdis seems likely to live a little longer than her ancestors. Nothing foreshadows the catastrophes that will mark the century's end.

*

From the age of six, Vigdis Adelaïs is tutored at home. Her parents are wealthy and cultured. She wants for nothing; her every need is catered for. A priest comes to the house to teach her to read and write. Not that her father's motivations are entirely religious; education for girls is, above all, a status symbol for the nobility. The more she learns of elegance, eloquence and good manners, the more attractive she will be to high-ranking suitors. To this end, her freedom is restricted. After her tenth birthday, she is allowed to play only indoors, and only for the few idle afternoon hours before vespers. She must learn to hold her tongue unless she is asked a question, instead of speaking first. Out in the streets, she must cast her eyes down and never stare. When she walks, she must learn to take small, graceful steps. Her budding womanhood is bound up in dignified garments made of rich fabrics.

One evening she hears her parents quarrelling at the table after the meal. She creeps into the room and sits down, unnoticed, on a bench against the wall. Her father is fulminating against Pope Gregory VII, who has plunged into a shameful power struggle with the Holy Roman Emperor, Henry IV. He lambasts the Church leaders and condemns in the strongest terms the corruption of some bishops, who systematically appoint their own relatives to powerful positions.

Her mother raises her voice, defending the Church and the priests with a ferocity that frightens Vigdis. She accuses her husband of having heretical ideas.

Her father snorts, slams his knife into the tabletop, and says that the priests are whipping up a growing hatred of Jews among the masses, and that he doesn't care for it because it leads to unrest and fighting in the city.

Her mother crosses herself and says that, after all, the Jews nailed their Saviour to the cross and besides, as a descendant of the Normans, her husband knows a thing or two about violence himself – with all those brawling uncles and cousins of his, is she wrong?

Her father retorts that just like the Norsemen, the Jews wish to live in peace, but that riots are often stirred up by priests and zealots acting in secret.

Her indignant mother mumbles that, in any case, the Jews are to blame for the destruction of the Church of the Holy Sepulchre in Jerusalem, because they let the Muslims into the city.

Her father snarls that he's sick to death of all the rabble-rousing nonsense about marching to Jerusalem and taking vengeance in the East.

Her mother snaps that sooner or later Jerusalem will have to be liberated from the Saracen devils, and that the destruction of the Church of the Holy Sepulchre by that demon Al-Hakim seventy years ago is a disgrace to the whole Christian world.

Whereupon her father, with a long-suffering sigh, replies that St Wulfram called Normandy the land where many peoples will be forged together.

He steps outside and growls at the stable boy to fetch his horse.

When her mother turns round, she finds Vigdis staring wide-eyed. Come here, she says, and takes the girl on her lap and strokes her hair. Vigdis doesn't grasp much of what is happening, but years later her parents' quarrels will resurface in her memory with a clarity that startles her. For now she and her brother Arvid play in the courtyard with rabbits' feet, stone marbles and pigs' bladders, and she does little dances in the shadow of the house before she is summoned indoors for her singing lesson and prayers.

2

She is fifteen when one day, on the way home from the great church with her mother, she passes the synagogue in Rue aux Juifs. A lad her age rushes past, pursued by a merchant from whom he appears to have stolen a bag. Huffing, puffing and swearing, the man runs after the quick-footed thief but soon has to give up. The boy is about to vanish round the corner when a young knight comes out of a gate, collars him and asks what is going on. The boy squirms in the knight's iron grip, drops the bag and starts kicking his adversary, who hits him on the head so hard that he drops to the ground like a rag. Right away, a few onlookers start spouting curses. One of them kicks at the boy, striking him full in the face. His head snaps back as though his neck is breaking. The fat merchant comes running up, panting for air. He grabs a stone and pounds it into the boy's bleeding head. A thin young man kicks the boy in the stomach, seeming half mad, shouting, Dirty Jew! Dirty, filthy whoreson of a stinking Jew! On and on he goes, cursing and kicking. The knight pushes apart the little crowd that has formed, telling them to stop. He picks up the boy, whose injured head falls back limp as his blood drips, quick and abundant, onto the ground. That is the moment when Vigdis and her mother pass. The girl looks straight into the mauled face, the blood-soaked lump that remains of it, the string of ooze from the burst eye, the swollen tongue bulging out between the lips, the blood from his belly soaking through the coarse linen smock. The knight, seeing them, makes an apologetic bow to the mother and her young daughter and withdraws into the gate with the dead boy. Vigdis is overwhelmed. She cries till her stomach cramps, her whole body trembles, and she seems about to faint; it's the first time she's witnessed violence from so close by. Her mother speaks soothing words, holding her upright and shushing her, but Vigdis doesn't seem to hear. She slides to the ground; her mother tries to pull her back to her feet; the girl cries out something unintelligible, swinging her head from side to side. Then she vomits on her brocade dress.

3

A couple of years after this incident, the chief rabbi of Narbonne, Richard Todros, the reigning Rex Judaeorum, sent his son David to the city of Rouen to study with a few of the most eminent scholars there. During David's studies, a great debate was in progress in the Jewish community. A few decades earlier, Rabbi Gershom ben Judah had issued an edict forbidding northern European Jews, the Ashkenazim, to practise polygamy. This prohibition followed from a strict, literal interpretation of the Torah. The Sephardim, the Jews of southern Europe and Muslim Spain, were more worldly in outlook and saw greater latitude in the scriptures. They went on insisting on a limited right to polygamy. In some places, the debate grew heated.

The yeshiva or rabbinical school in Rouen – or Rodom, as it was then called – was later known for great teachers like Menahem Vardimas and the illustrious Rashbam, men whose commentaries on the Torah remain authoritative in our day. Scholars came from far and wide to teach or study there, men like Abraham ibn Ezra from Al-Andalus. In David Todros's day, the Rouen yeshiva was still quite new, having been built around 1080. The city's Jewish community, which had existed since Roman times, had reached a considerable size.

When young David Todros arrived, the city had some five thousand Jewish inhabitants, about a fifth of the total population. Narbonne and Rouen were the two main *terrae Judaeorum* of the day. Besides the Talmudic school where young Todros went to study and debate, Rouen also had a synagogue and a ritual slaughterhouse. The entire Jewish quarter lay nestled between Decumanus – the present-day Rue du Gros

Horloge – and Rue aux Juifs. Traces can even be found of David's stay there; the name Todros appears in Rouen's Jewish archives.

During her walks through the city centre, Vigdis has often seen the stately yeshiva building, which was close to the Christian part of town. The young Jewish bag-snatcher was kicked to death just a stone's throw from the school. Now and then, she has exchanged a few words with a couple of students. Some greet her when she passes, though her escort – a tutor or chaperone – disapproves, and it never amounts to more than a nod of the head or a few words in passing. Maybe it was there, where she witnessed the boy's cruel death, that her attention was first drawn to this group she knows so little about, these people with whom she is never in real contact. But in any case, since the Christian neighbourhoods abut the Jewish quarter, the youthful David Todros, son of the chief rabbi of Narbonne, was bound to catch her eye eventually.

*

The old rabbi has warned his son of the dangers he will face while studying in Rouen. Each year, the Christians become less tolerant of the Jews. But because the Jews pay hefty taxes for the right to practise their religion, they are left undisturbed for the most part and don't often face anything worse than verbal aggression. Torah scholars can hold their own in a religious argument: What do you mean, our fault? Wasn't Christ's death on the cross God's will and plan? Didn't God send him to earth to atone for mankind's sins? Isn't that what it says in your own Christian Bible? Well, then, even supposing the Jews had played some part in his death, wouldn't they just have been carrying out God's will? And what could be wrong with that?

In the yeshiva, David hears the shocking story recorded by Jacob bar Jequthiel a few generations earlier. In 1007 King Robert II, a Norman warlord, proposed that the Jews become Christians of their own free will. The implication that they had a choice was somewhat misleading; if they did not convert, they were to be put to the sword. After debating the matter, the Jews decided to remain faithful to the Torah, upon which many of them were, in fact, murdered or driven to drown themselves and their families in the Seine.

Be careful, the elder Todros had told his son, just before David set out with a few other students on the long journey to the north in the spring of 1087. The old rabbi had no way of foreseeing the very different problem with which his son would return to Narbonne.

4

Seagulls wheel over the Seine; the morning sun shines over the roofs of Rouen. It is now the spring of 1088. David is about twenty; Vigdis Adelaïs is seventeen.

The Western world is a place of growing unrest. Prophets of doom, beggars and heretics roam the land, spreading tales that agitate and confuse the gullible masses. They denounce the priesthood and claim that the true faith should no longer be sought in Rome. Now and then a man is lynched, a peasant beaten, a farm set on fire, a score settled with blunt knives or an axe. The knights hold unchecked power over the countryside, and the commoners, after centuries of relative freedom, now feel their iron fist. The lords in their castles feast on what they have plundered from the farmers. The Normans watch for disturbances and riots. By maintaining order, they enhance their status in the eyes of both the populace and the seigneurs.

Counting petals, counting hours, counting days, counting moons. Vigdis Adelaïs, a budding Flemish-Scandinavian beauty, comes home from market with her governess. Her hair – oiled with butter, combed straight and gathered up in a chignon woven with pearls – shines brilliantly. She has the sharp features of her mother's forefathers: a small straight nose, an ever so slightly receding chin, chiselled cheeks and a high forehead. The looks of a woman with a rich inner life – the kind who nowadays would become an intellectual or an art-house diva. Her blonde eyebrows have largely been plucked away, in the fashion of the time, as found in paintings by the Flemish primitives or Jean Fouquet's renowned Madonna. Those who wish to picture her in a state of nature might imagine one of Lucas Cranach's girlish Eves. When she goes out in the streets, her light blue eyes are almost always lowered. She wears elegant, sharply pointed shoes of reddish-brown leather, open at the heel – with each step, one is concealed and the other revealed – which form a discreet contrast with the emerald of her dress and the deep blue of her coat. Her chaperone is dressed in black – an ageing widow employed by Vigdis's father to care for the girl as she reaches womanhood. Ahead of them is a servant with a mule, which carries the food they've bought. It's cool for the season.

At the gate of the Talmud school, a few young men are conversing in low voices. They pause as the young woman passes with her governess. Vigdis looks up for an instant and finds herself staring into two twinkling eyes. The young man, who looks like a southerner, sizes her up shamelessly. He wears a small yellow pointed hat of the kind often mandatory for Jews in those days. His mouth creases into a smile. Before she knows it, she's smiling back and blushing down to her neck. A Jewish boy, she thinks, a Jewish boy smiling at me. The memory flashes through her mind of the bloody, monstrously deformed head of the young thief. She feels foolish and embarrassed; for the rest of the day, she's peevish and says little.

*

Her parents must have marriage plans for her. Her brothers must keep an eye on her too; if she can make a good match, her marriage portion will increase the wealth and prestige of the whole family. Her speech is cultured and reserved. She is learning Latin and taking singing lessons, she plays a five-stringed viol (a novelty in those days), she likes to banter with the young knights who are always hanging around the stables, and she adores the beautiful horses. Even though she is forbidden by law to ride, a few of the stable boys have given her lessons. She stopped when one of them could no longer keep his hands to himself. She has learned to spin, to weave, to run the kitchen; when she sees the peasants who live in the cottage behind their house, she likes to stop and chat, even though her mother doesn't approve. She sometimes questions her father about the Scandinavian gods, the heathen doctrines of her distant ancestors.

Her governess escorts her to her singing lessons in the nearby church, just a few streets away. But instead of walking home through Decumanus, she suggests a little detour through Rue aux Juifs.

One early evening, this has the desired result: the young man is there again, talking to his friends in front of the Talmud school. Feeling her breath grow shallow with excitement, she moves closer till she is just a few steps away from the group. She must lift her eyes, she must, she must. She does, and looks straight into his. The shock is greater for him, because of the blend of diffidence and audacity in her gaze. She seems to bore into his eyes; she senses she's causing him pain. That knowledge brings her a strange, carnal satisfaction that makes her cruel and imperious for an instant, even as her heart races under her finely embroidered garments. The students are not only silent, but look with a kind of surprise at young David Todros, who stops halfway through his argument, swallows and blinks.

By then Vigdis Adelaïs has vanished round the corner.

For weeks, on her daily walks, she goes back to her old route along Decumanus. She doesn't know what to do with herself. At last, one evening, she confesses to her governess that she is sick with longing to see that young man again. Thinking back wistfully to her lost marriage, her governess shows enough worldly wisdom not to betray the girl's confidence. She warns her that desiring a Jewish boy is forbidden – more than that, unthinkable. When Vigdis starts to cry and pull her hair, overcome with anguish and frustration, her governess puts her to bed – but she too is torn, and lies awake that night brooding, with no idea what to do.

5

The risk the girl takes is, by the standards of her time, utterly irrespon-
sible. She has no right to decide her own fate. Nor is David, in fact, per-
mitted to propose to her. Young knights sometimes go so far as to abduct
the girl of their dreams to compel her parents to consent to the marriage,
or if they are rich and respected, they buy the parents' permission with
a large settlement. Marrying without parental approval is almost incon-
ceivable and a sure road to violence and slaughter.

So the marriage of a Christian girl to a Jewish boy is beyond the imagining of the upper classes. Yet forbidden love is ever-present in human
hearts – as it always has been. In that eventful year of 1088, the future
lover in the most famous of forbidden affairs, Pierre Abélard, is a nine-
year-old boy at play in the streets of Nantes, and his beautiful Héloïse has
not even been born. They will form one of the most renowned and tragic
couples of the High Middle Ages. Master Abélard will be able to hide
his love for the young abbess for a time; the theologian and his beloved
will meet in the relative safety of her uncle's house. Vigdis Adelaïs has no
place for her forbidden love but the streets.

*

There's no way of discovering how and where they finally spoke to
each other. The rules of propriety made things difficult; still, there were
opportunities for furtive encounters. The world was not dominated by
clock time the way it is now; stray moments could be found for stealing
away. And because the city centre was not so large and the church and

synagogue were close together, it was not hard to strike up a conversation in a busy street without anyone noticing right away.

After avoiding the synagogue and yeshiva for weeks, Vigdis – encouraged by her governess, since the girl has no interest in anything else – returns to the old Rue aux Juifs. She passes the school, sees the narrow windows of the yeshiva, and thinks of David inside, bent over manuscripts. She fears she will faint on the spot.

She is young and longs for freedom, a larger world than the stifling life of the city elite and the arranged marriage that awaits her. She starts dressing with greater care, and whenever she passes the synagogue and yeshiva on her daily walks, she tries to catch a glimpse of David, her head darting up and down. After all, there's no prohibition against greeting a Jew, though it's not really done.

Their first conversation cannot have been easy at all – her first true greeting stiff and formal, his more flamboyant, in the southern style. His *langue d'oc* accent must have clashed with her northern *langue d'oïl*. They must have had trouble understanding each other and found themselves shy and embarrassed. Fumbling and giggling their way through a series of incomplete sentences, waving their hands, feeling abysmally stupid – the addictive self-torture of youth. It has its funny, awkward side, but to the young it is deadly serious.

Seduction was a circuitous art in those days, a smokescreen of rhetorical devices and charming sidetracks that veiled the act of flirting, but without making it tedious or prudish. On the contrary, these cultural practices created a tension that only heightened the mutual attraction. On the other hand, Vigdis Adelaïs and David met a century before courtly love became common practice in privileged circles, and David was anything but the Christian stereotype of the valiant young knight.

Jewish boys inhabited a different planet: a world of ancient writings, erudite scholars and introverted study. The tradition in which he was raised did not show the same extremes of bloodthirst and piety; his world view was more placid, more timeless. His style of courtship would not have fitted the culture of a genteel Christian woman. His upbringing required that he resort to age-old formulas and rituals: 'O my Jewish bride, let me lead you to the altar as Moses led our ancestors out of Egypt.' He was supposed to promise her the joy of Sukkot: the bounty of the Feast of Tabernacles, the harvest of the fruits of the years. David Todros's fine words must have failed him completely. Vigdis can't have understood half of what he said. To her, it must have sounded exotic and a little over the top – not that an ironic, culture-specific concept like 'a little over the top' could have existed for her. We are groping in the seductive dark.

*

Does this girl know what she's getting into? Of course not, how could she? She is the one who will have to learn to live on a different planet, in a different calendar. She vaults into terra incognita, blind and overexcited, reckless and naive. She does it for those eyes and that little beard, for that smile and that strange excitement, for that yellow cap perched on the crown of his head, for the unknown and the adventure that draws her in, for that cloud of dazzling brightness in her muddled head. She has seen the white unicorn and wanders delirious through a wood of ancient prohibitions.

David's parents are far away; he lives in the yeshiva dormitory and can take certain liberties there. He is under supervision, of course; associates of the chief rabbi of Narbonne have seen to that. But there is also leisure time; he is free to laugh, to drink, to go out into the fields on days of rest. Truth be told, he is free to do all sorts of things. The city has its brothels and disreputable taverns. Even wealthy citizens patronise what are known as women's houses, private residences where girls who took the wrong path now play the courtesan. They are kept there for a while and then sent on to a convent, or else they remain ladies of easy virtue.

Why wouldn't the young men visit those houses, as long as they can keep their religion a secret? The only ones who know for certain they're Jewish are the girls themselves, who must enjoy having circumcised boys for a change – and who've learned to keep quiet. In any event, the young students dream of girls, talk about girls, joke about girls.

Until one day David Todros has had enough of jokes, turns moody, seems distracted in discussion, no longer takes any interest in going to taverns, frowns at obscene jokes, can't concentrate on his Torah studies, sits and stares out the narrow window in the study hall on the first floor, has no appetite, and arrives at morning prayer fatigued and dishevelled.

*

It's a mystery how they manage to start an affair, but it happens. They arrange to meet one autumn day in the market square. From there they sneak off to the home of one of David's friends, stammering at each other. Because their conversation makes her heart beat so hard she can scarcely speak, she soon runs off. Sobbing, she arrives back home where her anxious governess is waiting for her. Three days later they plan another meeting. He promises that the next day at noon he will come and sit beside her in the deserted church, unnoticed, with all traces of his Jewish identity well disguised from prying eyes.

In the cool shade of the church, she tells him in an agitated whisper that she'd like to learn Hebrew. He stares at her, dumbfounded, and tries to take her pale, delicate ringed hand in his. She pulls it away, under the precious linen that conceals her girlish form. Her confusion is so great it makes her dizzy. Blasphemy in the face of the beloved Mother of God, as the small flame of the Holy Spirit flickers in front of the tabernacle – what is she thinking? God, forgive me my trespasses; I have no choice. Her Jewish admirer is taken aback by her words, but also moved. Well before this moment, he fell for the young woman who has more or less put her life at stake for the chance to talk to him. He promises her he will teach her, stumbling over his words.

*

They arrange to meet unseen in the early dusk of the months ahead. David has told one of the rabbis about the girl, describing her as a proselyte. This gambit works: converts are welcome in the Jewish world. The line separating Jews from non-Jews is more permeable than in our day. Prospective converts can be accepted as Jews in the fullest sense, instead of remaining goyim all their lives. So whenever Vigdis summons the courage to go out in her veil and steal into the Jewish house where they meet, she can talk to him without much danger. Through David, she also becomes acquainted with the other Jewish students. Though always surprised to meet her, they offer polite greetings. Soon they all know that this young proselyte is studying, in strict secrecy, with the son of the chief rabbi of Narbonne and is under his protection. They also realise there is more to the story.

One day, as they sit bent over a Torah scroll – he is teaching her the Hebrew alphabet – what must happen happens. Their hands brush, their faces turn towards each other, the scroll falls to the tiled floor, there is not breath enough in the room for their breathless desire. Red-faced, David picks up the scroll and is obliged to kiss it right away, because it was desecrated by touching the ground. But Vigdis brings her mouth closer and shuts her eyes. On the Seine, the ships are tossed in the autumn storm. It is late November; fishermen are dragging their sloops up the riverbank; the swallows flew south months ago; the sky is clouding over again; people are rushing home before darkness falls. With red cheeks and unsteady feet, Vigdis Adelaïs returns home through Rue aux Juifs to an angry mother who demands to know where she was loafing about, all by herself. In church, Mother, she says, in church, that's all, and she endures the sceptical looks with inner trembling and patience.

6

As the weeks go by, her discussions with the young Jewish intellectual teach her that there is a religious alternative to the violence and turmoil of the Christian world. This tremendous shift in perspective throws her off balance and fascinates her. She pictures a different world, a different chronology – one that does not begin with death by torture and crucifixion. A historical sense not bewitched by apocalyptic delusions and millennial fears, by the return of the dreaded Beast, by hell and Devil and torment and Fall, but by a far more ancient calendar that begins with a creative act, the beginning of life itself: the instant when Yahweh created the world. The thought comforts her; no longer is history broken by any fault line. At the same time, she lies awake at night in her narrow alcove, agonising over the words of the Torah, comparing them to what she has learned from the priests. She is afraid of all her secret thoughts, hardly daring to open her eyes to her changing view of the world – which is, in fact, the worst of heresies. She says nothing to her governess about her growing doubt and confusion, and she certainly never speaks of it to her parents. In the church, during the Latin service, she bows her head like a humble worshipper, she sings the Christian prayers with the congregation, she still feels the pacifying power of the collective song and monotonous droning. Her hair is in a tight braid. Under her loose shawl, she shines with the fragrant oil that her chambermaid rubbed into her skin. Her grass-green dress of fine cloth is cinched tight and adorned with small glass pearls. An elegant fox fur is draped over her shoulders, discreetly covering her young bosom. As the service goes on, she regains her composure, drawn back into the safe world she's known as long as she can remember. She begs the Virgin Mother for guidance and asks forgiveness for her thoughts. She sinks into despair, but is buoyed up again by the changeless calm of the prayers and litanies. Her eyes burn and sting as she joins in with the old church songs. It's as if her consciousness and therefore her personal development are advancing by leaps and bounds. Her sudden, intimate feelings of alienation have turned her, against her will, into a young intellectual; she is bursting free of the certainties of her familiar world. By this time she is equipped to think for herself about her spiritual doubts. She has learned Latin as part of her Christian education and from hearing it in church services. Frankish is her mother tongue, and she's picked up a little Flemish. Who knows, she may even speak a smattering of Danish or Norwegian, used by her father during childhood games. In her lessons with David, she has already become more familiar with the *langue d'oc*, and of course he is teaching her Hebrew. Later, in Narbonne, in a household composed mainly of Sephardic Jews, she will prove a quick study in Spanish. But for now, she must learn to keep silent about all the thoughts that so confuse and consume her – an enormous effort for her young mind.

7

Every day for the past few weeks she has refused to wear the refined city clothing laid out for her in the morning. Instead, she wants a dark dress to wear over her simple undergarment. She even asks her governess if a black dress can be made for her, as plain as possible, with a matching hooded cape. The question raises immediate suspicions. It's like the daughter of a modern-day Christian family announcing she plans to start wearing a headscarf. When her mother hears of her request, she storms into the girl's room and demands an explanation. Vigdis bows her head, remains silent, lets the torrent of words crash over her, and then raises her head slowly, looks her mother straight in the eyes, and says nothing.

That vacant stare and stiff-necked silence are enough reason for her mother to tell her father about the matter that evening. The next day, he summons Vigdis to the front room so that he can speak to her with a priest present. The girl's explanations are confused; she's certainly not about to give away her secret, so she mumbles whatever comes into her head. The priest commands her to make the sign of the cross; she does, but with such a spooked look in her eyes that he launches into a harangue about the many threats to a young woman's spiritual welfare. He conjures up visions of hell and the Devil; she turns away, squeezing her eyes shut. Her father's intuition cannot be thrown off so easily. He snorts, throws down his hunting glove on the table, and brusquely informs her that she's not to leave the house for a month, and he'll send her to a convent for six months if she doesn't shape up. She stamps her feet, shakes her head in despair, wrings her hands, but still says not a word. She goes out into the garden and cries, convulsing with sobs; her parents will still be talking about it that evening. Vigdis is roughly escorted to her bedroom. She sits moping in her place of confinement, watching the rims of the clouds flare red in the twilight.

As soon as night falls she flees through the kitchen and the little gate in the back of their garden, leaving home on her own for the first time; her governess knows of her plan and will not betray her. Her heart pounding, she heads towards the parish of Saint-Lô, passes the Hôtel de Bonnevie, and then follows the familiar route past the synagogue again, past the Jewish bathhouse and slaughterhouse, towards the yeshiva. It has only one window on the street side, a small opening that shows her nothing. The first of the two heavy doors is still open. She goes down the stairs to the second door and knocks. Nothing happens. Dead silence, broken only by a cat's meow. For a moment, she stands in the gloom of the staircase, looking around in bewilderment. The half-moon barely illuminates the streets; her heart is thumping wildly. She doesn't realise how strictly women are forbidden to enter the yeshiva. She returns home, having accomplished nothing, sits on the old bench in the garden until her heart and mind stop racing, and creeps into the house with dew on her lashes. Back in her room she sits in the alcove, incapable of sleep, and feels something in her body burn and tear and pound.

She stays in her chambers for a month and tries to pray, thinking the whole time about the two irreconcilable worlds and attempting to decipher the few small scrolls that David has entrusted to her. After that, she resumes her walks with her governess, going to and from church, the market, the banks of the Seine, blind to it all, in constant, secret hope of catching a glimpse of her foreign beloved.

King William of Normandy is dead; his successor is a hothead, she hears from her father, who's worried about the country's future. What in God's name does she care?

Not long afterwards, news of their clandestine relationship starts to leak out. There are tales and rumours; the sexton has seen them hand in hand. Again, Vigdis is confined to her rooms. This time, her father does send her to a nearby convent for six months. When David is sighted near the convent one evening at dusk, the consequences are swift and grave. At the priest's request, the rabbi reluctantly orders a search of the yeshiva. This turns up a piece of parchment bearing her handwriting: a poem in calligraphy about golden butterflies in a garden, found on a rack for Torah scrolls among the personal effects of David Todros. She is told she will remain in her convent cell until her father has selected a suitable candidate for marriage. David receives a lecture from the rabbi, who threatens to send him back to Narbonne for his reckless behaviour. He promises to mend his ways, to search his soul; he shows remorse. But the next morning he's spotted near the convent again, with a piece of rich cloth under his arm. The rabbi writes to the elder Todros in Narbonne and asks him to summon his son back home for a while.

This is a turning point in their lives. But her prospects look much bleaker than his. A high-born girl's future tends to be mapped out well before she reaches the age of nineteen, unless she decides for herself by accepting a marriage proposal. Vigdis has already fended off three candidates while her brothers looked on in dismay. Her eldest brother comes to the convent to tell her that their father will soon name a knight of their acquaintance as her intended spouse. This leads to bickering, threats and shouting matches. She tries to bluff her way out, telling her parents she'll become a nun if they force a husband on her. In the convent chapel she prostrates herself on the cold stone, trying not to think of the Jewish prayers that David has taught her, doing penance, mortifying her flesh –

but she remains impure. Hunger, sleeplessness, waves of mystical rapture and panic, nausea and cramps, menstruation and self-mutilation. Prayer, but to which God?

And after a few weeks, a little miracle: the gardener, who has been eyeing her all this time with a lewd grin, passes on a message from David Todros. This illiterate go-between hopes that by delivering the note he can get into her good graces. The message is terse and factual: a date and time, at the back of the convent garden. No name. But she recognises the handwriting, the strange curlicues on the letters.

It is eleven o'clock at night when she slips out the back door of the convent's large kitchen, shivering in her thin clothes. She passes the stables, reaches the walled courtyard, and bangs her left foot into a line of rough rocks around the herb garden. Gropes for the little door that leads out into the fields. It is locked. Silence. The night owl; a dog in the distance. No moon, no light. Her breath quickens; her teeth chatter. Then she hears her name from the other side. A knife slides into the lock; the door rattles, creaks and flies open. She sees a dark shape in front of her. She hears her name. It is not David's voice. She stumbles over the small stone threshold, is caught in someone's arms, gasps. The man clamps her by the shoulder and grunts, This way. The grass smells chilly underfoot; moss and bitterweed, trampled nettles. The taciturn man leads her to a nearby house on the waterside. There a back door opens, and someone with a small torch lights their way in. They are brought to a room; no one speaks a word. She is left alone there. The door is locked. She lies awake on the small couch, listening to the sounds of the unfamiliar house. If she's betrayed now, her punishment will be merciless – maybe even interrogation and torture. She has to be gone before matins, when the nuns will find her cell empty. The door to freedom swings open, but it's a trap.

There's no way back.

III
Flight

1

I drive out of Brussels in the afternoon, heading south via Tournai and Lille to Rouen. I arrive in the evening. It is late March; a cold wind scours the deserted squares. I walk down Rue du Massacre, snapping a photograph of the street's name. A moment later, I'm in Rue aux Juifs – a long, straight street where two government buildings face each other. The one on the right is the Palais de Justice, the court building. In 1976, during excavation work for an underground car park, a bulldozer ran into a block of stone with a vague inscription. The foreman brought the work to a halt, and when digging resumed, it was at a slower, more studious pace. Bit by bit, a large structure was unearthed. Archaeological research showed it was part of an eleventh-century Jewish building. Was it a synagogue? A Jewish school? An aristocratic home? Rouen turned out to have once had a flourishing Jewish community. The American scholar Norman Golb threw himself into the subject, writing a scrupulously documented study. The building was found to have been a Jewish school, a yeshiva.

This is where I mean to begin my search, a search that will take me – like Vigdis Adelaïs and her Jewish lover – far from home.

The next afternoon at the appointed time I meet Annie Lafarde, an animated woman who offers tours, on request, of the remnants of the yeshiva. She seems eager to tell the whole story at once; ten people show up and are held captive for an hour in a little room opposite Rouen's cathedral. The view distracts me. This is the cathedral which so fascinated Monet that he painted it almost thirty times, each time in different hues, in his eagerness to grasp the fleeting light. His passion had an element of pathos, because the light on old stone buildings changes by the instant – like our perspective on the past.

The group follows our effusive guide outside, entering the courtyard of the Palais de Justice. In the right-hand corner, a glass door with a security gate gives access to the sanctum. Only now do I grasp that a thousand years ago the city lay about two metres lower. We descend a staircase, and what I see at the bottom makes my head spin. In the damp, stale air of this underground chamber, between concrete walls and metal shoring, in hazy neon light, there it lies: the astonishingly well-preserved yeshiva of Rouen. I run my hand over the rough walls pearled with moisture and think, *David Todros, a thousand years later I am touching the stone you knew*. I soon find the inscription describing this building as a *maison sublime* – a sublime house, because every yeshiva alludes to the Temple in Jerusalem, destroyed forever by the Romans in the year AD 70 during the Jewish–Roman War described by Flavius Josephus. Unlike Christians, who have rebuilt their great churches time and again, the Jews never erected another central holy place after the destruction of the Temple. Instead, that catastrophe is commemorated in and by all the world's countless synagogues, as scattered as the diaspora itself – and so all those houses of worship say an architectural Kaddish for the forever-vanished Temple.

It must have been somewhere in front of the facade of this *maison sublime* that Vigdis and David first met. I picture David Todros arriving here, but this time I have the actual details of the building in mind. In the wall of the central chamber, I see the round holes for the beams that held up the racks of Torah scrolls. The yeshiva had two doors: one higher up, on the street side, and one at the bottom of the stairs by the entrance. Those doors must have been heavy, considering all the treasures they protected.

There are traces of the great fire set during the pogrom of 1096 – by which year Vigdis had assumed a new identity, she and David were living in my distant southern village, and fate found them there all the same. Meanwhile, here in the north, the synagogue and this yeshiva burned down, bringing an end to a period of peaceful coexistence in Normandy. I notice the Babylonian ornaments and columns by the entrance to the building; the vanquished lion, symbol of evil defeated, and on the other side the dragon, symbol of life and struggle, both distinct even now in the worn stone. There is a narrow passage to the first floor, which may have been used for study. All these rooms are much more intimate than I had imagined. They remind me of the tall, narrow houses in my Provençal village. Seeing them, someone once quipped that Jews were given such small plots of land they had to invent the high-rise. Norman Golb has even suggested there may once have been a third floor here, which would have been quite exceptional back then. Annie Lafarde waves off that idea with a laugh.

I don't know; it doesn't matter. I'm surprised how strong an impression this place makes on me. Besides my southern village and a synagogue in far-off Egypt, it's the only place I can be certain that Vigdis Adelaïs once stood. This is where her heart pounded as she stood by the gate in the street, aware that she was strictly forbidden to pass through the entrance below. This is where she lingered and waited.

Knowing her life story and its tragic end, I wish I could warn her of what lies ahead. Walk on, young lady, find a different man, escape this destiny, flee what you most desire. But no: she is so much in love that she leaves her whole world behind. Again, I see her descending the Provençal hill near Monieux with her sprained ankle and muddied clothes, and I realise that not one of the other nine visitors to this crypt full of inscriptions and photographs knows my secret. I feel far from the present, deep in history, however much I might like to join their conversations, which,

I must admit, become more and more insightful and absorbing as the afternoon goes on.

When we resurface, I find it hard to put up with the crowds. I walk along the Seine; the evening rush hour has begun; the air I breathe is nothing but exhaust. The seagulls wheel above the waters of the harbour.

2

In the first glimmer of sunrise, she hears the lock creak again. David stands before her. He holds her in his arms for a moment, without a word. He has brought her clothes – plain black garments unlike anything her mother ever gave her. They leave the house on the edge of town through the back door. It is six in the morning; the city gates, normally guarded, are opened around that time for the peasants who come to Rouen with deliveries for the merchants.

The young couple leave the city through St Ouen's Gate, in the east, pretending to be poor merchants picking up goods on the outskirts of town. From there they walk a long way down the left bank of the Seine with their pushcart and some provisions and borrowed clothes, passing through the fields and meadows of Saint-Étienne-du-Rouvray and going on to Pont-de-l'Arche, then known by its Latin name Pons ad Archas. No farmers live in this deserted region; there is not a house to be seen for miles around, and the clouds hang low over the countryside. A few foxes and wild dogs cross their path in the early afternoon; rain lashes the earth and their faces. Near Pont-de-l'Arche, one of David's friends has arranged for a ferry to meet them. He is waiting on the other side with a harnessed mule that they can lead by the reins. He wishes them a safe journey; the friends embrace.

Vigdis abandons every form of security, her fortune, her social status, her future, and her good name, because a Jewish man has promised to marry her as soon as they reach his home town of Narbonne. David has to keep calming and consoling her; she often flies into a panic, bursts into frightened tears, crosses herself, prays to the God of her childhood, asks for forgiveness, thinks of the Jewish God, David's Adonai, feels sure of nothing, squeezes her eyes shut, loses her balance, and falls from their mule as it gallops across the fields. She has to be helped back up onto her feet; her wrist is sprained, and she's dripping with mud. She can no longer pray to the saints; they no longer exist. In the beginning was the word. It's been taken away from her now, and her young limbs are trembling.

*

The only document describing their fate is in the world-renowned Cambridge University manuscript collection known as the Cairo Genizah. At the end of my own wanderings, I will hold this almost thousand-year-old Hebrew document in my hands. It tells us that David and Vigdis arrived in Narbonne in the year 1091, having travelled nine hundred kilometres across medieval France, with innumerable dangers and difficulties along the way. They had the overconfidence of two young people who have struck out on their own. They knew that knights would be sent after them to track them down and bring them back as captives. Their lives hung by a thread; he would be put to death for abduction, and she would spend the rest of her life in a convent, under strict watch, if they were lucky enough not to be accused of devil-worship. In that case, they would both be burned at the stake. But they took their chances, as fugitives always do, because no other tolerable choice remains.

*

As I drive out of Rouen, seagulls are skimming over the small harbour. Traffic is heavy on the wide bridge across the Seine. An endless line of cars is crawling towards Évreux and Orléans. On this bright spring morning I try to imagine how two people who had to flee in secret could cross the wide river, their first obstacle. And how they went on from there – what an interminable trek, on foot or on horseback. Now the traffic rushes along the banks. There are no clues for me here.

I park the car at one of the first lay-bys along the route to Évreux and take in the view from a low hill: the roads, the suburbs and the line of lorries. On the left I see a wooded expanse in the distance. I drive on to where the motorway crosses the Seine.

Life is peaceful here; a woman sits with her toddler in a playground on the bank. An imposing house with a large car parked outside has a view out over the sandy river water. The Seine is shallow here; was it easy for them to cross? As pointless as it may seem, I want to see the landscape for myself, to absorb the details, the possible views. I want to find out what might still be visible a millennium later. Almost nothing, it seems – except the landscape, here and there. I can scarcely picture what their journey was like, even with the help of historical documents. My whole task is to cross out, take away, pare down to the essence: no bridges, no motorways, no buildings, no hard shoulders, no sound either, and hardly any human presence. To cross it all out with the care of an archaeologist, and then to find the wastelands underneath. *Tohu va-vohu* in Hebrew: everything still waste and emptiness, formless and void. The clouds and trees, the rivers and rolling hills, the early cities, the boundless woods. To be erased: filling stations, supermarkets, crowded suburbs, housing estates, rural planning, cultivated fields and pastures. Even the modern forests seldom give any impression of how it was then. Empty countryside, with here and there a stray house, a mud hut belonging to penniless peasants, dirt tracks full of bumps and potholes without any road signs or shelters, low church towers the only landmarks. At night, you couldn't see your hand in front of your face. To find your way in the daytime, you had to use the sun. You ate whatever you could get; sometimes, you couldn't find a sheltered place to sleep before sundown and had to spend the night in a ditch, in fear of your life.

Animals prowled at night: bears and wolves, wild dogs and the dreaded European wildcat. So did the other nocturnal predators: poachers and thieves, vagrants and swindlers – scum. In the daytime there were tramps, preachers, false knights out for personal gain, double-dealing pedlars, clairvoyant charlatans and zealots – enough rogues on their long route to keep the young couple vigilant in the extreme. They could trust almost no one; the news of their elopement preceded them, brought by her father's messengers and the abbess of the convent. So they couldn't take refuge in abbeys, churches or rectories, nor in forts or castles, and rarely with city folk. The safest places were the barns of uninformed peasants.

It must have taken them at least a month and a half, since their average speed was no more than twenty kilometres a day, unless they had fast horses – and they surely didn't, not until much later. That would have drawn too much attention. There were only a few places along the route where they could go from door to door in search of lodging for the night – concealing their true identities. They would have seized those opportunities to recover their strength and lie low, hiding from wandering knights. Such interruptions must have extended their journey to almost three months. At least until they passed Orléans, they had to be careful not to attract attention; they heard from a Jewish family near Évreux that the knights had already passed that way and ordered every Jewish household to confess if they had seen the two fugitives. They threatened to burn down the houses of anyone who aided the couple or withheld information.

*

Nowadays the distance between Rouen and Narbonne can be traversed in a nearly straight line on the French autoroutes. After poring over maps for potential signs of old country roads, I decide that the lines of the autoroutes would, with a few exceptions, have been sensible choices even in those days. For example, the most comfortable route that would have taken them far away from Rouen, fast, was the Roman road known as the Chaussée Jules César, which cut straight through the Bois de Vexin and was still in heavy use. But it curved south-east, towards the capital, and that would have exposed them to great danger. Messengers used the road to zip back and forth between Rouen and Paris. It was packed with people who might recognise them. No, the runaway lovers must have remained west of Paris, in the rural parts of Normandy and Eure-et-Loir. They went from Rouen by way of Chartres to Orléans, where courageous Jews gave them shelter despite the risks – their first chance to spend a few days resting and recuperating. By then they had already come a long way: the total distance to Chartres was 130 kilometres, and to Orléans 250. The same trip now takes me half a day by car on local roads, at the sedate speed of fifty kilometres per hour.

How many waterways must they have crossed on that ceaseless slog, if they kept detours to a minimum? Between Rouen and Narbonne, there are – at a rough estimate – fifty, including smaller streams. Bridges are risky, because they're bottlenecks. Just after crossing the Seine at Pont-de-l'Arche, they had to cross another river: the Eure, which merges with the Seine nearby.

Standing on the sandy riverbank, I'm assailed by fresh doubts about their escape route. Why wouldn't they have been smuggled out of the city in a nondescript boat by a helpful Jewish fisherman who lived nearby? They could have followed the looping course of the Seine southwards. No, then they might have been discovered and betrayed at any time. I imagine their pursuers conducting a systematic sweep of the river. The other stretch of the Seine, north-west from Rouen to the river's mouth in

Honfleur, was also combed by a number of small, fast-moving snekkjas, since Vigdis's father had just as much reason to suspect that his daughter and the Jewish southerner had taken the sea route from Rouen to Bordeaux (and travelled on by land). Of course, that's assuming he guessed that the young kidnapper was taking her to his home town. The Hebrew manuscript in the Genizah Collection in Cambridge, on which this story is based, at least tells me this much: her father's knights pursued her all the way to Narbonne.

*

I have let myself be carried away, she sometimes reflects. The words of the Torah wind around her childhood prayers like tefillin. Thoughts of rabbis and thoughts of priests are equally frightening; she sees her father's threatening hand lifted over her head. She has no confidante or adviser to tell her how to behave, how to handle this. She had a sheltered upbringing; now that she has obeyed her feverish impulse and taken the initiative, she is lost. The only thing that can save her now is her will, her force of character. After ten days or so, the tough Viking side of her personality surfaces. As the horse trots down the deserted roads, she gradually recovers her poise. The quivering of her heart transforms into tensed willpower. When it all starts to seem like too much, she clenches her teeth and studies the watchful young man beside her. They would like to hurry on, but that would attract the attention of passers-by. Suspicious peasants are quick to pick up rumours from the city: the daughter of a leading burgher has run off with a Jew! The important thing is not to flee as fast as they can, but to keep as low a profile as possible. So they travel in disguise, looking out for danger, and mostly stick to the early-morning hours. They skulk across the thoroughfares, trust no one, and pull their hoods over their heads when they run into horsemen on a country road. They make little detours to avoid the places where they suspect or fear that sentinels are posted.

One afternoon they see a colourful parade of fools passing by and decide to walk with them for a while. It's a procession of strange messiahs and would-be saints, stirring up the mobs of the poor and destitute with their speeches and sermons. They quote fragments from the Apocalypse of John, shouting that the Beast with ten horns is coming, that the Antichrist is already among them, that the world will perish by fire and by sword. The commoners respond with a fury of whoops and whistles, dancing around and racing on to the next small village to bang on doors. Everywhere this throng passes, people leave their hovels behind to join them, abandoning their homes and their possessions. Husbands, wives and children march together, in the hope of a better future, joining in the cries about the end time soon to come. They dream of plunder, mayhem and adventure. They have nothing to lose, nor will they gain a thing, but their sheer numbers make them reckless. They drink homebrew and get into fistfights. Here and there, the wounded collapse by the roadside. They are usually left behind.

David and Vigdis walk with them, their hoods pulled far over their faces, glad to be shielded from the knights pursuing them – since no one would dream of searching or interrogating the crowd of zealots. They keep quiet and try to stay with the women and children. Now and then, they are handed a hunk of bread or some milk. No one asks any questions. They sleep with the others. In the night, fires are lit to protect the group. This sees them across much of the most dangerous stretch of their journey, the first two hundred kilometres or so. But one morning, they wake up and see that their little horse is gone. They have to leave their cart behind and take whatever they can carry on their shoulders. As they shuffle onwards, they watch the unruly mob dwindle into the distance.

*

When they arrive in Évreux after that first, hectic stage of their journey, Vigdis Adelaïs has a chance to draw breath. An early cloudburst caught them by surprise, so their garments dried on their sweaty skin, and now they stink. They are taken in by a Jewish family, relatives of one of David's friends from the yeshiva. There they can finally have a full meal and bathe; clean linen underclothes are laid out for them. Vigdis is given an outfit that won't draw attention, a dress with a close-fitting top and full skirt. Over it, she wears a cape of plain grey cloth. Their own clothing is cleaned and hung in the garret to dry. They sleep side by side for the first time there, on a bed of felt in a clammy back room, but they barely touch. They lie pressed against each other in their underclothes, eyes open, bodies burning, staring in disbelief. Their heads spin with thoughts.

Tired, and in a strange blend of euphoria and panic, they hear the first cock crow around half past four in the morning. Next to her, Vigdis hears mumbled words she doesn't understand. *Modeh ani l'fanecha, melech chai v'kayam, she-hechezarta bi nishmati b'chemlah, rabbah emunatecha.* Then David rises to his feet. In the half-light of dawn, the girl watches the ritual she has heard described. The man winds one strap around his arm seven times, and the other around his head. The young woman stares at the strange box on his forehead and holds her breath. The young man recites the morning prayer in the bare, silent room. She watches from beneath the coarse sheet. She thinks of the Christian credo, which her father often recited in the morning hours. She is free and in mortal danger.

She has no way of knowing that, after her husband's murder, she will take his tefillin with her and leave them in the genizah of an Egyptian synagogue, to be discovered eight centuries later by Rabbi Solomon

Schechter, who will treasure them as one of the rare examples of medieval tefillin. A vague grey photograph circulates the Internet of these objects, lifted from the cold silence of their storeroom. The diaspora of things.

3

Beyond Évreux, the plains stretch out ahead to the horizon. They pass small villages, moving fast; the level landscape makes for easy progress. They arrive at the present-day site of Nonancourt, where the road rises, and climb the gentle slope to the higher plain. Looking back, they see the road they've travelled, a wide view under clouds and flocks of seagulls. Then they move on – undergrowth, thickets, a few pools of still, black water, the occasional shock of a wild boar, thorny brambles they sometimes have to pick their way through, fatigue, discouragement. A fit of crying in the dusk; hunger and thirst; the mistrust shown by the scattered denizens of the few low houses where they knock.

Here and there spelt has been planted. The fields are small, sloppy and irregular. Lean, dark pigs amble along an embankment beneath tall, old oaks, thrusting their snouts intently into the soil. In the Bois de Saint-Vincent, just south of Blévy, they wander through the enchanting serenity of a friendly forest: ortolans, shrikes, garden warblers, a golden oriole, a woodpecker's hollow rattle. The rustle of leaves, clusters of tall ferns, Solomon's seal, a pang of hope. They pick berries. David, who learned how to net birds as a child, outsmarts a few doves and slits their throats in a single stroke. He plucks and cleans them, rinses them in water and a little salt, and hangs them overnight so that the blood drains out – as required by kashrut, Jewish dietary law. The next morning, he roasts them over a fire. Flies buzz around the carcass of a young fox; Vigdis yearns to pray to some saint or other. Confusion. Nightly fears. Gentle wind in the morning twilight. They set off at once and by afternoon are close to where Méréglise is today.

Then, without warning, by the edge of some burgeoning young wood, he throws his arms around her, overcome by doubt and anxiety. She tries to shrug him off; he squeezes her tighter. It's like a flame rushing through their bodies. He presses her down into the grass and tugs her clothes off, panting. She is damp with sweat, and the scent of her skin makes him dizzy with lust. She has no idea what's happening to her. She is glowing; she feels herself grow wet with unbearable desire; he's already on her and, before she knows it, *in* her, hard as a nail, but what overwhelms her is nothing but softness. She sees the doves beating their wings; dots of light fall on her face; she is overwhelmed by the smell of the dry grass. David kisses her neck, his caresses are wild and clumsy, he murmurs words she doesn't understand, they heave in waves against each other, euphoria alternates with fear and trembling, frenzying their bodies. She feels something hot run down her legs. A thrush whistles in a wind-blown young birch. Everything turns vague, there is only this endless sky in her moving, then it ends, he is twitching and crying, she caresses him, they lie there a long while recovering their breath, they are dripping with sweat, they begin again, wordless and determined, it takes almost half an hour this time, she feels something so intense it dizzies her. She hooks her fingers into the grass, then into his shoulders, the scents of their love-breath mingle. Buzzing bees in their ears, ants in the grass below, she feels the acid biting into her skin. It only heightens her arousal, their feverish thrashing, she sobs and gasps and rubs and bites and licks, it begins again after barely stopping. They go on for hours before coming to rest, he is still heavy on top of her, she underneath him, dreaming, watching a stag beetle buzz over their heads. She bursts into laughter, with a silly, thoughtless happiness in her voice, and says, Now I am your wife.

*

She is right. According to the Jewish traditions of the time, their fit of passion in an insignificant field on the edge of the woods has made them man and wife for the eternity of their short lives. They lie there until dusk and, when they rise, are still unsteady on their feet. I want more, she says, laughing as if drunk. He holds her up; for an instant, she towers naked against the backdrop of the woods. In the distance, wild dogs are chasing each other. He wraps her up in his coat to protect her from the wind and the world, pressing his nose into her wild curls of blonde hair again, into her neck. She giggles, stops, stares at him, and plumps back down in the grass; he helps her dress. They fall asleep then and there and do not awaken until the next morning, by first light and the overwhelming sound of nightingales. They kiss again, their tongues playing over each other, biting each other's lips. Again they meet in long, furious waves, she claws at his throat, he buries himself in the warmth of her thrusting hips, they lose themselves in each other, it goes on till the new sun grows hot and they sweat again, the paradisiac scent of their mutual desire. Then they lie still, panting in each other's arms and listening to the sounds in the undergrowth behind them. The place where they are will later be called Illiers, and still later be given another name, Combray, the place where young Marcel Proust will dream away his legendary summers by the overgrown hawthorns, amid yellow fields under vast skies on which time seems to have no hold.

*

In the days that follow, their progress is steady but slower; they stop every few hours to dive into the tall grass, tired and aroused, groggy and ravenous, kissing and romping for hours. Love drains them and fills them with unfamiliar energy; they cannot escape this intoxication, they forget hunger, they sleep beneath the stars and no longer seek shelter. As easy as it is to survey the landscape, these are the riskiest days of all. The slightest misfortune – a run-in with a couple of surly vagrants – could mean the end of them, because of their good clothes and the wallet at David's belt. They lie unprotected, the evening wind runs over their sweat-damp skin, and now and then they hear a wolfdog howling. One day they see a brown bear by the edge of the woods. They laugh and shrug, their hold on reality has weakened; one moment they float free and the next they are trudging again. Navigating by the sun, they head south, but after a while they realise they've drifted eastwards too. After another week they see Orléans in the distance. They keep a few kilometres west of the city, reach the sandy banks of the Loire, rinse out their clothes, bathe, and are making love in the water when a man in a flat-bottomed boat comes floating towards them. He stares; you can see him working out his chances. David stands up straight in the water and fixes his eyes on the man till he has passed. Using Vigdis's underclothes folded into a net, he chases fish for an hour or so; once he's caught three, they eat one raw and save the others for twilight, when they make a fire and roast them. Their fingers, slippery with fat, slide over each other's bodies. They decide to go on to Orleáns that very evening and find one of David's father's friends, a prominent Jewish merchant with whom he stayed on his way to Rouen.

4

In those days, Orléans had a substantial Jewish community – larger than the one in Paris. According to the chronicles, the city had more than a thousand Jewish inhabitants around the year 1090. It was a sensible place for the two of them to seek refuge, but entering a city through a guarded gate was always risky. If they said they were Jews, they ran the risk of discrimination, abuse or extortion. If she revealed herself to be a Christian woman, she might become an object of suspicion, with so many knights out looking for her; a blonde woman travelling with a southern-looking Jew was not hard to pick out. But the Jewish communities, too, were in close communication. There was a network, which sent messengers ahead to a friendly house. The chosen host could then take security measures; someone would come to fetch them outside the city gates and smuggle them into town in his covered wagon. There were as many possibilities as threats.

In Orléans, the rabbi's house serves as a yeshiva. There, David meets the renowned Rashi of Troyes, a colourful scholar who has come to discuss gardening, French idiom, Hebrew manuscripts and circumcision. They spend the night in the Jewish merchant's home. Vigdis is given new clothes. She sits resting beside a well and feels love burning in her body – how far away her parents are, the quiet of their house, her first timid steps past the yeshiva in Rouen. In the evening, she walks along the riverside with David. Children play on the bank; fishermen with small nets wade in the shallows. A man plays a simple shawm; another beats a little drum. A pack of stray dogs lies beside the river, a drunk empties his bowels where the two of them were just sitting, a horsecart creaks onward through the dust. Mosquitoes, beetles, horseflies. The chaos of life surrounds them. They burn with exhaustion, itch with excitement. They sleep in separate rooms, prepared for them at the merchant's bidding. In the morning, David slinks into her room and pounces on her as if famished. They are caught by a housemaid, who giggles and tries to join them. David holds her off; Vigdis lies still and thinks, Why do I see so many dark spots in the light?

In the merchant's house, she receives her first lessons in kashrut, the law prescribing how to prepare kosher food. She learns that animals may be eaten only if they chew their cud and have cloven hooves, and that she's forbidden to boil a kid in its mother's milk. She learns that there are two rinsing tubs, one for meat and one for milk, and two sets of dishes and cutlery. She also comes upon a strange new thing: a two-pronged fork, a rarity in those days, which shows that her host family is wealthy and well mannered. Laughing, she stabs the newfangled object into a morsel of goat's cheese and brings it to her mouth. Nausea sweeps over her, she grabs the edge of the table to stay upright but is pressed down into a chair. The women around her whisper and shake their heads.

Later, she is walking with a few Jewish women past the city's Romanesque church. She feels a stabbing pain and wishes she could go inside the cool cathedral to pray. One woman says, 'That's for the goyim.' Vigdis stares at the carvings of saints in the stone and tries not to think.

While they're on the subject of Christians, the woman says, 'When my grandmother was a child, twelve heretics were burned alive here. It was the first public burning for heresy. The whole town still talks about it today.' The story also lives on in the Jewish community. The men in question were distinguished clerics, and the debate at the tribunal is said to have been scholarly and impassioned. The piety and dignity of the accused led to confusion. Maybe the strange fervour of their faith was in fact the most threatening thing about them. Their beliefs must have resembled the doctrines of the later Cathars. They showed signs of theological rationality, taking the transubstantiation of bread and wine into the body of Christ not as a literal truth but as a symbol, of denying the possibility that the Holy Spirit could enter a person at baptism, and of ruling out forgiveness after murder and manslaughter. They also rejected the idea – again, like the Cathars – that Christian marriage provided any divine sanction. The most fascinating thing about them may have been their vegetarianism; they believed it was unclean, and forbidden, to eat animals. Innocent of any ill will, they had thought of themselves as contributing to theological debate. In the end, the accused all confessed their heretical ideas. Outside, the crowd clamoured for their execution. They were thrown in a cell and, a few days later, brought to the edge of a forest outside the city, where they were locked in a wooden cage that was set on fire. The sight of those high-ranking churchmen screaming as they perished made a great impression on the common folk. Since that time, prominent Jewish citizens have been more careful, knowing how easily tolerance can give way to hate and purges.

Vigdis Adelaïs thinks of the changes in her own life. The story shocks her; when she asks for more explanation, the women shrug. A man with a hurdy-gurdy passes. The world seems menacing yet familiar, so close yet inscrutable. Not that she knows what that means – 'inscrutable'. Those are not the terms in which she thinks. In her parents' world, she is now a heretic. To her husband-to-be, she is a convert. It's so hard to learn the prayers by heart, she blurts. The other women raise their eyebrows and ask if she can say a Jewish prayer. She stutters and stumbles; she gasps for air. One woman says she will never really be Jewish. Another takes her by the arm and says, 'It's late, let's head for home.' In that instant, Vigdis realises there's only one person left in the world who can save her: the man who has put her beyond saving.

*

After three days they have to go. They've heard there were knights in the city, asking about them – fortunately, they only went to Christian households, but you never know who may have noticed the couple on the banks of the Loire and thought they might meet the description. They are sent off with a mule, new clothes and sheets, a skin of wine, one pouch of dried meat and one of flour and matzos – back on the road, rushed and apprehensive, watchful and sticking close together, hurrying down dusty byways. The first heat of June hits them as they reach the road running south to the town of Bourges, across the marshes of Sologne. On the way there, they are stung many times by insects. They use an ointment given to them by the merchant's wife; it makes them glisten, stinks and doesn't help. They scratch themselves half mad in the hot nights under the naked sky, lying awake and listening to the cries of small wild creatures, smelling the penetrating odour of droppings nearby. Most of all, they listen for horses trotting past in the dark. Because of the heat, they haven't built a fire to keep animals at bay; that would be too risky anyway. David has made a circle of pointed sticks around their sleeping place and draped animal skins over it. It surrounds them like a small, safe citadel, but they cannot sleep until the cold of morning comes. In Vigdis Adelaïs's young belly, something is growing that she does not yet understand.

*

For days they are surrounded by lush forests, pools and cascades, herons by the waterside, fish in abundance. They eat currants, wild strawberries sweet as honey, hard wild cherries. She has learned how to bake flatbread on hot stones. She guts fish with her coarsened hands; she is starting to look like a young peasant woman. Her face is sunburned, she sometimes falls asleep standing up, and one day she vomits out everything in her body.

Afterwards, her clothes spattered with sour slime, she hiccups, has to pee, and vomits again. David lowers her onto the grass by the road and covers her with a light sheet. She sleeps until she feels the first cool breeze of the late afternoon. Then comes a thunderstorm: in the wink of an eye, the rain begins gushing and spewing down from the dark black cloud bank; lightning flashes all around them. She shrieks, makes the sign of the cross, reminds herself she can't expect help from *that* God any more, and clings to David. The mule bucks and tugs at its leads, pulls loose, and runs off through the torrent. The rain is tepid and so torrential that it's like being underwater. She has the feeling she can't breathe, lightning strikes nearby, there's no shelter in sight. They huddle together, waiting for the storm to end. God, Vigdis thinks, God of my childhood, how much I miss prayer. She prays in silent Latin as David murmurs Hebrew phrases.

As the storm drifts away to the east, they see an iridescent mist rise from the empty landscape. Which God has sent this sign? she thinks. She pinches the arm of the young man next to her so hard he jumps and raises his hand in anger – and then, shocked at his own reaction, takes her in his arms. There is nothing to say. The first stars appear in the pale blue sky. They are all alone in the world, somewhere north of present-day Vierzon, nothing more in their time than a clump of houses. As vapour rises from their clothes, they reach an inn with a worn thatched roof, where they drink verjuice at a dark table and eat hard bread with sheep's cheese served by the innkeeper. The room where they sleep that night, on a sack of straw, stirs and whispers with mice, rats and dormice.

Following their trail, I leave Rouen – after an hour of studying road-maps and consulting Google. It seems I may as well head straight south towards Évreux on the smallest country roads. Rural France rolls out ahead of me in all its early-summer sweetness. Bunches of wild roses on weathered fences, stately swans drifting over ponds, market day under flowering lime trees, bluebottles dotting the fields of grain, fruit trees in blossom, distant views, kitchen gardens and old greenhouses. Endless concrete lanes without any opposing traffic. Once every ten kilometres, I take note of the changes in the landscape, keenly aware that almost nothing has stayed the same. Near Montigny-le-Chartif, I wander what's left of the forest where David and Vigdis made love for the first time. A motorcyclist zooms past, so loud in the quiet summer grove that my heart skips a beat. There are still bilberries in the woods today; I picture what they ate, wonder whether they walked fast or took their time.

In the early afternoon, I roam the quiet streets of Illiers-Combray, a place I first visited twenty years ago. Again, I nose around the home of Proust's Aunt Léonie. Out in the garden, I find a few moments of stillness. I remember how captivated I was, the first time I came here, by the patches of colour cast by the sun through the stained-glass windows on the tiles of the old floor, which inspired Proust's musings on light and time. Now I am searching for a different light and a different time, but some hint of his hunger for intimate sensations vibrates in the midday sun as I walk to my car. I drive on to Orléans as slowly as possible.

In the evening sun, I stand on the bank of the Loire myself, watching the flat-bottomed boats, the beautiful girls showering passionate kisses on ugly boys, the peace of this hectic age. In my head David Crosby sings, *Orléans, Beaugency, Notre-Dame de Cléry, Vendôme ...*

After that, I face three hundred kilometres of black, deserted highway, staring into passing headlights as if a film's opening credits were going on forever – soundtrack by Gregorio Allegri and the divine Josquin. I peer out at time as I imagine it: dark distance, a patch of light gliding out ahead. Arriving home under northern skies at 2 a.m., I wonder, did I learn or see anything more in the past few days than I have just now, in the dark, on this nocturnal trip through my inner world? My delusive longing to sense some genuine vestige of this woman has culminated in the awareness that she's no longer present anywhere, except in my imagination.

*

A summer morning in central France. The clop of horses' hooves, rolling barrels, hammers striking in a smithy, tolling bells, yellow pennants by a crude fort. David and Vigdis stand and watch a watermill for a while. Water gurgles and tinkles and gushes and drips and runs beneath their feet through the muddy streets, which are steaming in the sun. David buys a mule, a small, fierce mount, Asiatic in appearance. The man claims someone brought it back from Jerusalem. 'Yerushalayim,' David says with a dreamy look.

Vigdis tells him about her brother Arvid in Rouen, who danced up and down the courtyard, shouting, One day I'll go to Jerusalem! Jesusalem! and her mother who corrected him with a smile: Yes, one day you will go to Jerusalem, Holy City of the Christians, and I will go with you.

And David says, Your Church of the Holy Sepulchre wasn't the only thing destroyed there. So was our Temple, centuries earlier. To hear him, without warning, address her as a stranger, as one of 'you', consigning her in an unguarded moment to her father's world ... She is silent and thinks, I have never been so alone.

The world through which they fled was embroiled in sweeping, revolutionary change, with new ideas springing up at a furious pace. I have no idea how much they knew about all that. Had David learned, in his studies, that the great philosopher Avicenna was the first to describe the nature of infectious disease? Had he heard about the innovations in dentistry by the Arabic surgeon Abu al-Qasim al-Zahrawi? And would he ever discuss such things with her? The poetry of Omar Khayyám had not yet reached the West, the songs of courtly love had not yet been written, but the cultured young men of the Rouen yeshiva may well have discussed poetry together. And it does not seem unlikely that Vigdis had learned how to read music, using the notation invented by Guido d'Arezzo some half a century earlier. The churches of her childhood resounded with the first contrapuntal songs; polyphony was on its way. Architecture was on the cusp between Romanesque and Gothic; the construction of ever-taller churches was in full swing; the world was arraying itself, as the monk Raoul Glaber had written, in a white mantle of churches.

5

After Orléans they may have made swift progress, though the Loiret was trickier to cross than the Loire – narrower, yes, but faster-flowing, with eddies here and there. I pass through the forests of Sologne, where the insects buzz around the ponds. Many stands of young trees have shot up recently; they alternate with pools and open fields. On the bank of the Ardoux, I eat a sandwich and doze by the water. Over the centuries, the area has been drained; the terrain must have been much marshier in their day and difficult for travellers. The next stream, the Cosson, now runs just behind the seventeenth-century Château de la Ferté Saint-Aubin. It is a castle fit for a king, bright and very comfortable. In the capacious cellars, a portly woman gives a cooking class once every two hours in a kitchen with period furnishings and a stuffed boar on a hook. I linger in the large chambers, the entrance hall, the classical gardens, the tranquil and somewhat infuriating setting where aristocrats once enjoyed the fruits of all the underground labour in the souterrain.

On days when Vigdis and David could stay in cities with Jewish families, they may have eaten very well. When they stayed with peasants, David must have explained to Vigdis what she was no longer allowed to eat as a convert. In the Middle Ages, all social classes ate small birds of almost every kind, mostly in pies or roasted whole until even the bones were soft and edible. Pheasant, quail and thrush were served regularly. Haute cuisine included dishes like swallow tongue consommé. Copious meals were consumed by those who could afford them – a one-pan recipe for an aristocratic family might well have called for ten eggs per person. A well-to-do family had their pick of the produce of the tenant farmers and serfs living on their estate. The same is true of the feudal lords, but they collected many times more tribute. A great deal of pork was served, but David would not have touched that. Vigdis changed her diet to match her new faith. When they journeyed through fields and woods from one city or refuge to another, they brought provisions – watertight leather skins of wine and water, dried meat, matzos, hard bread and cheese. They found fruit everywhere; it was summer, and bilberries, blackberries and raspberries grew in profusion, along with early apples and pears, though these were often the hard fruit of wild, still-uncultivated trees. They also ate vegetables: carrots, peas, a lot of beans and beets, shallots, garlic and chives, and even leeks and watercress were on the eleventh-century menu. They could catch freshwater fish in ponds and streams.

All sorts of herbs were gathered for medical use. Almost every herb was good for something; there were large albums of dried medicinal plants, and a wide variety of extracts were recommended, and taken, for complaints of the most diverse kinds. Hildegard of Bingen – born in 1098, the year Vigdis Adelaïs returned from Egypt – later became the first to write a detailed medicinal manual. They may have had a small supply of medicines with them, ointments and sachets of herbs and grains.

*

For a while, they follow the Rère on its winding course through the Arcadian forest. They bathe in it, rest, catch a little sleep. He teaches her the Shema Yisrael. She sings old Flemish songs to him that she learned from her mother.

They're in the Berry region, which for me is associated with George Sand and Chopin. They travel on to France's oldest known vineyard, in Menetou-Salon, mentioned in chronicles as early as 1063. When David produces a silver coin from his wallet, they are welcomed by the

Seigneur de Menetou. He is mentioned in the archives of the nobility: a generous, big-hearted man, devout but broad-minded. He often donated wine to religious orders in the region, most often to Saint-Sulpice Abbey near Bourges. He gives the young couple everything they need to recover their strength; his cruciform garden, in full bloom, is a joy to behold, a private little paradise with square beds of herbs, flowers and vegetables. They stay there for five days, and in the evenings they chat with the seigneur, who wishes them only the best and gives them advice for their journey. When they leave, he returns the silver coin with a friendly nod.

Like a hasty pursuer, I stay there only one night. Just before midnight, I am still out wandering around the garden. The moon is full and shines in the brackish water of a pond fringed with tall bamboo. Light glows from the windows of today's château as in a painting by René Magritte.

*

To reach the city of Bourges from the north, they must have crossed three rivers: the Moulon, the Yèvre and the Yévrette. There were bridges over the first two even in their time; the third had none until almost a century later, but there must have been some kind of ferry.

I don't know who they stayed with; all traces of the medieval Jewish community have been wiped out. But the safe, civilised life of the city surrounded them. It would be another ten years before Bourges became a royal domain. Bells were ringing all around, reverberating from small churches, pealing from high in the cathedral, clanging in a cloistered courtyard. The cathedral was still a Romanesque, early-medieval building. The sculptures of saints must have been painted in vivid colours, the usual practice in those days. It made the church entrance look almost Oriental – a motley beauty that surprised even David.

There in Bourges, I recognise her at once in a double sculpture in the Saint-Étienne cathedral of a couple seated face-to-face, praying in utmost concentration like two figures engaged in performance art. The female figure on the left, executed in several kinds of marble, seems to me the perfect likeness of the girl from Rouen – even though I know it's a portrait of Jeanne de Boulogne, the fifteenth-century Duchess of Berry. This is the face, the expression, I had in mind in Rouen – no, even earlier, when I saw her limping down the slope to my mountain village in Provence. She too must have worn rich robes like this one in her younger years in Rouen – although the suggestion of rich brocade is more appropriate to the married noblewoman I have here before me. The marble of her outer garment is painted with intricate motifs; her small breasts are gracefully accentuated by the delicate pleating; and the unpainted marble that includes the cuffs of her lace undergarment reflects the great refinement of the artist's culture. Her hands are folded with serene precision, and the delicate thumbs pressed together suggest concentration in prayer. The pointed fingertips gleam. The high collar around her neck, emerging from under her robe to cover her up to her earlobes, conceals and emphasises the frail power of her neck and head, the force of her will and complete repose of all her hope in prayer. The back of her large belt sports a broad clasp, its leather strap dangling decoratively into the train of her robe.

I am not the first visitor to be smitten by the realism of this sculpture. When Hans Holbein visited this church in 1524, he made a meticulous sketch of the likeness of Jeanne in prayer. He too felt the intensity of this figure, just as I feel the urge to touch her, to lay my hand on her narrow shoulder. Vigdis Adelaïs must have kneeled the same way in the church in Rouen; these are the near-aristocratic hues she exchanged for modest Jewish garb, entering the world of a different nobility.

I take in the play of morning light and shadow in this immense space with its double aisles, the intense serenity of the perspectival patterns created by the huge pillars, the way the colossal scale of this architecture evokes the light, silent life of her inly muttered prayer. Through a high stained-glass window, an oval shaft of light falls, sparkling with bright dust on the old floor. In my head, Hildegard of Bingen's ethereal music.

6

They are sad to leave Bourges. Their hostess urges them to be careful. They nod and assure her they'll look out for danger. They follow a sandy, winding path, breathing in the summer air; they are almost halfway to Narbonne.

But this time, along the edge of a forest south of Bourges with impenetrable underbrush, things go badly wrong. An unbelievable creature leaps out from the brambles and stinging nettles and blocks their way. A scruffy farm boy, somehow grown gigantic, a large, impressive savage in a bunch of stinking rags, with a cap on his lumpish head, he swings his heavy fists, stammering, gurgling and raging. Samule, he growls, heh heh, Samule, he grins and draws a rough serrated knife, Samule, ay-oh, ay-oh, Samule. What in God's name does he mean? He cackles like a man possessed. Under the cap, his eyes have a lunatic gleam. The Devil, Vigdis thinks. It is the serpent from hell come to take me. She sees his feet, great, gross and bare in the furrows of the blocked road. They stand as if paralysed. Vigdis grabs David's arm, and he jerks it away, reaching for his dagger. Samule, ay-oh, ay-oh, the man howls, like an animal in pain. He throws himself at David, who kneels low and jumps at his attacker's belly, giving him the chance to plant his knife in David's shoulder. As Vigdis screams, two other men leap out of the bushes and grab her, tearing open her clothes and reaching between her legs. Their breath smells like rotten fish, she thinks as a fist hits her face, everything reels, she is lying on the ground, her nose bleeding, her clothes tugged and torn off her, burning pain, she doesn't know quite where, she hears the giant roaring, he falls back with his hands on his belly, blood running from under his heap of rags. Then the ravisher writhing over her topples forward like a log, his skull half shattered. The third man flees. She sees the panic in David's eyes as he stands over her, stabbing his dagger deep into her violator's back, twice, as he lies dying on top of her, beside her the giant's death-rattle, Samule, he moans, ay-oh, ay-oh, Samule, thick blood runs from his mouth, he regains his feet, rushes at David, misses, stumbles. David swipes at his throat, slicing it open in one stroke. The giant collapses on Vigdis and the man whose limbs are still twitching on top of her. She feels her breath cut off by the enormous weight. David tugs at the giant, who is choking on his own blood, a gulp of dark fluid welling up from his slit throat. He doesn't have the strength left to pull away that colossal body. Vigdis is being slowly crushed, she passes out. David pulls and yanks till at last the giant rolls off her with a final spasm. Underneath is the dying man, the rapist, still rolling his eyes. Vigdis wakes up again, tries to scream, can't. With a lurch of her hips, she pushes the man off her at last. He rolls into the dry grass beside her, spreading a stench of shit. David, bleeding from three stab wounds, his face bone-white and blood-smeared, his whole body trembling, tumbles to the ground. She cannot stand up to help him. There they remain, lying less than a metre and a half from each other. She sobs, he pants. Above them, a thrush sings in a tree, leaves blow, a church bell rings not far away, then she knows nothing.

It's pitch-dark around them, the deepest hour of the night. The Great Bear has drifted out of heaven's dome. From somewhere, an owl's melancholy cry. A few vague stars twinkle between the silent, wind-ruffled leaves. Something is moving, not far from her, she is cold, her whole body shivering. Then a figure teeters over her, dark and swaying. This is my death, she thinks. She hears panting. Only then does she recognise David. He falls again, next to her, they clasp hands, lie that way till morning.

The cold awakens them. The mutilated bodies next to theirs send them scrambling to their feet in confusion. The man feels the sting of his stab wounds, the woman the burning and chafing of the rape inside her. They stand shivering in the dew, then stagger a few metres away from the horror. Their mule is gone and their bags along with it. The wallet of silver coins still hangs from David's belt. They sink to the ground again, lie there till the sun brings warmth. 'Warmth of the dew,' he says, a long time after. 'In Hebrew, that's a girl's name: Hamoutal. That will be your new name, when you have your Jewish baptism: Hamoutal, warmth of the dew. He tries to embrace her; she twists out of his arms with a raw sob. Saying nothing, she stares at the passing clouds. Through her head runs an old prayer she dares not say aloud. Lustrous bluebottle flies are already buzzing around the giant's corpse.

7

Something inside them has snapped. They shamble on, broken and exhausted, to a large farmhouse where the farmer treats them with a herbal balm and shows them to a couple of hard benches where they can rest. They answer his questions in one or two words, unable to string whole sentences together. When he hears who stabbed David, he crosses himself three times and mumbles something they can't make out, except for the word Samule. David asks what he means by that, but the farmer shakes his head in a vigorous no, places his gnarled index finger over his mouth, and looks at them wide-eyed with warning.

They sit on a bench staring ahead till night falls. At some point, they notice their mule grazing in the field in front of the farmhouse, unflustered, the full bags still strapped to its sides.

Vigdis has nightmares. The next day she wakes with a fever; her whole body trembles. She knows nothing about infections but can feel that something in her pelvis is burning. Days go by before she begins to recover; David stays with her, his injuries healing. Only his wrist still bears a festering wound where the knife went into it. He cares for her and for himself. They bathe in infusions of herbs that the farmer's wife gathers on their instructions. They drink broth and eat chicken; Vigdis vomits it all back up.

After a week David finds her kneeling next to the hard bed, beset by fears and surrendering to the prayers of her youth, her fine lace undergarment stained by her dingy surroundings, her blood and her recurring fits of sweating, her hands folded and shaking, a rosary looped around her thin wrists, weeping: she wants to go back home, she can't do this, it's too much, she can't betray her God, it's all impossible, it's pride, and this is her brutal punishment for denying the God of her parents, in fact she deserves to die, she should join a convent to atone for her sins, the Devil will find her. David remains silent, kneels beside her, murmurs a Jewish prayer, closes his eyes, stays there by her side. Then says, There's no way back. If you ever return to Rouen you'll be burned as a heretic. She stands up without words, lies down on the bed, stretches out, and remains there motionless as an effigy on a Gothic tomb, her arms alongside her frail body. She hardly breathes. She shuts her eyes.

*

They are more than halfway there. The fields are barren; the scents of the north gradually give way to drier southern smells. There are small farmhouses roofed with primitive slabs of shale or thick layers of thatch, and now and then fences braided from supple willow branches, inside which goats and sheep or a few pigs roam. Then once again there is nothing at all but land, a road pocked with bumps and hollows, an old maple tree under which they rest, a ruin with a mean, growling dog. Then the dark wooded slopes of the Auvergne rise up ahead. Almost from one day to the next, it turns damp and chilly in the shade. They search for level routes through valleys and passes but sometimes have no choice but to go up or down a steep incline where their mule must feel its way forward, step by step. Near the Church of Saint-Éloy, they run into a huge boar snorting and churning the soil with its head. It looks up, startled, and charges; they flee into the church.

The road winds left and right, up and down. A light mist shrouds the forbidding gorge carved by the Sioule. The next day, the ground beneath their feet is black with volcanic ash. Here and there they stumble upon a menhir and don't know what to make of it. They move on. Small churches are often a refuge for the doubt-ridden woman, who has fallen silent. Then one day they see Clermont's two Romanesque churches in the distance. They fall into each other's arms and take heart again.

8

By evening, I am driving into the city of Clermont-Ferrand. The heat is still oppressive, cars swarm out of the market halls and *supermarchés*, it's hard to find a parking spot, I'm hungry and tired. Walking out of the parking garage, I see the black volcanic stone of the Cathedral of Our Lady of the Assumption looming ahead. This is not one of the Romanesque churches the two fugitives saw. A century before Vigdis and David arrived here, her Viking forefathers had destroyed the city's holy places. By the time the two of them reached Clermont, three successive churches had been erected on this site; they saw the third, built at the behest of Bishop Stephen II. Today's cathedral dates from three centuries later, but the tenth-century crypt has been preserved, though I won't have the chance to see it for myself. It's open to visitors for just one hour on Wednesdays; the old God must know why. The cathedral's lofty interior is too crowded; I step back outside. Among the paving stones are metal plaques depicting Vercingetorix and Pope Urban II.

I search for the Basilica of Notre-Dame-du-Port and find it in a small, enclosed square. The great age of the church is apparent from the fact that you have to descend more than ten steps, well below street level. What you find when you enter is stunning. The interior is tinged a surprising shade of light yellow; despite its brightness, the architecture is massive. The rays of evening sun fill the space as if it were new and weightless; there's something Byzantine about it. The basic structure dates back to the sixth century, but the church was rebuilt in the eleventh after being torched by Normans. It must have been a meaningful, poignant place for Vigdis, stirring up all her conflicting feelings anew. The church is so exceptional that in 1998 UNESCO added it to the World Heritage List.

I look around in amazement at the short, squat columns on the upper level of the central dome, and at the contrast between the massive pillars and the allegorical scenes in relief on their grey stone capitals. Austere chandeliers hang low like the outlines of six-petalled flowers, almost reminiscent of a synagogue. The stained-glass windows are intact and filter the light in a hushed, mystical way. A basin of holy water protrudes from one wall, so massive, dark and old that I feel new hope of touching something Vigdis once touched.

The sense of standing at a momentous crossroads becomes overpowering as I descend into the crypt. I picture the young refugee coming here to pray for the last time, to ask forgiveness for her conversion. She knows that soon enough she'll be immersed in the mikveh, the ritual bath, and become Jewish, and she knows she can't go home again. David is waiting outside; he has Jewish acquaintances in the city, people he met on his way to Rouen, and he knows that Vigdis must find her own resolution here. This is where Hamoutal must begin to say farewell to Vigdis Adelaïs.

But what she cannot know is that this crypt is the very place where, several years later, Pope Urban II will come to pray, the day before he goes to the fields outside Clermont – now taken over by supermarkets and petrol stations – to make his historic speech calling for the First Crusade. This will have the incidental, irreversible effect of ruining her life in the distant village in Vaucluse.

After the Rouen yeshiva, this crypt, with its columns more than a thousand years old, is the second place where I've come so close to what she saw and touched. One building is Jewish and the other Christian, but they stem from the same uncompromising age, built in the same spirit. Long before those tall, impressive Gothic churches, there was this austere, fundamental intimacy, which offers a strange consolation and shelter from the slaughter, fanaticism, poverty, misery and riot outside the doors, from malodour and decay, from all the foulness of the world that has left her scarred, from the whole of that violent, volatile, irresistible life that has brought her to this place – here it falls silent, here the stone of the basilica reaches out a hand to the stone of the Rouen yeshiva, and makes her realise how truly she is driven by love, by passion for the man who is waiting for her somewhere in this city. She forgets time, sinks into thought, and feels everything come to rest.

An hour later, she bobs back up into the light of the evening sun. She is walking a few metres ahead of me in black leggings, a light blue shirt and white trainers. She sees the crowd; she smells the stupor of the present. She enters a tall dark house, takes her lover's hand and feels encouraged. A few more weeks and they'll be in Narbonne. The twilight is brief and warm.

*

I spend the night in an old castle south-east of Clermont. Château des Martinanches is a dark and somewhat dismal building, some of which dates back to the eleventh century. It lies hidden in the wooded depths, encircled by a canal partly lined with stones from an earlier building. The forests of the Auvergne are dark and lonely.

9

David and Vigdis have now arrived in the Cantal region. Sometimes he affectionately calls her Hamoutal, though she'll have a different, official Hebrew name after immersion in the mikveh. She responds with a shake of her head and a half-smile, putting a playful finger to his lips: Narbonne is still far away, she says.

They see Saint-Flour ahead, a fortified town on a high rock. Something tells them not to enter, even though they cannot know that a few days earlier Norman knights passed this way and gave out their description. Clouds of butterflies and moths: peacocks, red admirals, hawkmoths, blues. Bee-eaters come out in flocks, swerving silhouettes with translucent wings against the hot blue sky.

They follow the bank of the Alleuze for a while, to the Bès river gorge, which they cross. Before nightfall they have reached the abbey in Nasbinals. As fugitives, they are entitled to spend the night at the monastery of Saint-Victor de Marseille. The next day they hike through the Aveyron region, passing the hill of Severus, named after its sixth-century Roman owner. The landscape opens up again; they are moving faster every day.

Not long afterwards, they stand at the confluence of the Tarn and the Dourbie, just before arriving in Millau. There they stock up on fresh provisions, cross the Tarn and make their way through the hills, where the road rises again. They must continue due south. They track the position of the sun and sometimes stop around noon to nap under an oak tree. Each day, the heat grows more intense.

*

Almost ten centuries later, I drive across the spectacular bridge high above Millau. It feels like flying over the valley in a miniature plane. Below, like tiny insects, they plod onward, past the Millau Valley now and searching their difficult way through the Causses. The pastures are dotted with rocks and boulders; there is fierce light, stinging sun, small white clouds dispersed by the hot wind soon after sunrise, arid grassland, low shrubs, palm trees, juniper bushes, wild apricots, under-growth. Hérault is close by, and David is feverish with excitement. They no longer travel in the afternoon now, but only in the morning, from the first hint of dawn to around eleven. Then they rest and eat, sleep until late afternoon, move on in the early evening, and stop at dark. Near Larzac, monks are hauling large stones for an abbey or hospital.

In the little village of Lunas, near the banks of the Orb, they rest for a few days. Just north of the village is a sixth-century church dedicated to St George. They sit down on a few Roman stones. Below, on the riverbank, a church of St Peter is being built. They hear the slow, tired rhythm of the stonemasons. Vigdís describes the churches of her childhood and how the Christian faith filled her with awe. David lays his hand on hers. He has a distant cousin here, who puts them up for a few days. They gather their strength for the unknown adventure awaiting them. From Lunas, they more or less follow the course of the Orb to Bédarieux, where for the first time the landscape becomes truly southern. At every step, swarms of locusts fly out of the dry grass on colourful wings. Just before they reach Bédarieux, they pass underneath the large Roman aqueduct, still in use in their time. David is in high spirits and relieved to feel the southern heat again; for him, this climate is a homecoming. The young northern woman finds it harder to adjust. So much is unfamiliar: she's never heard the chirping of the cicadas before, the scent of thyme and rosemary is sharp and bracing. She smells and tastes wild fennel for the first time, and something like homesickness mixes with jittery anticipation.

France has cast its spell on me: I'm behind schedule. To avoid a traffic jam, I drive through the sheltered Alagnon river valley, turn onto a still narrower road, and find myself in the tiny village of Blesle. Time comes to a halt again. Water murmurs behind small kitchen gardens; in the graveyard, lizards guard the souls of the dead; one old church has its doors open. Cool air, blue light. Ah, this is what I'm meant to see here; my detour has put me back on track, their ancient trail is under my feet. There's an ageing cartwright, who has a covered wagon for them. They buy it for a song; the man harnesses their reluctant mule and invites them to join him for supper. They feast on bread, vegetables and clear water and feel themselves breathe freely again, as do I. In the Abbey of Saint-Pierre, a convent, they pay for lodging; no one asks who they are.

I return to exploring the streets, drawing deep breaths. History is out here for the taking, a skittish thing, like a patch of light with a human shape, surrounded by dark, lost lives. Look, David scrapes his hand on a thick wall; it's not serious, but it swells and bothers him. They leave in their new wagon, rattling over the bumps and potholes in the old roads. They are a half-day's journey ahead of me. In that time, they could travel about the length of this line of cars inching along the hot highway.

*

A few days later, near the present location of Octon, they sleep amid unkempt vineyards in a kind of barn, a large building open on the south side, where the Salagou reservoir is today. A cooling breeze blows through it; they see the stars through the holes in the roof and curl up in stale straw. They nod off to the sound of wolfhounds howling in the distance. In the middle of the night, they hear voices. Vigdis, awake in a flash, shakes David's shoulder. The voices are rough, boozy and full of laughter, coming ever closer. What David does then is nothing short of absurd; his fear brings it welling up out of him. He barks, loud and gruff like a wild dog, growling and howling like a man possessed. He sits upright, and the noises he makes become more and more alarming. A devil seems to have taken hold of him. When he stops, he can hear the men walking away again, talking in low voices. He slumps back into the straw; Vigdis lays her hand on his thumping chest. It's been a long time, but they make cautious, tentative love, moving against each other in silence, slow and subdued, half undressed, pulling their clothes awkwardly out of the way.

The next day, as they pass Béziers heading west in the late sun, dusk comes sooner than expected. Not long after that, the darkness is complete – gone are the long northern twilights of her childhood. It takes them a while to find shelter; they grope their way towards a fire in the distance till at last they reach a group of drunk fishermen. One of the voices sounds familiar from the night before. Ha ha, a tall thin man says, there's a fine-looking thing. Isn't that the blonde bitch those two knights were asking about yesterday? The fishermen point the way to a barn, shouting obscenities. They walk on past, afraid the men will come after them in the night. A couple of kilometres further, they find a deserted reed hut where they fall fast asleep as the warm wind blows through the crevices. Around them, pine trees rustle. The wind is mild and tastes of salt.

They awaken with a start at first light to the braying of a wild ass next to the hut. Vigdis's body burns with the knowledge that today they will reach their journey's end. Excited, they take to the road. Later that day they pass the Oppidum d'Ensérune. Even there, so close to their destination, they must remain on guard. They've heard tell of the blood feud between the supporters of Raymond Bérenger and those of the vicomtes of Carcassonne. Vicomtesse Ermengarde was in power in their day. There is unrest in these parts; the Peace of God has been imposed but is often breached. The fugitives avoid contact with the locals. David is well informed about this conflict, which goes back several decades and has led to disputes even in Narbonne and Barcelona. His excitement grows; he is on familiar terrain. In a few hours, he will be home and can introduce his blonde, Christian, Norman fiancée to his Jewish family. But instead of cheering him up, this thought sobers and worries him. He is tense, squeezing her tight every time they stop to rest, as if trying to protect her from what's coming. After another ten kilometres or so, they bathe on the banks of the Aude. They are nearly there. Every horseman they hear in the distance sends them racing into the trees for cover. A church tower gradually comes into sight in the flat landscape, shimmering in the hot, salty air. Cicadas screech in the dry branches above them.

They sell the small black mule to a merchant and take a ferry across the slow-flowing Aude. On the other side, they find another, smaller boat, which carries them to the waterway in the heart of the old city, later known as the Canal de la Robine. This is where Vigdis, stepping out of the boat with shaky legs, overheated and tired, first sees, on the bank by the market, the famous Chief Rabbi Richard Todros, *le Roi aux Juifs de Narbonne*, the man who will become her father-in-law. And the moment she sees him, she knows she has become Hamoutal for the rest of her days.

IV

Narbonne

1

I'd never formed an image of Narbonne; maybe that's why I'm so surprised and charmed by this serene city, ten kilometres from the sea, bathed in Mediterranean light, founded long ago by the Romans, with a canal running through it. Leafy avenues and side streets. Aristocrats' houses and spacious courtyards. Yellow stone, blue sky. The intensity of southern colours seen through northern eyes.

The home of Richard Todros, direct descendant of the biblical David, is barely one hundred metres from the canal, which leads from the River Aude through the city to the sea. Halfway down the sleepy row of shops, I find a cul-de-sac: the Impasse Jussieu. Jussieu is a widespread surname in France nowadays, but its original meaning was 'of Jewish descent'. This alley must have been the heart of the Jewish quarter, right in the historic centre. Narbonne was still taking shape in the eleventh century, and its wealthy Jewish community was an influential presence. Numerous Spanish Jews who had fled the escalating tensions in Moorish Spain ended up here. They brought along Spanish and Moorish influences, which changed how Hebrew was written. A series of tolerant archbishops acted as their protectors – thinking, no doubt, of the high tariffs they could demand from Jewish moneylenders.

Jewish intellectuals in Provence were often highly educated and had absorbed the elegance of Spain's courtly culture. They were open-minded and got along well with their Christian neighbours. Furthermore, Provençal women in general enjoyed a high social status, better than in most other communities. I try to imagine David's sophisticated family making a place for the young Christian woman their son had brought home from distant Normandy. An appropriate response would require dialogue, tolerance and an open mind.

The day after their arrival, David's father invites the two of them to the synagogue. Vigdis, who is doing her best to become Hamoutal, trips over the seam of her robe and almost stumbles into the large candelabrum. The old rabbi takes her by the elbow, bearing her weight for a moment. She is mortified; her heart pounds. The men go on to the Talmud school, a yeshiva once built on Charlemagne's initiative, where they discuss how to handle her official conversion. But first, she has a great deal to learn; her future mother-in-law will take charge of her education. The other women in the house will teach her how to behave in social situations and manage a household. For the first few months after the wedding, the couple will stay in his parents' spacious home.

Through waves of panic and disorientation, Vigdis feels a confusing new power raging inside her. Deep in the night, she tries to adjust to the thought that after leaving behind her whole past, she is now leaving her lovely names behind too.

She dreams. A man with a long beard throws her a staff; she grabs it, and it turns into a snake. She throws the snake in the water; it becomes a staff again. The water parts. The man is young now, waving to her from the shore.

She wakes with a start, doesn't recognise the room, looks outside; the sunlight blinds her, almost taking her breath away. That same day a Greek Jewish woman named Agatha is assigned as her companion, an elegant lady from Alexandria with large gold rings on her fingers in the shape of tiny snakes.

*

Two major Roman roads meet in Narbonne: the Via Aquitania to the west and the Via Domitia to the east. Thanks to its location at this major crossroads, the city grew rapidly. For centuries, the Arabs considered it the spearhead of their thrust into Gaul. They were reluctant to give up Narbonne. As late as the tenth century, the Arab geographer Zuhri wrote that the Christians there would have to turn and flee to escape beheading, and could fight till the end of their days if they wished but would never take back the city. At that stage, his words were a mixture of nostalgia, wishful thinking and bluff, rather than a realistic report. But thanks to Zuhri, I also know that in those days there was a large bridge over the placid canal where, as I walk along the bank one sunny Sunday afternoon, a flea market is in progress.

Unlike in Rouen, it is impossible to determine the yeshiva's exact location. But we do know the site of the old synagogue: around the corner from where the shops are today, in the Rue de l'Ancien Port des Catalans. David and Hamoutal probably lived nearby. The cathedral, like the one in Rouen, was just a few steps away from the Jewish quarter; members of the two faiths crossed paths every day.

At the end of the Impasse Jussieu I find a short flight of steps and a fence. Beyond, I see a garden and, through an arch of greenery, a portal, probably a side entrance to the nearby church. The cool of the paving stones in the late morning, the sound of doves' wings flapping in the immaculate air. Silence. Here Vigdis Adelaïs, daughter of a Christian Viking, became the Sephardic daughter-in-law of Richard Todros, chief rabbi of southern France. Here she underwent the Jewish ritual of conversion, 'dying to her former life', in the words of the prayer that accompanies the immersion of proselytes. Here she descended into the living water of the Jewish bath, the mikveh. The ritual even specifies the volume of water: forty seahs. Each seah is about fourteen litres. That makes more than five hundred litres of water that had to be brought here from the River Aude, for the water must come from a living source.

Unlike a woman cleansing herself after menstruation, a prospective convert cannot carry out this ritual alone; three rabbis must be present as witnesses. David stands next to his father and reads a prayer. The girl is escorted by Agatha, who helps her remove her outer garments; she keeps her light underclothes on. Yesterday evening, she announced that her chosen name was Sarah. She has made herself beautiful, trimming her fingernails and toenails as this purification ceremony requires. She hears them reciting the blessing, *Baruch atah HaShem Eloheinu melech ha'olam* ... She sits down on the stone seat, probes with her toes underwater for the rough limestone step, and has never felt so alone. The cold makes her flinch and takes her breath away. She trembles from head to toe, closes her eyes, hesitates. She pushes off. As she sinks into the bath, it feels bottomless. In the synagogue, a slight sob is heard, something like a muffled cry, sloshing water. Then she vanishes, letting herself drop, deep, feeling her heart skip a beat in the bitter cold; she holds her breath, keeps her head underwater for the count of ten – it seems an eternity. Darkness surrounds her; she can feel the rough floor of the mikveh scraping her knees now. Her blonde hair fans out over the surface of the dark bath. A few air bubbles rise through the water. Will she stay down below, disappear from the face of the earth? It's as if a womb has swallowed her, a timeless womb that has borne her out of the world and into a lightless eternity. In a flash, she sees before her the baptismal font in the church in Rouen, not much more than a dish, just large enough for a newborn baby. Here her whole body is sinking into the ice-cold depths that draw her in, as if she will disappear through the bottom into another dimension. For an indivisible instant, she feels the violation deep in her body again, long ago by the edge of the forest somewhere in an empty landscape. Now she is so overcome by emotion that she sobs and breathes in water. Coughing and hiccuping, she surfaces, wipes the wet hair out of her eyes, looks around in a daze, and lets out a sigh; the echo rises to the decorated ceiling, past the burning candles in their holders, to the sunlight, the world, the intent faces staring down at her. Agatha reaches out, pulls her up, helps her back on the stone seat, and holds out a towel, in which she lets herself be wrapped up like a child. There she sits, dripping and panting. She hears prayer; the men's droning voices calm her. She thinks she sees a white dove patter through the patch of light by the open door. The slight swell of her pregnant belly, visible through her wet shift, is enough to tell the worldly-wise Roi aux Juifs that this ceremony of rebirth has acquired a double significance for the continuation of his own lineage; the proselyte, now reborn, has become Jewish through and through, and can carry on his line. The children of this fair-skinned foreign woman will be, in the fullest sense of the word, his grandchildren.

*

Hamoutal, having solemnly relinquished her Norman name, soon feels safe in the erudite community. Five weeks after her conversion ceremony, she again lowers herself into the mikveh in strict accordance with Jewish law, this time for the purification ritual preceding her wedding. She has already been separated from David for weeks, living in the closed women's quarters; she has laid out the prayer shawl that she must present to him; she recites Jewish prayers. She has found peace, aside from the few nightmares in which she seems to wander through a desolate landscape of rough limestone and keeps tumbling into a dark hole, calling for help. On the day of her wedding it rains; sheets of tepid water lash the building fronts, leaving her clothes drenched as she walks to the synagogue with the women. She is pushed ahead, a friendly push, a large hand in the small of her back; she sees the door to the little side room where her husband-to-be is waiting for her with the other men of the family. Entering through the low door, she finds David in the traditional robe she had made for him. She steps forward in her cream-coloured suede slippers; her amber gown rustles around her body like a skin slowly letting go. Together, they say the prayer for forgiveness, which she has learned by heart. On a marble stand lies the *ketubah*, the marriage contract she must sign with her new name Sarah; when her hand touches her husband's, the contact is like a knife that tears through her skin and makes her bleed inside. David takes a step forward and covers her face with a light gauze veil. She breathes like an animal in a trap; she is as light and fragile as a petal on the wind. Surrounded by men and women carrying candles, she is led to a *chuppah*, or canopy, at the synagogue entrance.

David is handed a glass wrapped in cloth; he crushes it ceremoniously under his foot. She listens as more blessings are recited. It all seems so unreal, as if everything she does is part of a dream.

The wedding feast is modest but in good taste. The guests include many Spanish-speaking Jewish intellectuals. She understands little of their abstruse conversation, feels exhausted and ill at ease, eats almost nothing, drinks the sweet fruit juices, looks around in a slight fuddle, watches the sun sink behind the swaying myrtles by the wall in front of the old house. Her nose is red with sunburn.

*

In the weeks that follow her wedding she keeps noticing, again and again, the many ways in which she's travelled to a different world. She has to adjust to the listless heat of the afternoons, which can go on till early October. She gradually learns her way around the city. She visits the market with other Jewish women and sometimes walks with her husband along the main canal. She thinks back to the seagulls by the Seine, to her tall, dark childhood home, to her mother, to her affectionate, soft-voiced governess. They must have felt so betrayed, those people, her loved ones. Only now, as her life here settles into shape, does guilt sometimes clench her by the throat. At other times, she is flooded with such energy that she feels like dancing through the streets. She sits in the large rooms and cool garden, studies Hebrew, takes up the needlework her mother taught her, shows her handicrafts to the women in the house, and picks up new patterns from them.

One day in late autumn the whole family rides out to the Gruissan jetty, ten kilometres away. It's her first view of the Mediterranean, and she's overcome by tempestuous joy. The sea is wild, deep purple with white breakers. The sun is merciless; the light blinds her. The tramontane scourges the few gnarled trees and shrubs. A couple of fishing boats bob on the white-capped waves. She squeezes David's hand so hard it hurts. Laughing, he loosens her grasp and kisses her quickly on the neck. How strange this high-spirited sea, unlike anything she remembers of the grey northern mouth of the Seine. The squat tower on the shore is imposing in its mass; the wind whistles through the arrow slits, a melancholy, other-worldly sound on a glorious day.

2

On Cours de la République, along the Canal de la Robine, a large market is in progress, with clothes and all sorts of objects, useful and useless. The atmosphere is friendly; there aren't many tourists, mostly locals shopping here and strolling past. On the other side of the canal, near Cours Mirabeau, is the covered marketplace, Les Halles, packed with thick crowds of people, stalls that serve ice-cold rosé before noon, the mingled fragrances of scores of foods, and all the rainbow-coloured bounty of the Mediterranean kitchen. Markets are timeless, a tradition going back long before the Christian era. It must always have been this way: dried fish, ham, heaped fruit, wine, olive oil, rosemary and thyme, vegetables of all shapes and sizes. The age-old feast of life.

When I leave the market the back way, I stumble upon the Church of Notre-Dame de Lamourguier, which was still under construction in Hamoutal's time. Now it has been emptied out and turned into a storehouse for ancient stones from the time of the Roman occupation. I'm the only one there. The treasured stones and fragments are piled up to three metres high, row after row. Sunlight streams down from the high windows; it's like stumbling into a heathen temple. Dionysian ox heads – *boukefalas* – grin down at me from all sides. All around are the lamented dead on stelae and in low reliefs. I'm surrounded by Apollonian sun wheels, cryptic votive stones, fanciful leaf patterns, countless Latin inscriptions, and even open tombs and sarcophagi. I sit down on a stone, astonished to find this unique collection stacked there so casually. I learn from a folder that elsewhere in the city a brand-new home is being built for this *musée lapidaire*. Lapidary – that it is. I may be one of the last visitors to see the collection in its haphazard historical context. Soon these stones will be carried into their chic mausoleum, carefully numbered, well lit and accompanied by illustrations, stripped of all the past life I feel weighing down on me here in this overwhelming muddle.

In front of the Hôtel de Ville lies another unchanging stone witness: a surviving section of the Via Domitia, exposed at the bottom of a depression in the square. Large stones, polished by feet and centuries, smooth and uneven. It must have been torture for horses with small hooves and thin legs. This tremendous project, a paved road hundreds of kilometres long, connecting Spain with the Gap and Sisteron region, included a raised footpath where you could even sit comfortably. Staring at the huge, primitive paving stones, I imagine the Romans racing over them, spanning great distances in a matter of days. Children play at the edge of this remarkable site. An American street musician sings Cat Stevens: 'Oh, baby, baby, it's a wild world …' The outdoor cafes smell of cappuccino and suntan lotion. I feel a slight, strange euphoria; the present seems exotic today. I am so immersed in Hamoutal's age that I feel as if a time machine has carried me into her distant future, where I have no right to be. Tomorrow I'll drive north-east through Arles and Avignon, into the Alpine foothills.

3

Because Hamoutal is pregnant, she is lavished with care and attention. After a mild autumn, winter drenches Narbonne in crisp brightness, a new and brittle beauty: the bite of the sea wind, purple morning skies, the abrupt warmth of an early afternoon, the just as sudden cold descending at dusk, the sparkling night skies, the comets on their mysterious, fiery paths – signs that seem to come from heaven, beyond human understanding. From far away, they hear many stories of rioting and of clashes between Christians and Jews. She scarcely listens; their happiness consumes them. Hamoutal has fine clothes to wear every day now. She has become intimate friends with Agatha from Alexandria, whom she tells long stories about her old life on quiet evenings. Winter is a festival of white light and clear mornings. Everything promises to turn out well; spring is already fast approaching, January brings warm days. Then the rain floods down again and for days on end Narbonne is as grey and damp as Rouen. She sits at the window, humming and staring out at the low clouds with her hands on her swollen belly.

Then, even before the swallows return, one afternoon in the silent hours of the siesta, Agatha runs into the room in panic; she was at the market and heard three men on horseback asking about a blonde woman from the north. They demanded that anyone with news of her tell all, without delay. They promised three silver pieces to whoever would help them find and capture the woman. The crowd swarmed around the horses; a man shouted, 'I know, I know, it's that blonde Jewess in the Todros house!'

Hamoutal feels the child kick in her belly; soon afterwards, David joins her, having heard the story from Agatha, and tells her they must go this instant, never mind how or where. The elder Todros calms everyone down; he has just come from the synagogue, where he spoke to the knights and convinced them that the woman fled for Spain on her own. The men galloped off after her. They're sure to return at some stage, but for now he has gained them a little time – a few days, perhaps.

Be that as it may, Rabbi Todros writes a letter that very evening on the skin side of a used piece of parchment, carefully scraped clean, to his friend Rabbi Joshuah Obadiah in the remote Vaucluse village of Moniou, a place no one has ever heard of, reminding him of the old bonds of fellowship between them. Bags are packed, preparations are made, all in utter secrecy – it's too risky even to harness the horses, they'll have to buy some later, somewhere along the way.

*

Very early in the morning on 15 March 1091, David and Hamoutal take flight for the second time, around half past three, while the city is sleeping and the Via Domitia deserted. Just a hundred metres from the house where they'd hoped to lead a happy life together, Agatha, whispering and crying, hastens to send them on their way. Earlier, Rabbi Todros and his wife embraced the two frightened refugees behind closed doors and gave them a considerable number of silver coins, along with provisions for a week. They assured the young couple that their stay in Moniou will be temporary, that they'll send a courier ahead to inform the village rabbi, that there's nothing to fear. Rabbi Todros used a surprising word for their flight: *aliyah*, a journey up to safety, something like an ascent – it's also the word for returning to Jerusalem. For the time being, all those connotations went over Hamoutal's head, but she'll later think back to that moment many times, without ever figuring out what the old rabbi meant.

They must hurry; Hamoutal is seven months pregnant, and it will take them three weeks or so to make the 250-kilometre trip in as straight a line as possible. They could follow the Via Domitia to Apt, but then they would have to be on constant lookout for horsemen. That's too demanding and dangerous; the Roman road is a trap. But scaling the heights of Saint-Saturnin would be exhausting. After some hesitation, the old rabbi has decided that only one route will allow them to leave unseen: namely, the sea. They are bundled as discreetly as possible onto a covered wagon bound for Gruissan. Hamoutal wears a black scarf pulled tight around her blonde head. That afternoon, they board a ship. A day and half later, it drops them off at the mouth of the Rhône, where a flat-bottomed boat waits to carry them upriver to Avignon. Three days of anxiety and dismay: there is almost no wind, the boat tacks a slow course up the middle of the river, against the tideless current, they eat almost nothing, and Hamoutal sits speechless, staring at the small ripples. In those days, Avignon is little more than a fortress run by the lords of Avignon and Forcalquier. It is not a risky area for them; no Christian knight would ever expect them to go in that direction. But the familiar sense of constant menace from their earlier journey now resurfaces. During her few hours of sleep on the boat, Hamoutal has nightmares.

They disembark by a waterlogged field out of sight of the fortress's watchtowers. From there, they cross the windy plains to Carpentoracte, a small walled town with a Jewish community. There they are taken in for a few days by a family informed by the courier of their predicament. They are given a small pack animal – a mule laden with provisions, clothes and a few blankets – as well as a guide to lead the animal by the reins. The next leg of their route takes them to Malemort, in later times part of the

Comtat Venaissin. Here and there they see ancient olive trees in meadows of tough, swaying grasses, wild fruit trees with deep black bark, the primitive slate slab structures under which the herdsmen sleep, and in the east a line of Alpine foothills: the Vallis Clausa, or Vaucluse. Jutting out beyond them is the bald summit of the Mons Ventosus, the desolate mountain of the winds. From Malemort they pass through uninhabited terrain, close to where Méthamis is today. Then they cross the mountainous woods and the desolate plateau of Saint-Hubert. Pain shoots through Hamoutal's lower back; she is heavy and slow now, riding the mule led by the servant. They hardly speak a word for days.

*

By this time the three horsemen have returned to Narbonne and laid siege to the home of the Roi aux Juifs. They pound on the heavy door, shouting to him to let them in before they set his house on fire. The door swings open, and they are startled to see the lordly old rabbi looking them straight in the eye and asking what business they have there. They demand entry to his house. He curtly refuses. They repeat their threats, but they are hesitant. He swears to them that the fugitive they seek is not in Narbonne and he doesn't know where she's fled, but he suspects she took the busy road to Santiago de Compostela to repent for her sins as a Christian pilgrim. Incredulous, they draw their swords, but when he offers them his neck with a wry smile, they realise it will not do the three of them any good to start a religious riot by murdering the chief rabbi. They spend another day patrolling the city, pester a few of the residents with their questions, check out the Via Domitia one last time, shrug, and head back north to tell her parents they found no trace of the two. Who knows, they may be in Santiago by this time or even further away, in Moorish Spain, among the despicable Saracens – where the knights know better than to venture without reinforcements. Under the Atlantic skies, her father bursts into a fit of Norse berserker rage, and her mother's sobs are mixed with Old Flemish curses.

*

I drive from Narbonne to Montpellier and on to Avignon, where I pick up their trail again. From the N100, I cross the Rhône somewhere near Les Angles. There a stretch of the river forks into western and eastern branches; nearby are the bleak car parks around the high-speed railway station. Busloads of tourists are dropped off at the city gate, by the Palais des Papes. A few pleasure boats drift on the wide water.

The road from Avignon to Carpentras has become a busy four-lane motorway passing through Le Pontet – once actually a bridge, now a garish collection of large stores like an imitation of an American sub-urb. The road passes through marshy terrain, the breeding ground of the swarms of mosquitoes that plague visitors to Avignon's summer festival. To the east of Carpentras, past the Roman aqueduct, the land-scape becomes more rural. Bit by bit, in a whirl of light and memory, I am coming home. The names have changed since then. After Mazan I take the southern road to Blauvac and Méthamis, where I spend a quarter of an hour at the high lookout point by the church, gazing out over a landscape of vineyards and cypresses. I drive on to the large Saint-Hubert farmhouse, about eight kilometres further, and walk along the remains of the plague wall in the woods behind it, dark and primeval in the lonely landscape. Churned soil, boar tracks, a gleaming snakeskin, a raptor's thin cry. Instead of returning to the car, I continue on foot the rest of the way through the Bois du Défens, reaching La Plane. The end of the gorge is now on my left. The bare tops of the twisted oak trees shake in the brutal wind on this blinding morning; the road is rough and yellow. This is where they first saw the Moniou plateau in the distance.

But before that, they lose their way, descending too early into the meandering canyon of the Nesque, becoming disoriented, cursing their guide, and wading through the fast-moving river. On a slope too steep for Hamoutal to ride the mule, she sprains her foot on a large slab of rock and cries out in the afternoon silence. She sinks to her knees, closes her eyes and lays her hand on her belly. It can't be much further, David says, surveying the wild, deserted gorge. They could just as well keep following the riverbed, but they have no way of knowing that. They rise to their feet again and hobble their way up the east bank and the slope, an exhausting route; their mistake costs them nearly a day. They fall asleep under a cold night sky, the ice-white Milky Way glimmering overhead; the dwindling moon hangs red above the black horizon.

Animal rustlings, fear and light sleep, aching muscles. Lying uncomfortably on the bare ground, shivering in the twilight. Awakened by the cold, they scrabble to their feet and move on in silence. Morning glows faintly over the line of hills to the east. They sip their water; the guide heaps their bags onto the mule's back. They trudge south-east, past the plateau of La Plane, and see, in the first rays of sunlight, there in the valley that opens below, the village, like a nest of stone clinging to the rocky slope. Small birds are fluttering in the hard, dry oaks. The three of them descend to the lonely, fertile plateau, to the village from which I saw them approach in my mind's eye. They arrive, exhausted but safe, at the Grande Porte. David knocks three times with his walking stick. It is opened. A cock crows, a dog barks its greetings. It is still 1091. The Western world is sliding slowly towards catastrophe, a fault line in history, and no one can see it coming. The contemporary knows nothing.

V

Moniou

1

Not long after Yaakov was born, the young couple were assigned a home in the village, a two-storey house narrowing to a point at its southern end. Standing next to its decrepit rear wall, Hamoutal was so touched and relieved to have a place of her own again that, on impulse, she pressed her lips against the stone. Her husband stared at her in surprise and then took her in his arms. You kissed a house, he said, laughing. It was an old house with rough, thick walls. David fixed it up patiently over the months, and by that winter it was a cosy shelter from the icy wind and freezing rain. The house had a large cellar with a deep well from earlier times, which supplied them with clear, pure drinking water. Tranquillity seeped back into their hearts. Now and then they received a message from Narbonne. They lived in hope of returning one day to that spacious house in the centre of the city by the sea.

Soon another year has passed. It's the summer of 1092, and somehow they never manage to leave the village. Is it the daunting prospect of the 250-kilometre route back? Are they reluctant to put their young boy through such an ordeal? Have they received word from Narbonne that they're better off there, in anonymity, now that more and more Norman knights are terrorising the coast on the way to the occupied territory of Sicily? By now, Hamoutal is used to their hard, secluded village life. She has learned over time to take pleasure in simple work. Sometimes she sets off first thing in the morning with a few other women for a market in nearby La Loge and comes home energetic and glowing. She helps take care of the synagogue when no men are there. She weaves and mends clothes and has planted a garden of medicinal herbs in crude boxes. In the early-morning hours, before Yaakov wakes up, she studies and reads with her husband. Her build is more robust now, and her fingers are thick and red from working outdoors. David looks out through the window into the dark night; the stars are brighter than ever. He leaps up and calls out to his wife, pointing at something that shines in the night, rushing across the firmament like a runaway star. It's the great comet of 1092 shooting through the sky, striking fear into the hearts of people across Western Europe. They preach and pray, predict the coming of the Antichrist yet again, and the Christians in the village call it the return of the star of Bethlehem. The comet causes a commotion, not to mention a lively traffic in indulgences. Some quacks sell salves made from stinging nettles and goat droppings, for protecting your skin from the hellfire awaiting one and all. Herdsmen have trouble keeping their animals calm in the strange cometary light. Now David and Hamoutal stand side by side at the window. They feel no fear, only surprise. They have never believed in the prophecy of the end of days, but now Hamoutal wonders in silence how much was true of the childhood stories about the Messiah's return a thousand years later. But didn't the reign of the Antichrist come first? She lays herself down and dreams that night that a child is born to her in a stable under the sign of that uncanny wandering star, then wakes like a shot, feeling guilty about her blasphemous dream. But who will judge her? What god sends signs no human can understand? She tells David to go back to sleep and lies struggling through the darkness in her mind. The next morning, she is at the wash house early. The biting cold of the water on her hands does her good.

*

Two years later. Hamoutal is pregnant again. She feels strong and healthy. The landscape, the pure cool air, the vast silence – they cure her, day by day, of her doubts and intimate wounds. She is in the fifth month of her pregnancy, which is much easier than her first. She is well fed and carrying the baby high. She roams the plateau, where a few birds of prey soar overhead in the late-afternoon sun.

One clear day in late October, she returns with three-year-old Yaakov from the heights of Saint-Jean, where they picked wild fruit and the earliest olives. The boy walks ahead with a pointed stick. Along the way, they search for walnuts, chanterelles and ceps, which they put in the coarse wicker basket on Hamoutal's back. Under a crooked oak, they rest. In the distance, they hear the pealing bell of the small village church. A few sheep and their shepherd are roaming the grassy expanse below. Yaakov is playing with the pointed stick, tracing the path of a yellow fly as it flits from place to place as if searching for something. All at once, the fly seems to plunge its proboscis into the soil. An instant later, it flies off in a straight line. A few minutes later, it repeats the ritual. The boy is paying closer attention to the insect now, placing the point of his stick on each spot in the soil after it flies away, keeping track of its movements. When it darts out of sight, again in a straight line, after thrusting its microscopic mouthparts into the earth one last time, the boy falls to his knees and digs away the soil with his hands. To his surprise, he uncovers a large black clump, which he shows to his mother. Hamoutal recognises his find straight away. She has heard of the power of the black, misshapen truffle and the healing properties ascribed to it. Jews seldom eat truffles because the Christians hunt for them with pigs or dogs, unclean beasts forbidden to touch food. But the boy dug up this truffle with his own two hands; she smiles at him in amazement. They wait for the next fly. Yaakov follows that one too, again placing the tip of his stick on the spot where it just took off. When the insect flies in a straight line out of sight again, the child digs, and soon unearths another truffle, which he hands to his mother in triumph. Without knowing it, he has rediscovered an age-old technique for finding truffles. Over the next few weeks, the mother and child learn to identify the crooked oaks that nurture truffles by looking for the bare oval patch around the roots, because a truffle oak is a sick tree; the truffle is a fungus. Some of the villagers see it as satanic food, saying it's shaped like a deformed devil's hoof and its penetrating odour, which contaminates butter, oil and milk, is a sign of witchcraft. So Hamoutal makes her son promise to tell no one in the village about his discovery. At home, she cuts one of the clumps into thin slices; the smell fills the house. They ward off disaster and illness, she reassures David, who scratches his head and reflects that his wife's mind sometimes leaps in very odd directions.

Above the village, an eagle glides in spirals on the warmest currents of air. The sky is spotless, but over the line of hills a strange, enormous cloud forms, resembling an oyster, umbilical pink and dark purple, veined and hollow. They stare at it, fascinated, as if it were an apparition, a divine annunciation, until the cloud dissolves, leaving only a small vestige like a shell drifting on the horizon. The plateau is as solitary as a dream.

*

In the night, as the Milky Way slides like a bright stripe across the heavens, the owls over the valley seem to call out louder. The fire is warm, but through the chinks in the walls they can feel the cold wind on their backs. Obadiah's wife sits with Hamoutal and tells her the tale of the shepherd who became obsessed with the owl's cry. One moonlit night he whistled back on a whim, knowing that owls could spend all night calling to each other. The owl responded to his whistle immediately. Amused, the man whistled back a few more times. The owl kept responding. The next night he was sitting outside his cottage, and before he knew it he was whistling back and forth again with the owl on the far slope. He went on for an hour and a half, and when it was time to turn in, he stayed outside, still listening. It took him hours to fall asleep. From that time onwards, he seemed to have fallen under some strange spell; he would stay out all night till the crack of dawn, whistling like a man possessed whenever he heard the owl's cry. His wife crossed herself and told the women at the market that she feared her husband had been touched by the Devil. She tried to persuade him to stay inside at night and was once even about to bolt the door. They ended up scuffling and cursing each other. The children cried and whimpered because their father spent every night wandering around somewhere outside while their frightened mother stayed in the house and prayed. No one could sleep; the stars sparkled with menace, and a ewe gave birth to a monster with a beard.

After a couple of weeks of nightly whistling, the shepherd became obsessed with the whimsical notion that God was trying to tell him something; he had been chosen, and now he had to keep responding or else he would miss God's message. So he sat outside every night and whistled back at the owl until morning. He grew thinner and thinner; his eyes were clouded but full of fire. He scarcely ate, refused to sleep under a roof, and roved the valley whistling like a demon. A few of his sheep went missing; a wolf had its eye on his flock. He hardly noticed. After a month and a half he stopped coming home and wandered, wild and solitary, in the grip of a strange ecstasy. His brothers avoided him and took charge of his flock.

Autumn came, the nights grew colder, and the shepherd would crawl up into a tree at night, so that from this higher perch he could continue his mystical communion with the owl until first light.

Because God's message was becoming no clearer, he decided one night that the Almighty must be calling him to the other side of the valley, where the message would be imparted. He left around five in the afternoon, walked for more than two hours, and arrived after dark among the trees on the far slope. He waited till he heard the first cry and then searched the bushes and fields for the place from which the owl was calling to him, trying to come as close as he could and all the while making certain not to miss a response. After every exchange, he would hold still for some time in the foliage before taking a few more steps towards the source. Hour by hour, he drew so close to the spot that he could identify the tree from which the bird was calling. He crept up to the tree, quiet as a mouse, so as not to spook the owl, and looked up. To his chagrin, what he saw perched there was no owl but a man – who, like himself, was whistling back at the other side, though with some misgivings that night as the answering whistle moved closer and closer. The shepherd was so outraged that he started to shake the tree and kick the trunk, hollering curses at the astonished man in the treetop; he ordered him out of the tree, slammed his weight up against it, picked up stones and threw them up into the branches. The other man climbed down, frightened and bewildered, but when he saw the shepherd, he burst into uproarious laughter. The shepherd, however, driven to despair by the thought that he could have misunderstood God's voice so badly, seized the man by the throat, strangled him and crushed his head with a large stone until only blood and pulp remained. Then he ran all the way back across the valley to Moniou, foaming at the mouth, up the steep, rocky path to the site where the tower was under construction, straight to the edge of the cliff, and made an energetic leap. Two days later, in the spot where he had landed – true story, the rabbi's wife says – they found not his smashed remains, but the nest of a short-eared owl, surrounded by feathers, bones and mouse fur.

Hamoutal shakes her head and laughs at the story, but that night she lies awake and listens to the call of the owl, out there on the far slope. It's like hearing the solitude of time itself.

2

A little more than three months later, her second child is born. This time there is nothing to it: the girl slips out of her. They call her Justa. Half-witted prophets are roaming the valley; the locals hear the shrill sounds of hornpipe and chalumeau echo from the hillsides, the drum rolls, the rhythmic wheezing of rumbling-pots, the incantation of threatening prayers. Strident preachers of doom, penitents, beggars and bandits are wandering the land, combing the villages and frightening their people. The villagers stay inside. It is the strange month of February, with its slanted, unearthly sunlight growing stronger by the day.

One late morning in April, she sees four Norman knights ride through the Grande Porte; she recognises them right away by their armour. The hooves of the horses scrape over the paving stones. Their bearing has a masterful, implacable quality. They dismount and appear to negotiate with the herald. Hamoutal abandons all her chores; she can't find Yaakov and doesn't have time to reach David in the synagogue. She flees for the hills in panic, with little Justa hidden in her apron. When she reaches the edge of the cliff above the village, she sits down and stares into the depths to see if they'll pass her house. The calm of the village remains unbroken, but as dusk fades into night, she wakes in a panic under an ice-cold sky. Their loud laughter rings in the small streets below, and her heart races as she hears the northern tongue of her childhood. The child lies still and limp, bundled into her shawl. The madness of it stabs through her body and mind – what is she doing up here, for God's sake? The moon has gone, but everything is alive and quivering with an energy she cannot comprehend. The cold remoteness of the stars far above the dead quiet of the forsaken village sends chills down her spine. Somewhere in the spring leaves of an oak tree, something rustles. She waits till the drunken voices vanish through a slamming door and the silence returns. Then she steals back down along the steep, rocky path; in the darkness, it takes her almost half an hour. She shivers from head to foot as she walks, rubbing her baby girl to warm her up. At home, her husband opens the door and stares at her in horror. She creeps inside and lays the child by the fire, which slowly revives her. Hamoutal is frantic; her fear erupts in a flood of tears, almost unstoppable. Then she drags herself into her dark bed and falls asleep with her arm around her child.

*

On warm mornings in June, she bathes with the children in the wide pools formed here and there by the Nesque. The water is cool and invigorating; she can wash herself undisturbed among the bushes. After Yaakov heads for home, as her little girl sleeps on the bank, she removes her clothes and goes deeper into the water. She can't swim, but she enjoys the feel of water up to her chest. She leans back and lets herself float for a brief moment, her long locks bobbing on the ripples. Then she stands up straight again and feels some foreign object in her hair, a smooth weight sliding down her back – it's a large water snake, an albino reptile more than a metre long, which wriggles between her legs back into the water and disappears among the swaying water plants. She just manages not to scream as she watches the creature fade into the depths. She steps out of the water and dresses, still in shock. Between two bushes, she glimpses the grinning features of a peeping Tom. She is seized with worry about Yaakov. She sprints all the way

126

home. When she gets there, gasping for breath, nothing is wrong. The boy looks at her in surprise when she throws her arms around him and hugs him tight. That night a shepherd's young son is nabbed by a wolf in the field where, not long before, Hamoutal and her children were lying asleep together.

In early 1095, she realises she is pregnant for the third time.

3

These days, the old rabbi delegates more and more duties to young David Todros. Word is sent to David's father that his son will assume the care of the Jewish community in Moniou, and that the couple have decided to stay there for good. They have built a life there, David tells his father, their children are young and healthy, they have a sturdy house near the synagogue, and country life in their small community is a rich source of unexpected happiness. Hamoutal has found peace and quiet there, far away from all the ferment and intrigue of their age. They are safe from Norman knights, he explains; such knights often pass through Narbonne, but are almost never seen in this remote valley. Hamoutal shudders at the thought of returning to Narbonne only to be recognised and dragged off, after all these years, to some place far from her husband and children. David makes sure not to mention the knights who recently came to the village.

A few years earlier, after a long strategic tussle, a brilliant churchman from the Champagne region, Odo de Châtillon, was elected pope. He took occupancy of the Lateran Palace in Rome and called himself Pope Urban II. This new pope showed a good deal more talent for diplomacy than his reckless, bullheaded predecessor, Gregory VII. He established the Roman Curia, a body that broke with the tradition of papal infallibility and was thus capable of consolidating Rome's power and prestige. Urban felt deep concern about the safety of the many pilgrims headed east to Jerusalem, who were running into more and more hostility and aggression along the way. He understood very well that his first task was to restore the Church's tattered reputation in the West – and to that end, he cast a covetous eye on the East. Since the Great Schism with Constantinople forty years earlier, the Roman Church had been compelled to struggle with the Orthodox Church for influence. Urban was determined to do some great deed that would prove his power and boldness. Wherever he turned, people were calling for the liberation of Jerusalem from the accursed Saracens. Why not turn that into an instrument for restoring the glory of the Roman Church, still exhausted from its struggle with the Holy Roman Emperor? How was he to unite all those different forces? The social unrest grew, and not only among the masses; the knights, too, needed some high purpose to serve as an outlet for rising social tensions. Could the Normans who held power over Sicily be of use to him in a campaign for the ground on which the Church of the Holy Sepulchre once stood? How would the Christian knights cross the Mediterranean? The pope had sleepless nights, but a brilliant strategy was budding in his pious mind. He would go out and preach to win support for his plan. He was thinking most of all of his fatherland, France, where the unrest was greatest, but may also have sensed the interest in mounting a military campaign in the East. At night, he would fling himself to the floor of an empty church, pray, and plead for insight, feeling the cold creep into his spine.

*

Even in the peaceful valley that David described in his letters, such people passed through now and then – pilgrims and adventurers en route to the Holy City. They could be identified by their excited tone, their religious zeal, their eagerness to proselytise, and their loathing of Saracens and Jews. David preferred to keep such visitors out of the Jewish quarter, but the priest of the Church of Simon Peter at the other end of

Moniou liked to have them in the village as long as possible; by putting money in his coffers, they enhanced his status in the region. Not long after David's light-hearted letter to his father, this friction began to cast a shadow over Moniou. The Jews avoided going too far beyond the central Grande Porte; the Christians were less cautious about mingling but, even so, spent less and less time on the south side of town, near the Portail Meunier and the Jewish quarter. This opened up an invisible rift in the small community, a reflection of what was happening in many parts of Europe. Everything seemed to be propelling them towards a confrontation that no one wanted. The aggression usually went no further than insults, curses and provocations, though once in a while, things got out of hand, and yes, the Jews took most of the blame, so be it. But no political leader, no high-ranking official, had a clear view of the aggression and violence flaring up all over – except perhaps for the one man who saw the potential of that unfocused energy, if properly channelled: the new pontiff of Rome, the sly, worldly Frenchman who had already, in the second year of his pontificate, made his planned tour of France. He had studied in Reims, become a monk in the Cluniac Order, and climbed the ladder until he attracted Rome's attention. He was the ideal cement between the fragmented kingdom of France and the Holy See; he also formed a tactical counterweight to the power of the Holy Roman Emperor.

By the time Pope Urban arrived in the city of Clermont in 1095, after a long journey, he was ready to issue the great call to arms which he had been contemplating for such a long while, and which he hoped would unify the Christian world again.

His strategy involved shattering the relative peace between Muslims, Christians and Jews in the East; the dividing lines had to be clear and firm. Christ's tomb had to be hacked out of the Muslim world and made an integral part of Christendom. The only possible course of action was to reconquer Jerusalem. Urban, the brilliant tactician, turned his new idea over and over in his mind, a strange and novel concept to his contemporaries: the 'holy war'.

He went to Clermont to pray in the crypt of the Basilica of Notre-Dame-du-Port, and just a few days later, on 27 November 1095, he launched his holy war, somewhere in the fields outside the city, making his historic appeal to join the First Crusade.

His impassioned speech triggered a response he could never have anticipated. As Urban spoke, several knights echoed his repeated words, God wills it! The prelates and knights in the front rows fell to their knees and thundered in Occitan, *Deus lo volt!* Preachers shouted it, flung their arms into the air, men wept; horses reared up amid the jostling and tumult, and some knights tore long strips off their robes to make large crosses, which they sewed to the backs. The uniform of the crusaders was born. And when Urban promised his followers that if they defeated Christ's enemies they would receive a plenary indulgence for their sins, the crowd went wild, cheering, praying, chanting, singing. The enthusiasm spread so fast among the many lost souls in the throng that Urban himself was taken aback. His promise of a plenary indulgence meant that even a murderer could escape eternal damnation by committing other murders during the crusades – as long as the victims were foes of the true faith. We do not know Urban's exact words, but multiple witnesses mentioned in their summaries of the speech that Urban said they must not wait till Jerusalem to strike down the enemies of the Lord. This was a transparent reference to the Jews; his words gave sanction and legitimacy to the anti-Semitism of many preachers, such as Peter the Hermit in the north.

Under the feudal system, the gap between rich and poor had grown ever wider. Popular frustration and resentment were mounting, aimed at the wealthy, the clerics and the aristocracy. But the knights were undefeatable, so the people and their priests chose an easier target for their discontent: the Jews who had grown wealthy by lending money and charging interest, the Jews who had murdered Jesus. Wearing old pots and pans on their heads in a laughable attempt to emulate helmeted knights, they formed gangs armed with flails, pitchforks and blunt knives, and shod in clogs or clumsily knotted strips of leather. They trailed after the orderly horsemen, who looked so glorious in their shining armour, with their helmets, their plumes and the colourful trappings on their steeds. They besotted themselves with drink, fornicated by night with the women in their companies, and prayed by day for a plenary indulgence – the more enemies of their Saviour they could kill, the surer their salvation.

Among the excited believers stood an experienced, capable man who knew his way around Jerusalem: the fierce one-eyed adventurer and commander, Raymond IV, Count of Toulouse. He was placed in charge of the expedition at the head of the Provençal troops, together with the Bishop of Le Puy, who went along as the papal legate. Right away, these two leaders began the mobilisation and missionary work for the great campaign, determined to show the world how great and resilient Christianity had once again become. They promised the Saracens a 'holy war'. It would be another few years before the Muslims, in outrage at the barbarous attacks on the illustrious city of Antioch, adopted a counterpart to this expression: the word 'jihad'. Its original meaning was religious zeal or devotion, but from then on, it was haunted by an echo of Urban's words in Clermont.

The crusaders mobilised and waited till spring, when the first armies set off for Jerusalem. Raymond's great force, some 25,000 men, would not march until after the summer of 1096.

4

For three days, the mistral blows hard and unrelenting under a cloudless, pitiless sky. The wind is so hard that dogs, sheep and goats squeeze their eyes shut in the glaring sun, turn their hindparts to the gale and lie down behind low walls, rocks and tree trunks, waiting. The evergreen oaks rustle as the wind whistles through their rough branches, solitary and shrill; it presses at walls and shutters with a growl. The lizards stick to their nooks; the gaunt cows low in complaint. Throughout the plains of Provence, the flags and pennants are waving. People drag each other along, cluster into crowds, arm themselves with whatever is at hand. They are poised for action, a rising flood of humanity, afflicted with wind-madness. Plagued by headaches, they sink to their knees on the hard ground. They chant and sing; some villagers retreat into their houses. Cheese crumbles in clenched hands; the wine tastes sour and the olives sharp. At the top of the cliff, to the loud cawing of the circling crows, two Jewish workers, adding one of the last massive stones to the tower, are crushed beneath it. They tumble from the wooden scaffolding and break their necks. Is it really an accident? Their formless bodies roll down the mound of sharp pumice stones and into the bushes, leaving a trail of blood. The mutilated corpses are carried down the steep path to the village and given a simple burial in the Jewish cemetery by the road to the gorge. The villagers pray. They gossip. They curse under their breath.

It is October 1096. After years of cutting, carving, hauling, sorting, stacking and building, the proud tan tower on Mount Jupiter is almost complete. It catches the first rays of dawn, and as evening falls you can faintly see – coming into the valley from Saltus or standing on the high Plateau d'Albion – something like God's middle finger glowing in the gathering darkness above the medieval eyrie. The top of this fortification offers a view of the Tour de Durefort on the other side of the valley. At night, an emergency signal can be sent with bronze mirrors and fire from peak to peak, travelling from Marseilles to Moniou and onwards in less than an hour. The region is safe from invasion by the Moors.

But it's not the Moors who come. It is an army straight from the core of the people – not an external enemy, but one that was hidden in their hearts, now breaking free, undefeatable, nourished as it is by years of witch-hunts, minor vendettas, vengeance on neighbours, rabble-rousing, mutual accusations, and tall tales of ritual Jewish infanticide, cannibalism, demonic possession, satanic rituals and innocent people abducted by rabbis. A ten-year-old boy is found beaten to death at the entrance to the gorge. The Jews are blamed; there is violence in the streets; the rabbi and priest band together to bring the villagers to their senses. Hate clenches like a muscle in the heart of the community; its energy threatens to swell out of control, burst loose and destroy everything in its path. An armed guard post is set up at the synagogue entrance. The Christians call it a disgrace.

*

Raymond of Saint-Gilles, Count of Toulouse, was a respected man. He was born in 1042, the second son of Pons of Toulouse. By the time Pope Urban II gave his fateful speech in Clermont, Raymond ruled over the whole of rural south-eastern France. All the chroniclers of his day extol his many virtues; he surrounded himself with the noblest of knights and was held in greater prestige than any other military commander. During an earlier visit to Jerusalem, he had lost one eye in a fight. This only strengthened his unassailable image and authority. Knights came from Limousin and Languedoc to join him, even though the Norman armies mocked 'those Provençals'. His retinue included not only his spiritual guide, the Bishop of Le Puy, Adhémar de Monteil, but also such men as Gaston, Viscount of Béarn and Lord of Saragossa; Seigneur Pierre, Viscount of Castillon; Guilhem V of Montpellier, Raymond's protégé, who had already been to Jerusalem twice; Pierre, Lord of Avignon; Girard of Roussillon; and numerous other men of high rank and station, the elite vanguard of the troops that were now on the move. Behind them came the armed warriors, the armed civilians, and after that the farmers, their carts laden with provisions, equipment and assorted junk. Bringing up the rear were the whooping children, who sometimes walked a long way with the army, the women who decided to follow their husbands, and the sutlers and provisioners with their tempting concoctions; right at the back, a few leathery, desperate old fellows tagged along on the journey to the Holy Land to liberate their Saviour's hallowed ground from the Saracen Satan. It took days before the whole train was finally in motion, a human snake slithering its way to the heart of the Vaucluse en route to Italy.

*

After three days of mistral, one twilit morning the wind abruptly dies. Everything is motionless. The sun rises; it's a glorious day. The plateaus and valleys, the heights and gorges exude deep peace. A light veil of mist drifts up and over the Arcadian land. This day is a gift of God, Raymond tells Adhémar, we must go. They kneel and pray in the morning sun. Horses whinny and tug at their reins; knights drop to their knees in prayer all over the camp, crossing themselves and bowing their heads. A song rises. Many of the rugged men are deeply moved. Tears run down their faces; their hands are folded in devotion. The banners hang still, as if spellbound; late butterflies flit through the dry oak trees. The world holds its breath.

5

Since the weather is so mild, Hamoutal decides to go out into the hills alone. Her children stay with Agatha, her Greek attendant from Egypt, who came from Narbonne to join their household in the mountain village as soon as she heard the young couple planned to stay in Moniou. That day, Hamoutal plans to pick blue juniper berries from the thorn bushes, to be alone for a few hours. She sits down on a rock and daydreams, enjoying the beauty of the countryside in its mellow autumn mist, through which low, raking light is beginning to glimmer. She takes the road along the rim of the Nesque gorge, on the right side, and then makes a gradual climb through low shrubs and over sand-coloured paths strewn with pebbles. She draws a deep breath of fresh air. The fragrances are overwhelming. She sits down on an old Roman milestone jutting out from the sand. From there, she can see as far as the high Saint-Hubert plateau. The sun is warm and generous for the time of year; the last bees buzz in the wine-red vineyard. She closes her eyes and is immersed in memories of childhood.

When her head nods to her chest, she wakes with a start; looking around in confusion, she sees a shed snakeskin under the stubby palm trees. But when she looks up, she sees something glint in the distance, out towards Saint-Hubert, something else that resembles a serpent – an enormous silver serpent. It's moving, and it must be very large, hundreds of metres long, shining and glittering in the bright sunlight. She watches in fascination, without understanding what she's seeing. She drinks a little of the water in her wineskin and eats a hunk of bread with some hard goat's cheese. She feels contented, but also a bit concerned about whatever is moving there in the distance.

Half an hour later, she gains a clearer view of what's coming: an army on the move. Her astonishment turns to fear as she watches them marching straight towards the Saint-Jean plateau over the rough terrain now known as the Champ de Sicaude and then on to Malaval, past Vallat de Peisse, until more than an hour later the front lines reach La Plane and begin their descent into the valley of Moniou, following the same winding road she once took with David when they first arrived. There seem to be hundreds of horses. Countless riders are on the road, followed by foot soldiers. Their cuirasses, shields and lances shine in the sun. She can't stop staring; over the past months, she's heard all sorts of rumours from passing pilgrims, but she never expected to see an army like this for herself. Her thoughts leap to her father. She remembers his squabbles with her mother; she pictures him coming out of the swallow-filled stables, leading the skittish gelding on a long rein. She wonders whether he too will leave for Jerusalem, the city that now means something so different to her than it does to him.

As those images play through her mind, she watches the front lines coming down from the plateau into the valley of Moniou. She leaps to her feet, sprints down the long road to the village, and arrives panting. Meanwhile, on the other side of the river, about half a kilometre away, the first knights have come to a halt. Their shouts and cries rise from the valley; their horses rear up and make a racket. All the villagers come out to watch, open-mouthed, from the low rampart. Moniou's five soldiers stand guard at their lookout points near the gaol, choking back their anxiety. High in the tower, a hundred metres above their heads on the rock wall, the horn is sounded. The soldiers on the plateau respond to the signal with their trumpets. That's reassuring, at least.

Barely an hour later, a knight in glorious raiment with a silver cross on his armour fords the River Nesque, still called the Anesca. His horse ascends to the Portail Meunier. The knight knocks at the gate with his lance, and the sheriff enquires what he wishes from them. Not much, the herald says with a grin, just food and lodging for the honourable leaders of our holy army. How many men would that be? the sheriff wonders. About two hundred in all, the herald replies. The other knights and the foot soldiers can find what they need in the wilds around the village. You'd better start preparing. *Deus lo volt.* Slaughter all your cattle, build fires and fetch all the food stored in your cellars; the men are hungry and tired. They set off at five this morning and have barely slept for days. This valley is the perfect spot for a one-day bivouac; then we'll head further north, towards the *castrum* in Digne.

Without waiting for a reply, the knight turns his steed around and rides back down the road.

The sheriff is in a panic, afraid the small community won't be able to provide for all those men. After hasty discussion, a messenger runs up to the fort, taking the stairs in the wooden tower by the northern rampart. When he arrives panting at the top, he reports to the castellan, who's on lookout with several armed men. The castellan comes down the tower stairs, and the priest and rabbi are summoned. Trying to meet the demand for provisions would ruin the village. Without delay a messenger is sent through the northern Portalet to La Loge, the hamlet below Saltus, to request reinforcements. The villagers are in utter confusion, gaping in astonishment at this matchless display of power and prestige. Some fall to their knees, cross themselves and pray. Others stare in deep disquiet at the endless human snake winding into the valley. The knights all reached their campsite a while ago; they were first joined by the lancers, and now by the foot soldiers. From the Saint-Jean plateau, a disorderly rearguard is now coming into sight. The villagers can hear them singing, shouting, laughing and roaring. Barking dogs jump up and down around a herd of sheep, which break into loud bleating. A huge cloud of dust obscures the view; silvery motes rise into the unmoved blue. A strange odour reaches the villagers' nostrils. They huddle against the rocky slope, underneath their towers and lookout points, which are quickly manned. A few mothers with children flee to the caves and recesses in the cliffside, hidden from sight by wild bushes. The whole valley seems to quiver with unprecedented energy.

Hamoutal has run home and bolted the door behind her. She tells her trembling son Yaakov to keep quiet, soothes the little girl on her lap, and holds her youngest child, still an infant, to her breast. Should she hurry to the synagogue, not far away, to see if David is all right? A large crowd has now formed outside the village's lower wall; one colourful group of men is trying to climb the ramparts. Where the peaceful Chemin de la Bourgade runs today, horses are snorting, carts are rattling, and soldiers are roping poles together to batter down the central gate. Only now does it become clear to the people of Moniou that there is no escape from this; not until years after the coming catastrophe will they build a high defensive wall with reinforced gates. For now, they are helpless against this invasion of their small community. A second herald, accompanied by five knights, pounds on the Grande Porte around five in the afternoon, demanding to inspect the sleeping quarters. The guards reluctantly open the gate, and the five knights hurry to block the opening with a log so it can't be shut behind them. In the narrow streets, the villagers cluster together behind the sheriff, the rabbi and the priest. Some houses are bolted shut, and their fearful, stubborn occupants exchange curses and threats with the knights before opening the doors. One knight slices a flimsy door to pieces with his sword, stamps the pieces to smithereens and storms into the low, dark house. He re-emerges with an aggravated look. Almost no one has prepared for their visit at all. The knight turns up his nose at the decrepit hovels and cramped, malodourous dwellings. He demands the homes of the priest and the local worthies. He also demands the church, which is just outside the wall near the Portalet, as an additional place to sleep. The priest sputters in protest and is walloped with an iron gauntlet. Fine, he stammers, *Deus lo volt*.

Then the herald, irritated by the poverty he sees on all sides, wheels around and points to the synagogue on the far side of the village, near the little watchtower to the south, the Petit Portalet.

So ... what's that? he asks, smirking. Are there Hebrew dogs among these rats? Where are they hiding? They must have luxurious beds for us, those usurers, right?

Yaakov, who has been listening, runs up the hill to warn his father. David comes out into the street with Joshuah Obadiah, and they ask the herald what he wants. The man makes an ironic bow, spits on the paving stones, and says he hasn't asked them for anything, and they should keep their mouths shut till he's finished speaking. His first demand is the synagogue for the night: they have one hour to remove their furnishings, because Christian knights will not sleep under heathen symbols. Joshuah Obadiah straightens his back and says with dignity that it is unthinkable for them to desecrate their place of worship. He too is struck with the iron gauntlet. The old man staggers; blood flows from his lip. David holds him up and snaps at the knight: you can hardly call that kind of behaviour Christian. The knight responds by drawing his sword and shouting, One more word and you will die here, betrayer of Christ. *Deus lo volt!*

He turns his back on the frightened crowd that has gathered around him. You have until the sun passes behind the cliff, he snarls. Don't disappoint God's army, you pack of idiots.

He leaves the village through the Portail Meunier, which is closed behind him with its large draw bar. The iron portcullis is lowered behind it, but that won't do much good, since the Grande Porte below has been forced open and is under guard by several knights with drawn swords.

The villagers break into whispers, hissed conversation and moans of despair. They crowd together, at a loss; some are saying they should start slitting the throats of their sheep, building fires and preparing their bedrooms. Others say they'd rather use their knives for something different. The priest bellows, Have you lost your minds? We have no choice. These are the knights of God on their way to Jerusalem, and it is our sacred duty to serve them.

David and Rabbi Joshuah confer. They are willing to open up their houses, but not the synagogue. They will pass the night there themselves – almost the entire Jewish population, some hundred people, packed together on the floor of the synagogue to sleep, guarding their holy place while offering their hospitality. This plan meets with general approval. Everyone runs home and starts preparing. The women straighten up the rooms, fetch pillows and arrange their best sheets as neatly as they can on their primitive beds. Soon the air is filled with the wailing of sheep led to the slaughter; the smell of blood rises, the butchering begins, and not long afterwards the scent of roast meat permeates the village. Several knights have hiked up to the entrance to the village and ask to be let in. Their foot soldiers roll barrels of wine off a cart and carry them inside. The men drink their first toast and growl at the villagers not to stand and gawk. People retreat into their houses, not daring to take any food for themselves. Hunger gnaws as they smell their roasting sheep, which were grazing the dewy fields by the village just that morning. From the plateau comes a tremendous noise. The soldiers are felling trees; the entire bank of the Nesque, normally so peaceful, now resembles occupied territory. They strip the bark off the trunks and use the logs to build frames for large cloths, the roofs and canopies of their tents. Fires are built all around; they sing, yell, shout. As far as the eye can see, the valley churns with activity, all the way to the hills on the far side. Soldiers are setting up places to sleep for the night. The moon rises, large and fast, over the hills. Its silvery light makes the dusk glimmer. Below, the red and yellow fires burn, flaring and crackling up into the sky as the first stars come out.

The village is now overrun. Knights and horsemen drift in and out, brazenly inspecting the rooms and shoving the villagers aside. Some cross their spears at the entrance to show that the house is taken. Their mood soon turns boisterous. They laugh and drink, and the heaps of food quickly dwindle to nothing – there's nowhere near enough. Some of the knights raise a fuss, roughing up a few scared villagers. A fifteen-year-old boy tries to protect his father, who has taken a punch. He jumps up at the knight, who draws his sword and slices the boy's head off. Blood spurts onto his armour. A group of villagers rushes at the horsemen who are telling tall tales of their exploits by the fire. The knights plunge their swords into their attackers' throats.

The violence ends as abruptly as it began; the onlookers, trembling for their lives, retreat into their houses. No one dares to pick up the young boy. David steps forward.

A knight asks him what he wants.

I want to give the boy a final resting place, he says.

His southern, Sephardic accent betrays him.

So you choose to provoke us, Jew-boy?

No, David says, I choose to bury a dead man. The same as you Christians.

Yes, but we don't chuck them straight into the ground like you do, the knight says with a sneer. He turns back to his two drinking companions.

Then one of them, a man named Guy from Carpentras, asks, Where do the usurers sleep? Have we seen their houses yet?

The three of them jump to their feet and head for the synagogue, where Joshuah Obadiah and several other villagers are making beds for the Jewish community. Guy, well into his cups by this stage, says that these beds are fit only for dogs, not for knights. Obadiah explains that their honoured guests are welcome to sleep in their houses, but not in the synagogue. The knights don't like that idea. They'd demanded the synagogue too. Their words turn threatening; they swear Joshuah hasn't heard the end of this, cross themselves and stride off. Other knights swarm through the streets, all in search of something; a foot soldier grabs a woman's skirts. Her husband puts his arms around her and tells the drunken man he won't put up with such depravity. The man and woman flee into their home and barricade the door.

Now more and more men are wandering around the Jewish quarter. It stinks of Hebrew dogs here, one of them shouts. The others laugh.

Forget about those vermin, another one says, and a third retorts, Sure, but they won't let us sleep in their synagogue. Who do they think they are?

By midnight, the moon has risen high above the valley and casts its pale light on the rocky slope, which looks rugged and eerie. One by one, the fires on the far side go out. The stars sparkle, cold and bright. The shouts and laughter just below the ramparts go on for some time. Then it grows quieter. Some knights are still roaming the village in search of a place to sleep. They break down doors and drag villagers out of their homes. In the Jewish quarter, there's a commotion by the synagogue. The Jewish villagers have bedded down on the planks, sheets and rags; they left the doors of their houses open, but those have all been taken.

A few men break into the building, draw their swords and shout, Everybody out, now!

Joshuah Obadiah stands up and tells them that all the houses are open to the knights, but this place is theirs and sacred to their religion.

You'll pay a heavy price for this, Jew-dog, one man hisses.

A short while later, they hear the door being barricaded from the outside. Heavy stones are rolled down the streets, and beams of wood are wedged against the doors. They hear shouting from different directions and soon notice a burning smell. Someone is stoking a fire in front of the entrance, and the smoke is trickling in through a narrow window. The sleepers wake up and start praying. The children are crying; their mothers are rocking them. The noise outside has swelled to an uproar. Clanging swords, more cries and whoops of delight. They killed our Saviour, and now we'll burn them alive, someone yells. Cheers and whistles, screams and singing, *Deus lo volt!* A rhythmic pounding on the old door, which soon catches fire. The people in the enclosed space panic, run for the exit, realise they are caught in a trap.

Rabbi Obadiah, seeing that they are on the brink of catastrophe, has two other men help him gather up the simple menorah, the chanukiah, the old Torah scrolls, his Torah mantle, the ram's horn, the list of the names of the faithful in the village, the letters he has received from the distinguished Rabbi Todros of Narbonne, other documents, and, finally, a few sets of tefillin left in the synagogue and a leather bag holding twenty silver pieces. They put it all in a large sack, which the youngest of the three swings onto his back. Then they open the secret exit in the rear of the synagogue, a small door that has been bolted as long as anyone can recall. Intended as an escape route, it was installed after a fire a century ago, which they've heard old stories about. Now it creaks open, and they step out into an alley that runs in a semicircle along the southern rampart. They climb the stairs to the Petit Portalet, where the guard has left his post in the noise and confusion to join the fray in the village. The three men slip through the gate, where to this day a narrow goat path circles around to the left and up to the tower. After passing the great rock, the three men head south and then slide down the steep slope, ending up in a thicket somewhere in the Combe Saint-André. From there, they descend still further into the narrow, almost impenetrable gully, reaching two shallow caves, one above the other. They hide the objects from the synagogue in the darkness of the upper cave and then scramble down to the other one, so that they can follow the gully back to the road. A bear comes out, roused from sleep; in a heartbeat, he grabs one of the men, snapping his spine with his strong paws. The other man shoves the old rabbi out ahead of him, and they escape, gasping for breath, scratching themselves on the small, sharp palm fronds, the juniper bushes and the tangled branches. They run back up the slope and then down again, towards the village. They hope to return through the Petit Portalet, but there's a fight going on there between some guards and a couple of drunk men. There's no way through. They hurry all the way up past the fort, out of which dozens of heavily armed men are pouring. They reach the northern wooden tower, but the stairway is barricaded. In panic, the younger man throws aside a few boards, wiggles through the opening, and runs up the stairs. Joshuah Obadiah can no longer follow him. His heart is on the verge of giving out. Panting, he crumples to the ground, grabbing his chest, dizzy with pain. There's a scrape on his head so deep that he has to wipe the blood out of his eyes. Up here, from the edge of the ravine, he can survey the disaster unfolding in his peaceful mountain village. Near the synagogue he hears shouting and screaming; some men have crowded onto the stairs and are using a large beam of wood to ram the doors. Flames rise high in the darkness, sending up thick clouds of sparks into the black night sky.

By this time most of the women and children have fled through the small emergency exit and reached the rampart, where they run into more soldiers. Inside the synagogue, a few of the strongest men have grabbed whatever came to hand and, shoulder to shoulder, are trying to force open the smouldering doors. After a while, the flames burn their way inside. A moment later, the doors collapse. A few men leap outside, right onto the swords and lances waiting for them. At the sound of their dying groans, the other villagers in the synagogue back up as far from the entrance as they can; the rear exit has now been blocked from the outside. Someone smashes it open with the base of a heavy candelabrum, and they rush out into the night through the upper alleyway. A few foot soldiers, aided by peasants who have also forced their way into the village, soon overtake the fugitives and stab them to death.

Now the bloodshed begins in earnest – a massacre that continues till morning. A wailing child has its head dashed against a wall; the blood splashes onto the killer's coat. Women are raped at knifepoint. Men who fight are beaten down with clubs and then kicked and skewered. One large villager, Roger de la Loge, normally so good-natured, hurls himself at a few of the murderers, taking down three. A dozen men swoop down, grab him and put his eyes out; another plunges his dagger straight into Roger's throat. Spewing blood, he tries to stand up again, howls something incomprehensible, and falls at their feet. They crush his head with a large stone.

Deus lo volt! More and more screaming villagers run out of their hiding places, trying to reach the gate and escape. They are followed by a howling mob, which strikes them down. The soldiers seize the women, and the act of rape drives them into a frenzy. The streets are filled with a rising wave of shrieks, whimpers and screams. Bloodthirst becomes lust and lust becomes ecstasy. They stab, hack, pound and kick. Human gore runs down the paving stones where in a different season the snails mate; the moon is high and silent over the valley, and the Milky Way sparkles in eternal enchantment.

Alarmed by the women's shrieks, Yaakov runs away from the synagogue, shouts for his mother, hears her respond from somewhere near the Grande Rue, and hurries to her side. In the darkness, Hamoutal flees with her infant and the two older children for the rocky slope, where she knows of a cave hidden in the shrubbery. She is stopped by two armoured men with torches.

Hey, look at this, a blonde bitch crawling out of the Jew trap, one of them says. What are you doing here? You look like a Christian woman.

He draws his dagger. Hamoutal presses her infant to her chest, stands in front of her other two children, and begs, Let them live, let us live. She holds out her hands, palm to palm, and before she knows it she's reciting a Christian prayer in the *langue d'oïl*, the language of the north, the language of her childhood.

The man looks at her in sour suspicion. Get out of my sight, he says, but the two whelps stay here, just in case I change my mind. What's your name, anyway, darling? he adds with a sneer.

Without hesitation, she tells him her Christian name.

Oho, Adelaïs. And who's your husband?

He's back there … somewhere, she stutters, waving her arm at the far end of the village.

The man's sneer turns even meaner.

Oh yeah? And the children? Are those dark Hebrews yours? That can't be right. Give us their names, quick.

She chokes up, too flustered to think of any names but their real, Jewish ones. Only after she speaks does she realise she has betrayed them; she bursts into tears, weeping, Oh Yaakov, oh Yaakov, my boy, stay with me.

What's this now? the bumpkin snaps, as all around them people are dying and keening in agony. A Christian woman trying to save Jew-spawn? Get out of here, fast, or I'll show you a thing or two.

He drags the children off into the dark. They are crying their hearts out, calling for their mother, who is still clasping her baby to her chest. By this time, a figure from the darkness behind her has wrapped her tightly in his sniggering grip. She feels him rubbing his pelvis against her rear until he spasms, lets go, spurts onto the stones and walks away.

David is one of the last to rush out of the synagogue, where he was trying to defend the villagers still trapped there. Drawn by the sound of his screaming children, he runs in blind panic after the men who are dragging them off. He dashes straight into a sword held out by an enormous brute, who pulls it from his chest, laughing, and then deals the death blow. David falls to the ground as his wife races towards the cave, where she hopes to hide her baby before going back for the other two children. But the way is blocked. She turns her attention to her infant, taking him to her breast to calm him down.

By the time the pandemonium ends, dawn is near. The village is strewn with corpses, the synagogue is still smouldering, the whole Jewish quarter is in shambles, and dogs are wandering among the mutilated bodies piled pell-mell. Only then does Hamoutal awake from her panicky trance. Her heart pounding, she thinks of her children and husband and sets off in search of them, her sleeping baby swaddled tight in her long shawl. She goes back down the road through the Petit Portalet, sees corpses everywhere, runs through the narrow streets in confusion, calls out to her children, discovers her maimed dead husband among the other bodies. She falls to her knees and wails like a woman possessed. In the quiet morning, it sounds like an animal howl. Nothing and no one is moving in the village. The gate of the Portail Meunier has been ripped half off its hinges and hangs suspended in the morning light. All the village gates are wide open. Down on the plateau, horses are whinnying. The sun pops up over the hill, casting a stark light on the night's horrors.

Raymond of Toulouse, who has passed a fitful night in his richly decorated tent a kilometre and a half down the left bank of the river, rides out of his camp. He spots some of the smouldering ruins in the village and asks his lieutenants what happened there. When he hears there was fighting in the night, he demands an explanation. All he gets are a few muddled reports of villagers trying to murder the sleeping knights, who responded in self-defence, Your Merciful Lordship.

The army breaks camp, a trumpet sounds, the improvised tents are taken down again. The horsemen who spent the night in the village come out of the houses, make their way down the streets, and leave the village through the Grande Porte. Down on the plateau, the countless soldiers who slept in the open are waking. From all around them comes the cry to join the march: *Toulouse! Toulouse!*

Dogs bark, the surviving sheep bleat, the children bawl with them, oxen low, carts squeak into motion. The knights inspect the ranks of foot soldiers, issuing orders. Then the whole procession sets off towards what is now Grand Vallat, headed for La Loge and further east. Raymond of Toulouse, after saying a heartfelt morning prayer with Adhémar of Le Puy, kneels, receives a blessing and rides manfully at the head of his troops towards the highlands of the Plateau d'Albion. On top of the cliff far above the Chapelle Saint-André, the exhausted Rabbi Joshuah Obadiah is weeping. He struggles to his feet, limps past the northern tower, notices the Petit Portalet half demolished down on the far side of the village, descends, finds Hamoutal there frantic with sobbing, and sees the ruined, burned-out synagogue. By the Romanesque arch to the left of the stairs lies the dead son of the chief rabbi of Narbonne in a patch of black-clotted blood.

6

I too see the sun come up over the horizon, sudden and stark. I've been writing all night; I'm tired. I open the shutters and window in my study, slowly, so as not to wake my sleeping wife. Below me are the village's lower streets, and beyond them the valley of the Nesque, the lavender fields and the tall grass mingled with wild spelt – swaying heads of grain by the winding river. I hear the first swallows chirp.

In my mind's eye, I see old Rabbi Obadiah, who fled into the hills with two other men that night to hide the Torah scrolls, the contents of the genizah and the synagogue's gold among the rocks. Having stumbled back now, broken, feeling his way like a blind man among the dead, he has found the young rabbi's blonde wife stretched out sobbing over her dead husband. The smell of blood is unbearable; all around them are bodies slashed open, a wild dog is gobbling down brains leaking out of a skull. A metre away, the infant lies on the paving stones crying. The old rabbi, weeping in silence, lays his hand on the woman's shoulder.

The valley echoes with the blast of horns and the noise of horses and men breaking camp. As day comes, the soldiers sink into devout prayer with hung-over heads, thanking God for the great mission with which He has entrusted them. Obadiah puts his arm around the broken woman, helps her to her feet, and guides her to his house, where the front door has been kicked down. There he finds his own wife in the cellar, scared half to death and shivering. Her face is scratched and her clothes singed.

I amble down the narrow street to the bakery for bread and croissants. It's late August, and the valley is at its most idyllic. Above the ruins of the Chapelle Saint-André on the east rim, the sky is deep purple and spotless, cool and pure. Over the twisting riverbed lies a white snake of rising mist. Everything is deserted and peaceful; it's like waking from a nightmare.

The baker sees the circles under my eyes.

You had a little *fête* last night, *monsieur*? he asks with a twinkle in his eye.

A *fête*, I mumble. Yes, that's right. A *fête*.

Back at home I brew a pot of strong coffee and go outside to sit in the sun on the terrace. Swarms of bees are buzzing around the grapevines. Above the Plateau d'Albion, where France's nuclear arsenal was kept underground until about twenty years ago, two fighter jets seem to rip the sky open. They leave a thundering echo behind, as if the air is thicker than usual for minutes afterwards. Then the silence returns. A few sheep bells ring near Le Viguier.

A door slams. Then it's quiet again.

After breakfast, I climb the rocky slope. The old path to the former site of the Jewish quarter is still there.

Ten metres up the path, I turn left, climbing seven crumbling stairs half concealed under dry grass. To the left, I see the large Romanesque arch of a basement. The stairs lead to a grassy field where I've spent many a quiet summer hour happily reading in the warm breeze. I've known for years about the well there, covered with a sheet of corrugated metal and a few heavy boards. I look up into the immaculate blue sky; a few crows fly away over the tops of the rocks with loud caws. As if in a dream, I head for the ruins of the Petit Portalet. From there, I take the path up to the level of the tower.

The path is steep, and before you know it your view extends all the way to the Montagne de Lure, with your back against one of the many slopes of Mont Ventoux.

The *météo* predicts a heat wave. The postman is driving his small yellow car down the road under the lime trees towards the gorge. I'm nearing the large boulder that once tore free of the rocky slope and still weighs down on the ruined wall, in a heavy, shaky balance of its own, a mighty weight with shallow caves behind it.

So where did Obadiah hide the synagogue's treasures?

Not a living soul can say, but the stories are still told.

Obadiah took his secret with him to his grave.

After the crusaders rode north-east towards Digne and their whole ragtag band of followers disappeared into the distance, he tried to take care of the distraught Hamoutal. He couldn't do much. The whole village was suffering – even the Christians, who hadn't been massacred. All the livestock had been slaughtered; barns, sheds and cellars had been plundered; some stables had been knocked down for the wooden beams. No grain left, no meat left, their small flocks almost wiped out, the freshly filled casks of new wine drained. It is autumn, all their stockpiles are gone, and famine lies ahead.

Obadiah doesn't know what to do; he and his wife have no way of providing for the chief rabbi's daughter-in-law in a manner suitable to her station. He sends a courier to the Todros family in Narbonne with the terrible news of their son's death and the kidnapping of their grand-children. A week later the courier returns: Hamoutal cannot go to Narbonne. It would be far too dangerous under the circumstances.

The grieving woman spends weeks in a room hung with black sheets, sitting on the bare ground. She wears only a coarse garment of sackcloth, and is uncertain how Jewish tradition permits a high-born woman to express her grief. She prays and mutters to herself the whole time; twice a day she is served a simple meal of watery soup and a hunk of bread. She slides her bedpan outside her door before shutting it and drawing the heavy bolt again. Obadiah's wife sometimes hears her moving furniture. Opening the primitive window at night. Talking to herself. After weeks of this, the stench in the room is intolerable. She is absolved of the duty to mourn any longer. She comes out of her room, a spectre with burning eyes, emaciated and emptied, lost in the madness of her solitude.

The rabbi and his wife recoil at the sight. Water is heated for her. Herbs over the fire. Their sharp scent. The howling of wolves in the forests near Saint-Jean. The silence. She blinks her eyes in the brightness of the unrelenting light over the forsaken highlands. The muted sounds of the village. Her child, who has been cared for by the old midwife, is laid in her arms. Life returns to her, but she shows almost no sign of recognition.

By messenger, Richard Todros asks Joshuah Obadiah to write a letter of recommendation for Hamoutal and to send her away – eastwards, discreetly, and in any case not back to France. Narbonne is full of Norman knights on their way to Sicily and southern Spain; the Reconquista is flaring up again.

Obadiah writes the letter.

*

Time passes as I sit by the large, loose rock that was just above the synagogue. The silence is endless. There is no time, only space. I watch the village waking up; a man in blue shorts stretches on his terrace and looks out over the valley. A tractor rides down a narrow country road, slanting into the sunlight, on the way to a lavender field; I see it but can't hear it. The bakery's bell jingles; someone says *bonne journée*. A dog barks; a cock crows; a woman's voice cries, Mathieu!

I climb back down, passing the ruin, where I stop again in the tall grass by the well. A strange, deep peace has come over me. My wakeful night has left me in a slight trance. I'm tempted to lie down beside my sleeping wife, but I'm too awake, too alert. I sit down at my small writing desk and look up. A frame on the wall straight in front of me holds a copy of a faded Hebrew manuscript almost a thousand years old. There are holes in it. It possesses a sad, unearthly beauty.

7

MNYW 1096

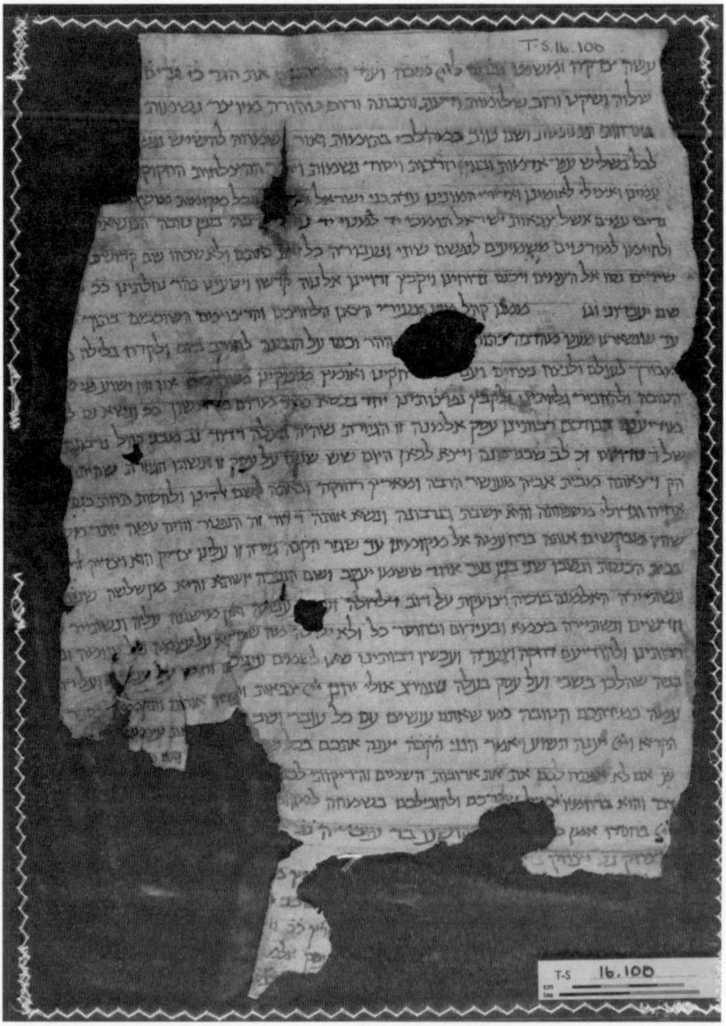

'To do righteousness and justice is more acceptable to the Lord than sacrifice' (Prov. 21:3). And further: 'Ye shall love the stranger, for strangers were ye in the land of Egypt' (Deut. 10:19). Repose and quietude, an abundance of peaceful tidings, knowledge, wisdom and bounteous purity from the Creator of Spirits to all those who tread in faultless paths; a good name for those who walk in perfection; light and happiness to make glad the souls; the granting of inheritances to all, through a third of the dust of the earth; and the building up of ruins, the foundation of spirits and the uniting of the inscribed happinesses. To our people, the nobles of our nation, the mighty ones of our masses, the congregation of the sons of Israel who reside in all their places of settlement, benefactors of nations, the tamarisk of the hosts of Israel, supporters of those in despair, offerers of benefits with goodly countenance, who 'lift up their bodies to the smiters and their cheeks to them who make bald', to those 'who have said to their soul, "Bow down that we may pass over"' (Isaiah 51:23). All this has come upon them, yet they did not forget the Name of their Holy One, the Lord of Israel. May He lift up His ensign to the peoples, may He gather in our dispersed ones and bring together our scattered ones to His holy habitation, and may He plant us upon the mountain of our inheritance, as it is written, 'For in My holy mountain, saith the Lord GOD, there shall all the house of Israel, all of them, serve Me in the land' (Ezek. 20:40). From us, the congregation of MNYW, the 'young of the flock' (Jer. 49:20), the oppressed and broken, who reside amidst d[ogs] until we have been left, a few from many, 'as a beacon upon the top of a mountain, and as an ensign upon the hillock' (Isaiah 30:17), 'to the heat by day and the frost by night' (Jer. 36:30), henceforth may the Name of the Lord be blessed forever and unto all eternity. Yet despite the badness of our oppression and the might of our distress, we offer pleadings, entreating the countenance of our King to hasten the tidings of gladness, to bind together our exiles and gather our dispersions together in the 'Throne of glory on high from the beginning' (Jer. 17:12), as it is written, 'And He will set up an ensign for the nations, and will assemble the dispersed of Israel' (Isaiah 11:12).

We hereby inform our honourable lords of the matter of this widow the proselytess, whose husband was R. David, his soul rest in peace, who was a member of the family of R. Todros in Narbonne, his memory be for a blessing. He came here six years ago to the day because of the matter of his wife, this proselyte, who had been a Christian and entered the Covenant of Holiness; she went forth from the house of her father, from great wealth and a distant land, and came on behalf of the Lord, and to take refuge under the wings of the Shekinah. She left her brothers and the great ones of her family, and was living in Narbonne; and R. David, the deceased person just mentioned, married her and was with her more than six months, when he heard that they were seeking her. So he fled to our place, until the Holy One decreed this persecution upon us, righteous is He and righteous [...] The husband was killed in the synagogue and two of her children were taken captive – a boy named Yaakov and a girl named Justa, she being three years old, and all they owned was plundered. The widow remained alive, weeping and crying because of her great degradation and poverty, there being no one to care for her; and there also remained alive unto her a son of [...] months. Thus was she left, in thirst and nakedness, lacking all provisions, and with no funds to pay for her daily needs and those of her orphaned son. So we have sought to turn to our lords, to inform them of her oppressed state and her sorrow. And now, O our lords, lift up your eyes to heaven and take pity upon her poverty, her great degradation and her children who have been taken captive, and with regard to her husband who was slain. 'Perhaps the Lord will be gracious' (Amos 5:15) so that she may redeem them. So accept her with friendly countenance and treat her in the same goodly measure as you do every wayfarer and passer-by and you shall merit for yourselves life in the world to come, as it is said, 'Call and the Lord will

*answer, beseech and He will say, "Here am I"' (Isaiah 58:9). May the Holy
One, blessed be He, answer all your requests [...] as it is said, 'If I do not
open unto you the windows of heaven and pour out upon you a blessing,
more than sufficiency' (Malachi 3:10) [...] The Lord God has spoken. He
in his mercifulness will double your reward and will surely lead you in joy
to the place of His glory; [... Blessed] is the Lord in His lovingkindness.
Amen, Selah. Joshuah b. Obadiah, peace be with him.*

VI

The Crossing

1

The survivors pass the months after the pogrom in a state of collective shock. They pick and press olives in deathly silence, doing without the old songs. The winter is near, and they have lost all their provisions; their fields have been trampled and ruined; felled trees lie scattered over the landscape; life seems to lack all meaning and direction. In some houses, the groans of dying villagers with infected wounds go on for weeks. Hamoutal can't leave yet; the nights are bitterly cold. So she starves her way through December with the rest of them. On Christmas Eve, she hears the fervent prayers in the streets. The half-ruined synagogue remains sunk in icy silence. Hamoutal has had David buried simply, without any ceremony, in the Jewish graveyard. Later she'll have a stone cut and his name carved into it. For now, hardly anyone can get anything done. Wood is gathered in the hills. The villagers hunt quail, rabbits and pheasants. They sleep by their smouldering fires. They keep breathing, so they do not die.

Her father-in-law in Narbonne has not been sitting idle. After the death of his son, he pondered how he might have the body brought home for embalming; the cold put off the moment when the remains would start decomposing. He soon realised his plan was impossible; the traffic on the roads made it too risky. From Narbonne, he sends word to several Jewish communities along the route to Jerusalem, asking for news of his kidnapped grandchildren.

Where is Hamoutal to go? In his letter, Obadiah mentions her extreme distress. In her sorrow, she clings to childhood memories. Nostalgia carries her through her darkest moments. She considers sneaking away to her in-laws in Narbonne. She considers joining a convent. She considers returning to Rouen and praying for forgiveness. She is only too aware that if she returns, she can expect to be burned at the stake or tortured to death. She doesn't know that at almost the same time, in her home town of Rouen, there was another pogrom, just as gruesome: nearly the entire Jewish community was driven into a church by a band of crusaders. Anyone who refused to convert was slain then and there – young and old, men and women alike. In Rouen, too, the synagogue was set on fire.

She is living with Obadiah and his wife again, as she did for her first few weeks in the village. She goes through the motions of caring for her nursing child; she hardly has the strength to take care of herself, and the shock has dried up her milk. The child is left for whole days in a small alcove, which is cold and clammy. Hamoutal has searched for her helper, Agatha from Alexandria, but found no trace of her. She has gone all the way to the top of the rocky slope to search and spent a difficult hour there crying and praying, tugged by the temptation to hurl herself into the depths. She stood at the edge, dizzied, the wind in her face. Then she let herself fall backwards into the bushes. She returned to the village below and took up her household tasks, saying nothing.

The villagers eat what they can find. The whole wounded and distressed community struggles back to its feet. Winter can be fickle at these heights; temperatures can plummet far below freezing in the early morning and then climb to around 18° Celsius by noon, giving you the chance to warm yourself for a couple of hours, out of the wind behind a sheltering wall. On days of hard frost, the smoke from the oak fires curls out of the old chimneys as if in a dream. In January and February, the cold is biting. When snow falls, the village is hard to reach; it blankets the roads and the mountain passes. Impenetrable fog sometimes covers the highlands, lingering day after day. For weeks, hardly anything moves. Peasants sleep side by side with sheep or calves for warmth, but few of those animals are left alive. A couple of shepherds were wandering the highlands on the day of the catastrophe and came back down the slopes with their sheep soon afterwards. Their animals are offered up one by one to supply the whole village with meagre rations. The last small stocks of dried fruits, nuts and truffles are brought down from the attics. Turnips, carrots and swedes are dug up. Herbs and the leftover grain are harvested and ground; infusions are brewed of sage and thyme. The few remaining goats and sheep are milked, and cheese is made. All this in small portions for the scarred community. The children catch small winter birds with their lime twigs. They pluck them, throw them in hot ash and gnaw off the meat but can never fill their stomachs. Around the ruins of the houses and the synagogue, the stench of fire and carrion persists for weeks.

In the first flush of spring, the villagers catch trout from the fast-running Nesque. Now and then someone has the good luck to bring down a roebuck or hind with a small wooden spear or a large stone. Then he drags his prey back to the village, where he receives a hero's welcome. On the other side of the river, they can see the wolves prowling the grasslands near the rocky slope. Sometimes they howl all night, especially when a cutting wind races through the valley from the north-east. From over the hills, a few merchants arrive with a cartload of figs and melons preserved in sour wine. The villagers scrape some coins together, get drunk by the fire that evening, and say nothing. In the Jewish cemetery below, along the road to the gorge, a few flat stones lie in a jumble. The stonecutters haven't yet had the time to carve names on them. The corpses, treated with herbal oil, lie wrapped in crude linen shrouds in their shallow graves and are slow to decay in the dry cold. That spring, nettles and cleavers run riot over the arid field.

A thousand years later a few primitive chisels remain, almost rusted away. Amateur archaeologists on holiday in the area are surprised to find this type of tool just lying around in the underbrush. In 1979, the American scholar Norman Golb writes that he has heard a few villagers in Monieux mention a Jewish cemetery, but no one can tell him the exact location.

2

According to Obadiah's letter, there was no one in Moniou who could care for Hamoutal. With no funds, he adds – which must mean that the silver coins that David had received from his father in Narbonne had been stolen in the pogrom. Or had David hidden the silver in the synagogue, and did Obadiah bring it to safety? That can't be, because then he would have returned it to David's widow soon after the pogrom. Broken and desperate, 'in thirst and nakedness' – under those circumstances, how do you decide which way to run?

Hamoutal, worn with uncertainty about her children's fate, decides to go in search of them. She has thought long and hard and sees only one possibility: the knights have dragged her children off to Jerusalem. So she must go after them, even if that means putting her own life in danger. The rabbi and his wife try to persuade her that this would be folly, a pointless path to nothing but death. But she seems determined and barely listens to their arguments. The next day, the rabbi hands her his letter of recommendation, addressed to any Jewish community in the world, entreating them to care for her. He pleads with her to be careful and not rush into anything. That night she tosses and turns, consumed by worry. She decides to run away while everyone else is sleeping. Goaded onward by despair, she steals off in the early morning with pain in her heart, leaving the high valley that has grown so dear to her. She has Obadiah's letter, along with David's tefillin, tucked into a pouch she wears around her waist. She goes without saying farewell to the two survivors who have taken care of her.

*

On her own, with her sole remaining child on her arm, Hamoutal crosses the valley towards Saint-Jean-de-Sault. It is 5 April 1097, and the weather is fine. She plans to trek south and reach Marseilles in a week. The landscape consists, at first, of gently rolling hills; as she passes through it, she turns for one last look at the greening valley of the Nesque as it sinks away behind her in the sprawling freshness of the spring day. She passes through the Fôret de Javon and over a hilltop where wild olive trees are turning a light grey. The child at her breast sleeps in the warm wind. It's still too early for jasmine; the first wild flowers sway, small and colourful, in the grass. She is at the mercy of chance, space, landscape, and could meet with misfortune anywhere. To survive some nights, she will have to go without sleep. She is numb to everything around her. She finds the path over the high crags, sometimes creeps behind a stone when she hears animals, and lives like a wild creature. At night she can't stop rocking back and forth, reciting Jewish and Christian prayers combined. She sings a lullaby to the baby, cries herself to sleep and is roused by the morning sun.

She chooses the heights – the fastest route, with views. After Saint-Saturnin-lès-Apt, she reaches lower, open terrain, and from there she makes quick progress. Though weak and underfed, she trudges on till her feet are bleeding and then slumps to the ground wherever she is. Begs for food. Lies down, now and then, to catch an hour's sleep under a holm oak. After crossing the plain near Villars, she heads south till she is near the gates of Apt. Two humble peasants take pity on her and offer her a bed; she stays with them for a couple of days. She doesn't tell them she's a Jewish convert; for the second time, she has the uneasy feeling she's abandoned her new religion, but she has no real choice.

Her baby is still weak; she's glad the peasants have goat's milk for him. For weeks, she's been almost unable to breastfeed under the weight of her grief, and because her own diet is too poor and meagre. She sleeps on straw in a little stable, next to the animals quietly shuffling their feet. In and around her, everything is dark; she feels the child's small breath against her chest. Her husband's mutilated head sometimes lunges out, monstrous, in her dreams; then she feels like howling. She sobs herself through difficult patches and falls asleep again.

The third morning, the concerned couple give her a few days' provisions. She leaves early, crosses the large smooth stones of the Via Domitia and recalls her last flight, when her husband was still with her. Her heart races; the dark woods of the Luberon rise ahead, looking like an insurmountable wall she must pass over. High in the sky, crows gather. There are not many easy routes even in our time – she must pass Bonnieux and head towards Lourmarin, where today Camus's readers lay stones on his simple grave. She has to move fast, crossing straight through desolate woods and valleys; around Cadenet she finds herself on more level terrain. She wades across the Durance, wide but shallow in spring. The ice-cold water takes her breath away. At some point, she loses her balance and falls flat into the current. Soaked and shivering, rubbing her crying child to warm him up, she reaches the vast reed fields on the other side – which a century later will inspire Cistercian monks to name one of France's most famous abbeys Silvacane, from *silva cana*, the forest of reeds.

What did she do when she ran into clergymen? Did she seek refuge in Romanesque churches along the way? How hard was it for her to keep changing her religion and identity to fit in? Rognes, Éguilles, Cabriès, Vallon de la Femme Morte. She walks like a woman possessed, through the rising heat on the salt flats, more than thirty kilometres a day. Somewhere near L'Estaque, she spends the night in a women's house and tends to her walk-wounded feet. In the morning, she prays in the small chapel, asking the Christian God to forgive her for now belonging to the Jewish

God. Yet some part of her knows that she's always calling out to the same God: that quiet, desperate voice deep inside her. The next day, she enters Marseilles, salt air on her chapped lips, her child sucking his thumb in a shawl on her back.

*

I sit down in the sun, which shines brightly on this plateau for more than 250 days a year. I pore over hiking maps and gamble on Hamoutal having reached Marseilles in less than two weeks. Two fighter jets tear through the sky with a deafening roar; disoriented birds flutter around in circles like confetti for a moment before flying onward. As I sit musing, my neighbour Andy comes down the narrow street and knocks on our small terrace door. Come on, he says, follow me, I want to show you something. I know where to find the base of that huge wooden shaft that connected the village to the tower above in the Middle Ages, like a big fire escape. We spend the rest of the morning scratching our hands and legs on juniper bushes, rocks and stiff palm leaves. Like panting schoolboys, we stare at the stone base, huge and rough, on top of the ruined rampart, near the rocky slope, where snakes roam free on the sun-warmed limestone and in the caves, and we watch where we step in our light shoes. In my mind's eye, I see the old rabbi on the night of the pogrom, collapsing beside the blocked stairway.

3

On the same day Hamoutal leaves Moniou, 5 April 1097, Robert of Flanders and Stephen of Blois arrive in Brindisi, where they will set sail for the eastern shores of the Mediterranean. It is a day of sunbursts, wind and spectacular clouds. At the same time, the Provençals led by Raymond of Toulouse are toiling their way towards south-western Slavonia, where they plan to push on to the Dalmatian coast and there to continue by sea, perhaps from Zadar. This plan will not succeed, either this time or in later crusades. A century afterwards, in the Fourth Crusade, Christian knights will vent their fury on the proud Croatian port, plundering and torching it. The northern armies will not join up with the armies from Provence until more than a hundred kilometres beyond Lake Ohrid – past Macedonia. For now, in northern Croatia, they lose their way again and again, stray into mountainous enemy territory, meet with delays, and have trouble resupplying.

Raymond of Aguilers, the embedded journalist of his day, describes their dreadful journey, through weeks of cold and mist, through thick woods and mountains, plagued by uncertainty and growing unease, attacked more and more often by locals warned of earlier atrocities committed by the unruly rearguard. The attacks targeted that vulnerable horde of plunderers, although Raymond of Aguilers portrays them as innocent victims. The vagrants who followed the knights and foot soldiers often didn't know which way to go, sometimes went days without seeing a single bird or animal, had almost nothing to eat, cut shoes out of birch bark, and hunted snipes and small game to survive. The locals refused them any form of support, providing food only under duress – in other words, after being assaulted and brutalised – and retaliated in the night, taking the worn-out mob by surprise as they tried to sleep on damp moss. By the time the crusaders arrived in Ragusa (now Dubrovnik), many had been weakened by overexhaustion, infections, broken bones, lacerations, intestinal complaints, undernourishment, pneumonia, hunger and stress. Raymond of Toulouse had learned his lesson by then and offered the local king all sorts of gifts in return for fresh supplies and logistical support. But Raymond of Aguilers complains that this had little effect; the crusaders were subject to constant attacks from the rear. They had an especially hard time in narrow gorges and along rough mountain paths – landscapes unlike anything they had encountered before.

The fate of little Yaakov and Justa can hardly have been anything but tragic. They were Jewish children, even if the girl had inherited her mother's blonde hair. They were too young to take care of themselves, and far too young to escape on their own. If they survived at all, they may well have been sold as slaves in northern Italy. But it's no less conceivable that they couldn't keep up and were left behind to wander the land like so many other children, starving to death or falling prey to infections or wild animals. Is it also possible one of the knights helped them out? Now she almost hopes that someone knows of her distinguished Christian background and will make sure the children are sent to her parents in Rouen. But she has never told the children anything about them – if only she had. Such thoughts torment Hamoutal. Day and night, the image of her Jewish husband's horrific murder vies for attention with her maddening worries about the children. When she conjures up a vivid image of Yaakov and Justa in the arms of the parents she'll never see again, she sobs for hours in misery.

Then one night she dreams of the snake that lay in the gravel next to Yaakov when he was born. She sees it creeping closer and tries to pull the blood-soaked newborn between her legs away to safety, but the child is stuck, attached to the ground by repulsive white roots. She pulls and tugs in desperation as the snake slithers closer, closer, looking as if he wants to creep inside her. She squeezes her legs shut and jolts awake with a shriek. She feels her heart on the brink of giving out. On the lonesome plain, she hears the monotonous rush of the wind through the pines. The stars look like pinholes in an impenetrable black sheet spread over the world. She dreams of the divine light beyond it and prays. She prays, but without words, a timeless murmuring to stems, stars and stones.

*

I drive up from Monieux towards Saint-Trinit and see the valley sink away behind me. I reach the lonely Plateau d'Albion, site of the mysterious *avens*, pits in the calcareous rock so unfathomable that if you toss in a stone you'll never hear it land. Sometimes you see birds fluttering through the dark depths in search of blind insects. An icy draught rises out of the complex of underground passageways; somewhere beyond reach, there must be an opening to the other side. These enormous limbos, lying precipitously on the arid plateau, draw you in; your head reels as you near the edge, the archetype of the entrance to the underworld. Some are surrounded by rusty barbed wire, knocked down by the rare adventurers who visit these hidden places. There are stories of collaborators hurled into the pits after the war, gangsters who pushed their rivals into them. A lean black dog approaches, swaying its vicious head back and forth. I get back in the car.

The road leads through a wide mountain pass, the Col de l'Homme Mort. The views are endless: Mont Ventoux behind me, Montagne de Lure far ahead.

I hike down the lonesome motorway to the lifeless village of Séderon, lose my car keys along the way, and wander the many desolate kilometres back over the row of hills, grimly scrutinising every patch of ground until, out of breath, I see something glittering among the wild stock flowers and sink to my knees as if I've found the Holy Grail.

I drive on. La Calandre, Serre des Ormes. Birds of prey. Crushing silence, thudding gusts of wind – *les rafales*.

Here's the narrow Méouge canyon. I follow the tortuous course of the near-dry river. The landscape here is prehistoric and utterly deserted. Challenging, perhaps even punishing terrain for an inexperienced army. The crusaders didn't have much choice; if they headed for Montgenèvre, the mountain pass near Briançon, as most historians suppose, then they must have come this way. Slopes and pits, shifting scree underfoot and steep cliffs towering above that might conceal all sorts of dangers. Here and there, a thin trickle of water loses itself in some dark crevice.

I follow the smallest byroads, sometimes going for hours without running into another living being. The poetry of place names: Laragne-Montéglin, Ventavon, Col de Faye, Barcillonnette, La Saulce. Jean Giono's beloved highlands. At the Château de Tallard I get out and visit the impressive castle, every detail of which attests to the crusaders' overweening pride. But it wasn't built until the fourteenth century. Flapping pennants in an elevated courtyard; bucolic views through glassless windows; tall Gothic arches. The stuff of medieval fantasies.

Should I drive towards Gap or take a more direct route east, towards the large Lac de Serre-Ponçon? The latter, I decide. The heights, with their thin scattering of pines, exude the atmosphere of a cheap skiing holiday. Think of all the human effort spent on that First Crusade. Where are Yaakov and Justa? Bumping along on the back of a cart? Have they already been left behind? Were they still alive when the armies passed this way?

I have to head towards Briançon. Massif des Écrins? Not an easy path for an army trailed by a migratory multitude. Imagine the exhaustion. I follow their route through Embrun to Mont Dauphin. Why did they cross the Italian border so far to the north? Did they hope to join the armies going by way of Germany? In the Durance Valley I see snow-caps on the Alps. After the Gourfouran canyon and the wild landscape around the impressive Gorges du Guil, after La Roche-de-Rame and just before L'Argentière-la-Bessée, they have nowhere to go but into the forbidding mountains. Puy-Saint-Pierre, Croix de Toulouse, now it's getting serious. Lugging, wheezing, pushing their carts uphill, beating their straining, baulking horses, scraping their arms and legs, aching with fatigue in every muscle, pierced with cold when it rains, bedding down on inhospitable ground.

I choose the road to the west of Briançon, drive as far as Serre Chevalier, and am astounded by the view. Wind in my face. A dead end, I have to go back. Finally, the Montgenèvre pass. Bad weather, poor visibility, dark clouds, danger. What an idiotic venture. The second large castle designed by the architect Vauban, after the one on Mont Dauphin. A car park, entrance tickets, school picnics. Knights' footsteps, imagination. Steep mountain paths, majestic views when the sun breaks through again. Approaching the Italian border. Below lie Sestriere and the Passo della Banchetta. After that, they'll have to pass through the Po Valley. I lose their trail and, exhausted, check into a small, musty hotel. The next day I drive all the way back to Monieux.

Yaakov and Justa? No idea.

*

The whole Mediterranean rim is afoam with the confused activity accompanying the recent waves of migration. More and more refugees are on the move. There is plunder and pillage – not only by the army's embattled rearguard, where anarchy and cruelty prevail, but also by locals chased out of their homes and onto the roads, who are out for vengeance. Sometimes they simply join the passing mob in search of adventure, easy women, an indulgence or a better life. Some people try to escape the raids by setting out to sea in small boats. Many drown, overcome by the waves, dying unremarked in the stiff wind and glaring sun.

These bands of migrants bring many prostitutes, abandoned women trying to survive by hawking their bodies. There is no way Pope Urban could have anticipated the moral turpitude, the atrocities, and the general callousness that would issue from his high-minded urgings to join the crusade. The northern routes, where fanatical leaders like Peter the Hermit are in charge, are no better: robbery, rape, sadistic pogroms, violent resistance by the plundered populace – retaliation and counter-retaliation.

The chaotic rearguard are struck down pitilessly, their meagre provisions stolen. One large group marches towards Macedonia; others scatter, or rush to find boats along the steep coasts of Montenegro – usually an impossible task.

The old world has been thrown out of joint; the delicate balances of earlier days are teetering. Where oh where are her children?

4

Marseilles bathes in bright sun. I've visited ten times or more – this is the city that ties me to the start of another world, radiating a feeling of hope, a sense of freedom, which need never be pinned down but is simply present, a form of relief and joy. I walk among the hipsters with their unlovely tattoos and the Ethiopians selling fake Ray-Bans, past the pot-smoking backpackers, the sharp-eyed dealers and the old men who take their first measured sips of pastis around ten in the morning, through the polychrome souk with its live chickens and its pervasive odour of marijuana, mint, stockfish, olives and cinnamon. Water runs over the old paving stones in the blue shade; the plane trees are gathering dust. I feel a hankering for a cup of strong coffee, and my throat itches to start smoking again. I think of the ports across the sea – how could I not? I feel like boarding a boat and slipping out of my life. In the morning paper, I read yet another article about dozens of migrants drowning off the Greek coast.

*

At the start of the Seventh Crusade – yes, six crusades later – the thirteenth-century French chronicler Jean de Joinville wrote, '*Au mois d'aoust entrames en nos nefs à la Roche de Marseille*' – in the month of August we arrived in our ships at the rock of Marseilles. The words evoke iconic scenes of ships sailing through the narrow entrance to the ancient harbour, where the Quai de Belges is found today. The rowers can finally rest after their ordeal; the rigging creaks, the first mate hops on shore and throws huge ropes around the mooring post. From the waterside, I try to get a sense not so much of how it was to arrive but of how it felt to depart. Warm salt wind, white-crested waves just beyond the break-waters, a colourful crowd waiting and jostling on shore.

Here Hamoutal enters another world, in no way resembling the sedate, conventional city of Narbonne where she lived with her husband's family, and even less like northerly Rouen, her childhood home. Marseilles is Greek in origin; in those days, the city was sometimes called Massilia, and it was known throughout the Mediterranean region as a cosmopolitan destination, kaleidoscopic and easy to reach. Even back then, the city and harbour were teeming with Maghribis, Africans, Byzantines, Montenegrins, Albanians, Syrians, Sardinians and Sicilians. Jews, Copts, Muslims and Orthodox Christians lived side by side. The city's districts were dirty and chaotic; life there was intense and edged with danger – the same images still reinforced with some regularity today on the French TV news. Since long before the Christian era, it has been a city of soaps, exotic woods, olive oil, imported Oriental spices and textiles, and a city of fishermen. Then as now, passers-by stopped to watch large tuna being cut on the wharf. There was shipbuilding, a lively black market, open prostitution. Street musicians stood along the quays; there were acrobats, conjurors, preachers, shady dealers and con artists. You could buy rough home-brewed spirits, drown your sorrows in a murky tavern, or pick fights in dangerous brothels. You might catch a disease or live on fleeting excitement, brawls and religious delusions, amid a cacophony of countless tongues. *Veni Creator Spiritus!* the adventurers would shout before going to church to pray for forgiveness of their foul sins – which, after absolution, they returned to with undiminished enthusiasm.

Unworldly Hamoutal hopes to board a ship bound for Jerusalem that very day, but of course no such vessel exists. The galleys crossing the

Mediterranean go to Tunis or Alexandria. From there, she can arrange to journey on. She tucks away her unwashed blonde locks under a black shawl, screws up her courage, and approaches sailors to ask which ships sail where. Since she has no money, she can't travel with the better classes; the remaining option is to be crammed into the hold of a cargo ship among crowds of paupers and to find some way to survive the trip unharmed. She sleeps in a run-down building in a labourers' district, barricading her door with a heavy stone for fear of being raped. The next morning, she walks along the docks. Three ships creak into their moorings: one is leaving for Cagliari and Tunis in two days. From there, she hopes to go on to Alexandria. She is nervous and restless, eager to move as soon as she can. A round-bellied man with just one brown tooth left in his grinning, unshaven face tells her she can travel with them – refugees hop on the boats almost every day, he says – but she'll have to render services in exchange. He gives her a lewd wink, squeezes his crotch and leers. Her stomach churns, and she walks away fast. The baby she holds to her chest protects her from most of the unsavoury characters who shout filth at every passing woman. It seems a shard of respect for motherly virtue is still lodged somewhere inside them; she is treated with more pity than she had expected. But she can hardly imagine knocking on the door of some upper-class family, as dirty and penniless as she is now. Yet in her desperation, she does precisely that. Like a beggar, she goes to the portal of a wealthy Jewish shipowner she's heard stories about.

As soon as the guard who opens the door looks at her, he tries to slam it in her face. Hamoutal mutters a few words of Hebrew, and he leaves it ajar. She pulls out the letter from Joshuah Obadiah. The illiterate man takes a quick look and motions with his head for her to enter.

Half an hour later, the shipowner's wife comes into the blue-tiled room where Hamoutal is waiting. Again, she produces the letter from Rabbi

Obadiah. The woman reads it and takes a long look at Hamoutal. Her eyes growing moist, she smiles and says, Come with me.

Hamoutal is led into the opulent back room of the house, where a fountain splashes in a blue limestone basin. Light is filtered through pearl curtains; a linen sheet is stretched over the courtyard. There are budding oleanders in large pots and, against a wall, a hibiscus in blossom. An ice-blue bird in a wooden cage under an orange tree lets out strange cries. A maidservant takes her child, who is rolling his head feverishly, washes him, tends to the scabies rashes forming on his skin, applies herbal ointment, wraps him in fresh linen, and lays him down to sleep under netting on the cool side of the courtyard. Hamoutal is given warm milk with saffron to drink. She means to start telling her sad story to this refined woman, whose eyes are full of questions and compassion, but she cannot: with every word she tries to utter, she has to gulp so hard that nothing coherent comes out of her.

She is shown to a cool room where a copper bowl of lemon water awaits her. Through the open window, the heavenly fragrance of orange blossom drifts inside. A dove is cooing on a roof. Now, as she washes, the tears burst out of her in a kind of dumb, primal relief. Sobbing, she washes herself and combs the tangles out of her hair. Simple black clothes have been laid out for her. As soon as she lies down on the bed, exhausted, she sinks away into a large warm darkness.

When she wakes up, it's pitch-black.

Somewhere close by, she hears the small, familiar breath of her one remaining child, the child whose name is unknown to posterity.

She falls back to sleep.

5

Seagulls and storm winds the next morning; pounding gusts, harsh sun-light.

She takes her baby to her breast to soothe him. She stays in her room until she hears stirrings in the house.

When she slips into the back room, the maid is already at work. The shipowner's there too. They exchange greetings; he has read the letter. He treats her with measured respect and assures her that he will help. He doesn't give her much hope of finding her children but acknowledges that Jerusalem is the only good bet. When he hears of the galley bound for Tunis that she'd planned to board, his words are harsh: most women passengers are abused or sold as slaves by the scum on those freighters. Tunis and the whole North African coast is a preposterous route, in his opinion, because of the dangers; she must avoid all the old pilgrim routes through the Maghrib and Syria in view of the recent tensions through-out the known world. One of his ships will set sail for Genoa in a week. There's a closed deck for well-born Jewish travellers, his main customers. In the meantime, she can stay in his house and regain her strength. Ham-outal listens without speaking. She bends her knee and reaches for his hand to kiss. The man waves her off, saying she owes him nothing, and is gone for the rest of the day.

She sees him only once more, just before she leaves. He shows up by the harbour to escort her to her ship and hands her a purse of silver coins and a second letter of recommendation permitting her to travel from Genoa to Palermo at his expense. And there comes the maid, with a bundle of clothing prepared for her. The shipowner's wife comes to see her off too. It's a tearful farewell; Hamoutal has latched on to these people like a drowning woman. They say little; the wind has died down a bit, and the bobbing ship remains docked until well into the afternoon. She hears shouted orders and banging below deck. Then the ship casts off and raises its sails, which immediately swell. The wind has soon carried it out of the harbour, past the rock later known as the Château d'If. The sea blinds her, endless dots of light shine in her eyes; she holds her sleeping baby close and takes deep breaths of sea air. But she feels no relief.

Nothing of Genoa will remain in her memory except that one Norman knight from Rouen she recognises at once as a distant cousin, who also seems to recognise her. He is grooming his horse; he gives her a long stare, and it seems he intends to approach her. She turns to go; he calls after her, but she lumbers down the street as fast as she can with her child and her bag, slips through an open gate and squats behind the bushes in a courtyard, covering her whining baby's mouth with her hand. She thinks she can hear his steps as he passes; the wild racing of her heart makes her feel sick. She waits there, curled into a ball, until it grows dark, then creeps back to the harbour, rents a room in an inn, and lies in bed, sleepless, alert to every noise.

The city echoes all night with footfall, back and forth, and men's excited voices. The dockworkers trudge and toil without stop, preparing ships to carry crusaders and adventurous zealots across the sea. Light flickers on the ceiling from the torches carried through the streets. Hamoutal dives deep under the coarse sheets with her child in her arms and cries herself to sleep.

The next morning she pulls her shawl over her face like a veil. She lugs her travel bag through the streets; the child is whimpering again and throws up in the sling as she crosses the plank. She reels for a moment, between ship and shore, at the sight of the water below, its dark and frightful churning; she smells the sour odour coming from the child and stumbles onto the galley, almost tripping. The sea is calm; the sun is rising over the harbour, which reeks of dead fish. The ship moves forward into the wind; she can hear the drumbeat and the chanting oarsmen in the darkness below deck. The mast creaks, gulls fly low over the rubbish drifting offshore, and above deck, people walk back and forth. She is on her way to Palermo. The galley is called the *Pomella*; according to the chronicler Caffaro, Godfrey of Bouillon took the same ship to Alexandria a few years earlier, in 1093; but David Abulafia, a leading historian of Mediterranean navigation, has shown that to be a mere fiction.

The voyage takes a week.

The ship follows the Gulf of La Spezia, staying close to the Italian coastline, and passes Livorno, heading towards Piombino. The winds are favourable; all the ship has to do is follow the strong current that meanders all the way around the Mediterranean rim. Near Follonica, she sees an island to starboard; it's Elba, a rocky protrusion in the form of a giant fish flashing its tailfins at the Italian mainland. But she can't see that from the ship, and certainly not on eleventh-century maps, which look much like the doodles of a dreamy child. The sailors are nervous as they pass the island, a notorious base for pirate attacks.

After two days, they dock in Porto Santo Stefano, unloading cargo and taking on fresh supplies. Hamoutal walks on the beach with her baby, the only constant in her life, sleeping in the shawl on her back. Somewhere in a small garden under a tall tamarisk, she sees a short, bald man bowed over a writing desk, the very image of calm and quiet. It is the great scribe Guilielmus of Hansea, who is staying in the port town. The man looks up, and his lips curve slightly into a refined, ironic smile. It throws her off for a moment. Long gone are the days of delicate fabrics and white fingers; her hands smell of fish and salt. The wind is mild and gentle; the sky above is filled with dazzling sunlight. No crusaders here, not even any Normans: quiet and calm. She sleeps for an hour under a myrtle tree with her baby beside her, returns to the harbour, and spends the night in her berth on board, which bobs, creaking peacefully, under the star-strewn darkness.

Over the next few days, they sail past Ostia and Naples, putting in at Sorrento. Hamoutal gives herself over to the rolling of the peaceful waves on the purple-tinged Tyrrhenian. The thin line marking the edge of the Italian peninsula is always shimmering on their port side; dolphins leap in silhouette as the light fans out behind them. A man plays a simple hurdy-gurdy and sings lewd ditties. An abbot on the ship has words with him: he is doing the Devil's work, he must stop at once.

Past Amalfi, off the coast of Salerno, the ship makes a sharp turn to the west. The sea is choppy, and the wind sends high waves over the bow, spattering white foam on deck; she feels seasick. The woodwork creaks; the prow sometimes plummets several metres from the crest of a wave, and the paupers emerge from the dark bowels of the ship to throw up in the sunlight. The oarsmen have to go back to work; the sails are lowered. From below deck comes a muffled drumming as if the old ship has a heartbeat. The next night, the sea calms. From a distance, they see Stromboli's hellfire raging in the darkness. Some of the more devout passengers are struck with terror and call it the Gates of Hell or the Devil's island. They kneel on the deck and pray. A man pounds his chest, long and hard, until he collapses in exhaustion and bursts into tears. Hamoutal joins the feverish prayer. Her baby is too young to have any idea what's going on in his mother's heart.

Malfa, Lipari, and then the Sicilian coast heaves into view: Capo d'Orlando in Messina, Norman territory in her day. Where could her brothers be now?

6

Palermo

Looking out over present-day Palermo from Monte Pellegrino, you cannot imagine how the harbour must have looked then. Of course, the mountains on the far side of the bay must seem just as dark and impassive on early mornings, outlined against the piercing blue of the sky, and if Hamoutal ever climbed this hill, she must have felt the sea wind full in her face, just as tourists do today. But the harbour could not have been more different: instead of a long, crowded wharf lined with tall cranes, it was a sandy shore with a few inlets crawling with merchants, sailors, traders, horsecarts and depots for the mountains of goods arriving from the Orient, which were shipped on from here to places further north. No rows of high-rises back then; small, primitive houses still stood shoulder to shoulder around the harbour, and behind them rose the mansions of the wealthy shipowners and citizens. In those days, Palermo was already a major city with more than 350,000 inhabitants. The mixture of Arab and Romanesque architectural styles made the city an impressive place. Visitors never failed to express their admiration for its pleasant, healthful atmosphere. A century after Hamoutal's passage, the Arab geographer Ibn Jubayr praised the city's mosques, fountains and grand squares, likening its splendour to Córdoba's. Yet for many years there was also friction between the Byzantine Christians and the Arab rulers, who jockeyed for power over both Christians and Arabs. Hamoutal's stop in Palermo may have been the most foolish risk she ran in all her travels. She put herself in serious danger of being spotted, captured, interrogated or otherwise harassed by someone who knew her from her childhood; she saw Norman knights literally at every street corner, shouting orders.

*

When I think of the city of Palermo, I will always remember how impressed I was by the catacombs of the Capuchin monks.

The Catacombe dei Cappuccini are in the centre of town, in the Piazza Cappuccini, near the order's monastery. In Via Cappuccini, the vegetable and fruit vendors sit amicably side by side in the shade of the old trees. Vespas vroom by, weaving around each other. Exhaust fumes blow past two dead olive shrubs in cracked pots. The husky voice of Gianna Nannini blares from a window: *Meravigliosa creatura!* One detail strikes me: a long, ugly concrete wall along Via Cipressi, spray-painted with the word YAHWEH, twice, in large capital letters.

Against a backdrop of stolid residential blocks, the bizarre tombs resemble an unrelentingly dark fairy tale from bygone days. Next to the endless rows of posed corpses in the crypt, an ageing guard stares into space in the cool shade of the entrance. The wordless parade of costumed mummies on display here is enough to strike you dumb. It's like descending into a burlesque of Dante's Hell and finding a chorus line of skeletons wired together: a showy prelate, a bishop in his mitre, an old peasant couple, a fifteen-year-old boy, a disintegrating patriarch. There are children's bodies in almost perfect condition, decked out in frilly lace and dusty silk, and a woman who died young, her surprise still apparent in the hollows where her eyes once were. Some empty sockets seem to glare at you darkly as the musty odour addles your brain. Under the pale, whitewashed archways, they form a vast showcase of death, a shameless peepshow. Children's dolled-up corpses, skeletons pointing cynical fingers, an elderly couple leaning towards each other as if death had done nothing to stop them quarrelling. A skull on a wire that has almost rusted away, dangling over a mouldering jacket. Four skeletons positioned so dramatically that they call to mind an excited crowd or Rodin's bronze burghers of Calais. Sometimes they're on shelves high in the wall; sometimes they stare at you from behind iron bars. When their jaws have dropped open, they seem to be emitting silent screams or cackling with pleasure at the idiocy of the living. There are Roman arches composed of skulls with three dead Capuchin monks in front of them; an entrance gate on one wall, a *trompe-l'oeil* effect with frivolous patterns of joint, arm and finger bones; row upon row of shoulder blades stuck to the ceiling in baroque motifs. A half-decayed face seems to give you a cynical wink, but it's just the warping skin, which will soon tear, reveal-ing the skull beneath it and making room for its broad grin. A monstrous monk with a thick rope around his neck tips forward slightly, as if ready to pounce at any moment. His name is Fra Domenico, and he died in the August of a long-gone summer. Four open mouths, filled with dust, appear to sing some holy song, their heads cocked so theatrically that you imagine them aiming for different pitches. An aged mother grimaces maliciously, her hands tied together with wire; a cardinal lies with folded bones on his own tomb, his mitre still pinching his skull but his mouth wide open as if he can't help laughing at himself. The obscene show never ends. When you return to the noise and heat of the outside world, it's as though you've arrived from a different plane of existence, an ancient past waiting with a grin to gather in all the people on the streets. The darkness clings to me as I down an espresso at a lively outdoor cafe, and I'm still a bit dazed as I walk on to the Zisa, the Norman castle attesting to the presence of the kinfolk of Vigdis Adelaïs, who cautiously shuffles past me in the form of a Jewish woman, her dark shawl tight around her head. In the square where the cathedral now stands, a few dry palm trees wave in the balmy sea wind. Tourists take selfies; nothing can shake them; everything speaks for itself.

*

The ferry to Cairo, *signore*? No such thing! And she laughs, the girl with green eyes and yellow nail polish. Who wants to travel to Cairo by sea? You can hop a plane if you want, the airlines offer direct flights. What were you thinking?

Yes, what was I thinking? That I'd discover some vestige here of the ancient maritime route? I'd scoured the websites of shipping companies and found only tedious cruises that went nowhere near the path I had in mind. I'd searched for freighters, but they never seemed to follow Hamoutal's route either. Imagining I would re-enact her voyage as accurately as possible, I'd overlooked how completely the world has changed. Yet that illusion was the thread I continued to follow as I walked along the harbour, realising the only way to come closer to Hamoutal was by forgetting everything I saw around me – except maybe that dressed-up woman's skeleton in the catacombs which reminded me of her and which, like the sculpture in the church in Bourges, gave me the feeling it *could* have been her, that this was the spark to light my imagination and make her reappear before me, a mummy come to life, flesh on those bones, muscles and veins, alive again and none too comfortable in her skin, toting that whimpering baby on her arm, on her way to Yerushalayim, the mythical city she will never reach. What could she have been thinking?

Here in Palermo, Hamoutal decided to board a ship bound for Fustat-Misr, as Cairo's predecessor was called in the eleventh century. The shipping line would have offered quick passage to Alexandria and, upon request, a connecting boat up the Nile. The vast collection of ancient

Hebrew documents found in the Cairo Genizah includes numerous business letters and ships' papers that show how heavy the direct traffic between Palermo and Alexandria was in those days. The trade route between Egypt and the western Mediterranean was controlled mainly by Jewish merchants. With Hamoutal's letter of recommendation, she must soon have found a captain willing to help her, and with one of the silver pieces from the shipowner in Massilia, she could pay him handsomely. So she didn't have to spend the voyage on deck, among passengers packed together like sardines, but had her own private cabin where she could care for her child and lay him down in a bed of his own. Thanks to the sailors' familiarity with sea routes, winds and currents, 90 per cent of those eleventh-century vessels reached their destinations unscathed.

Yet the voyage was rough, and even though Hamoutal had a few privileges, conditions on board would have been hard. Fresh water supplies were often contaminated. The provisions were salted meat, flatbread made with musty flour, the occasional fish when the seas were calm, a great mound of root vegetables, hard dried fruit and nuts. With this inadequate diet, malnutrition stole over the passengers, regardless of class. Dysentery, diarrhoea and stomach complaints were widespread. When the summer winds were favourable and the ship was quick to find the current around the Mediterranean, the crossing went faster. A powerful flow ran west to east from around the Pillars of Hercules, passing not far from Sicily's southern coast and leading all the way to the shores of Egypt. When the wind was fair, the rowers could rest and life on board was quiet.

The days go by in wave-rocked waiting and rumination, in nightmares and memories of all those places: Rouen, Orléans, Narbonne, Moniou, Marseilles, Genoa, Palermo. It all whirls together in her dreams; sometimes she sees her distant, impossible love at the gate of the Rouen yeshiva, and hearing the cries of the large terns over the water, she thinks of the small black-headed gulls from the harbour where the snekkjas lay, or of the short, peaceful days in sunny Narbonne. The old ship reeks of life and of the goods it carries. The men turn to the bottle to ward off homesickness and boredom; a few women sport with them for food or drink. They creep out of sight under bales of wool, giggling, their mouths toothless at the age of twenty-five, but their legs outspread in the shadows; the men thrust and twitch their way to a hurried release and a minute later are spitting over the taffrail in contempt. Above them a heavy sail flaps with slow, dull thuds; straight ahead a school of flying fish are leaping. Tales are told of demonic beings that flit back and forth under the bow and keel. Sometimes a strange creature is caught in the nets, with a hideous, toothy face, wild eyes, and fins like devils' feathers. The few children on board shriek, the women cross themselves and rattle off prayers, and the men look on as the monster fish writhes in the net on deck, gasping for air, a sight to see as it perishes, look at that, it comes from Satan's *caccabus*, the infernal cauldron *de profundis*, the Devil shouts in forty tongues but no one understands them. As the fish drums its tail savagely on the wooden deck and its eyes cloud over, the men shout *Vade retro Satana!* and roar with laughter.

The stars are brighter than any Hamoutal has ever seen. The dark vault of the sky seems to sway without cease to the monotonous surge of water around the bow. Are the stars pinholes, letting through light from a heaven above the black dome of their mortal night? She's sometimes seasick but lies flat on her belly until it passes. Her child is ill again and sleeps in a fever, oblivious. One day she wakes up and sees that the whole ship has turned blood red in the night. Warm wind from North African shores has brought red sand far out to sea, along with a light rain. Later that day, the sailors seize the occasion to sand the deck. The red seeps its way into the smallest cracks and crannies.

A few days later, they see another ship in the distance. Agitation, fear of being boarded. It sails closer, a light Arab vessel; they can make out people on deck. Shouting, back and forth. Then the ship vanishes like a dream, trimming its sails and sinking below the horizon. The bobbing goes on forever. Luckily, there's no storm; the sea is calm this time of year. When the rowers go to work, she can hear their muted voices far below, their rhythmic, droning song, the supervisor's cries, the splashing of the great oars in the rocking sea. Other days, there is nothing but the flapping of thick sailcloth, the voice of the man on the mast, the smell of wood, rope and salt. She settles into a state between dream and waking.

After many uncounted days, the lookout on the starboard mast points out a sandy, forsaken coastline in the distance. They must have already passed Benghazi. Alexandria is calling. There they will change to a smaller vessel. A few men become gravely ill. There's no end to their puking; the whole crew fears infection. They are dragged off, wrapped in sheets – limp and docile after two days' illness – and laid on the stern between a few improvised bulkheads and the rope. Their faded eyes track the movements around them in mortal fear. Others have already closed their crusted eyes and are no longer there. The next morning they've disappeared. Food for the devils from the watery hell, the merchant Embriachi says to Hamoutal with a grin. He's been leering at her for days. Sometimes when he sees her, he grabs the blue broadcloth of his crotch and makes faces like a dog on heat. She shuts herself in her small cabin, mumbling indistinct words as her child looks on in silence, sucking his thumb. There's a rabbi on board; she takes him into her confidence. He reads the letter of recommendation in her cabin, says nothing, and after long pondering tells her he will accompany her to Fustat. This brings her some relief, a sense of not being on her own.

The sea is purple and immense; above their tiny heads, one sky seems to slide through another, a colossal shift. Nothing remains of her, nothing remains of them all, that swarm of insects bobbing on a nutshell, a nothing in a greater nothing. But they advance. Each day, they advance. They are already well south of Crete; the wood of the ship creaks and bends in the strong current. They sail along the bare white coastline for days; heat pulses above them. Everyone is exhausted. Their supplies are almost gone; another man dies of dysentery. The rest of them starve out the days that separate them from Alexandria. Sometimes they catch fish; the sailors eat them raw, and the ship's cook throws the remains into boiling water. Small cups of watery fish soup are handed out to the passengers. After another two days, they dock by the ancient lighthouse, blinded by sunlight, their split lips encrusted with salt, their clothes threadbare from sliding back and forth on hard benches, their hands dry and skin papery, their souls leached and wasted. Even in those days it was a white city, a Fata Morgana, a dream of hot, ancient stones, Alexander's city.

7

Alexandria

'The sea is high again today, with a thrilling flush of wind … the city which used us as its flora … beloved Alexandria!' Thus begins the first book of Lawrence Durrell's spellbinding *Alexandria Quartet*. 'What is this city of ours? What is resumed in the word Alexandria? In a flash my mind's eye shows me a thousand dust-tormented streets. Flies and beggars own it today.'

I was consumed with curiosity about this mythical place, and I imagine that Hamoutal, likewise, squinted tensely at the shoreline as her ship neared the city. In her time, you could see the famous lighthouse, the Pharos, on its small spit of land projecting from the coast. More than 125 metres high and a thousand years old, it was deemed a wonder of the world. According to Euripides, Menelaus was shipwrecked here with a strange phantom of Helen of Troy; Cleopatra committed suicide a few steps from the site where today the post-colonial Cecil Hotel still gazes out over the sea in old-fashioned grandeur. Two obelisks from her palace, known as Cleopatra's Needles, stood here in Hamoutal's day; here the poet Cavafy wrote of the queen's lover Mark Antony abandoning the city as the city abandoned him. Durrell describes the mythical Justine, like Cleopatra reborn, drinking coffee in elegant gloves in the hotel lounge as she looks out over the flickering of the sea.

I have come here by train from Cairo. I get off at the central station and am plunged into thrilling chaos; in the streets around the square, a large market bustles; hundreds of vendors shout through small, tinny mega-phones over the deafening roar of traffic. This city was once known as the great wine-press of love, overflowing with ephebes and Oriental maidens, with fortune-hunters, passionate lovers with fiery blood, wealthy recluses, and potentates obsessed with the perfection of young bodies; with secret lovers, slowed by wine and hashish, lying tangled for hours in their lovemaking, to the sound of the crashing waves and the wind snuffling like a dog at the tops of the plane trees.

That is the exotic image, the Orientalist dream, which according to Edward Said was about a make-believe world invented by the colonial cultural elite.

How different it all was in Hamoutal's day. In the eleventh century, Alexandria was going through a period about which little is known, regarded by some historians as a time of stagnation and decay. Yet Amr ibn al-As wrote in the seventh century that 'it is impossible for me to enumerate the variety of its riches and beauty; I shall content myself with observing that it contains 4,000 palaces, 4,000 baths, 400 theatres or places of amusement, 12,000 fruit shops, and 40,000 tributary Jews'. The city was brought back to life by the comings and goings of the crusades, the international connections, the arrival of intellectuals and adventurers, beautiful boys, wealthy women and jealous lovers.

But even all the way back in the eleventh century, the fabled library of antiquity was long gone. I walk the whole length of the Corniche, the waterfront promenade – first from right to left, starting in the middle and ending at the Fort of Qaitbay, where young boys sell candyfloss in inflated plastic bags, which they hang from rods as if flying transparent fish from a cord. Then I walk back, past the central Saad Zaghloul Square, all the way to Alexandria's new library. Under the high, slanted ceiling of the spectacular reading room, I see two girls in niqabs huddled over a book; their kohl-lined eyes fly over the pages of a Michel Houelle-becq novel as they giggle and elbow each other.

Just as there is now an express train between Alexandria and Cairo, there was a high-speed courier service to and from Fustat in the eleventh century, delivering mail from one city to the other in less than a week. A ceaseless current of travellers moved between the two cities, bring-ing family members, distant relations, marriage candidates, goldwork, scrolls, spices and gifts. There were even families who took up residence in each other's homes, the house-swappers of their time.

The sea is calm and peaceful; the largest waves break against the tongue of land that protects the coast, leaving the basin of water behind it as smooth and unruffled as an inland lake. A man in a caftan walks to and fro, urging women who bare their shoulders, however briefly, to cover them again. Then he says a polite thank-you and moves on. A whole family is camping in a hut on the sand; the girls leap up when they see me and cry photo, photo. I duck into the old streets, a few of which remain unpaved to this day. In some dusty corners of town, I can daydream that maybe not so much has changed in the past thousand years. I return to the railway station in the evening sun and wait with crowds of commut-ers for the train back to Cairo.

In the Nile Delta, I had expected to find some remnant of the original landscape. A jungle of slapdash buildings is what it is, an indistinct agglomeration of endless non-cities, half-finished districts already decaying, metropolitan tendrils, vacant concrete skeletons of abandoned projects, each with its scrawny rebar crown stabbing up into the sky – a sign that construction is still in progress and the building is therefore tax-exempt. But whole families live on the lower floors, uncertain what each day will bring.

In between are scattered fields, some parched, some muddy, thanks to sloppy irrigation. I see grain and rubble, deserted farmland, hundreds of white ibises in a dead tree, crumbling industrial parks. In the suburbs, unemployed young people walk among smouldering trash heaps and grazing buffalo. I see women in the fields, swinging hoes into the fertile soil of the polluted Nile Valley. Then the beauty of orchards veiled in light mist, slender bridges over brackish waters, palms, eucalyptuses and tamarisks, the strange, bulging barrel vaults of ancient cemeteries lost in the sand, a small football pitch by the roadside, thin cows along a pasture's reedy fringe, goats in a field of clover, a grand house next to a rubbish dump, six horses on a patch of mud drying in the sun, endless silhouettes with unsteady edges.

8

There are not many ways for a woman in Hamoutal's position, with her baby in her arms, to traverse the more than two hundred kilometres from Alexandria to Fustat. Flood waters flowing down the Lower Nile sometimes fill what are known as seasonal canals, creating a number of fast moving waterways. One such waterway, the Alexandria canal, makes it possible to travel from Alexandria to Fustat in less than a week.

But Hamoutal learns the canal is not yet navigable; the season runs from August to October. She has heard tales of the dangers awaiting ships that try to enter the river from the open sea through the tumultuous mouth of the Nile's western branch, the Rosetta estuary. The accumulated sediment from the enormous mass of water forms ever-shifting sandbanks just under the waterline. The north wind whips the seawater into towering waves, which crash and churn against the current. Countless light ships are caught there to sink or be carried away by surges of mud and torn to pieces.

The tenth-century Arab chronicler Ibn Hawqal described how perilous it was to travel in the northern delta. Documents from the Cairo Genizah also shed light on the risks. The historical record leaves no doubt that navigating the Nile could be a hellish venture. Even in the late seventeenth century, visitors to Cairo preferred to travel by land as far as the southern Nile oases. In 1697, the French cleric Antoine Morison heard Turks claiming that anyone who did not fear the Bogaze, the mouth of the Nile, did not fear God. Day and night, sailors stood watch along the turbulent banks, honking horns to warn reckless skippers of the water's fickle currents, and many boats waited as long as two weeks for the north wind to die down before daring to sail upstream through the estuary.

The Nile is like a lotus, the elders say; its stem is the southern Nile Valley, the northern delta its curved flower, and the Faiyum basin sprouts from that large stem like a closed bud. Herodotus called Egypt a gift from the Nile, no less, but this colossal lotus, bringer of life to the country, is also a violent, death-dealing organism. All ships that sail to Cairo must fight the current, because the river's enormous volumes of water flow from the heights of Ethiopia and southern Sudan out into the Mediterranean. If you make it through the estuary, you might have the wind at your back; the meltemi, the near-constant north wind sometimes felt as far inland as Cairo, might propel you upstream without too much trouble. But on calm days, the feluccas – traditional sailing boats, often unstable – have to be towed. The tow-men toil their way down riverbanks littered with obstacles, or stand in water and mud up to their waists, sweltering against the current and making next to no progress. If the ship runs aground on a sandbank or one of the river's countless grassy islets, in the reeds or in the weeds, it's dislodged with bargepoles. When the southern khamsin blows masses of sand from the hot Sahara into the Nile Valley, sailing upstream is hopeless. The wind is too strong for some smaller craft, like the traditional *jarm*s or *germe*s, which keel over; the passengers and crew drown in the waves or under the vessels. The complex conditions on the Nile lead to a constant nervous hubbub in the ports. There is ceaseless discussion of the wind direction, the season, alternative sailing routes, the situation at the Rosetta estuary, the expected delays, and the number of *saq*s (a unit of measurement then used in the Arabic world, of uncertain length) that the boats hope to travel each day. But there are also fast-moving caravans available from Alexandria, which give travellers the option of going by land. Hamoutal settles on this safer route for the first leg, to the calmer southern stretches of the river. After a few days of fretting and walking back and forth between merchants and mariners who are at constant pains to swindle her, she chooses – for reasons of safety – the Jewish merchant caravans, which travel what is known today as the genizah route. After she presents her letter of recommendation, she is granted special protection and a better deal. The world in which she is now immersed seems to her like a hectic dream. Dust billows in the hot wind, people shout on all sides, the stench is excruciating, the bustle never ends. Along the dusty streets, she sees food sellers who have put out their wares next to piles of camel droppings, dried fish crawling with flies, beef tripe next to dishes of dried dates. She mounts a kneeling camel for the first time, with her child in her arms. She falls straight off the other side; the child rolls through the sand and wails. Onlookers laugh; a man helps her up and points to the end of the street; she can't understand him. He takes her by the arm and brings her to his wife and daughters, who smile at her and all start shouting at once. She is shown to a dim passageway in the back of an old house and offered a small room with a couch and carpets. They bring her a dish of water and olives. The next morning she is awakened; a man is waiting in front of the house. He speaks to her in Aramaic: her caravan is leaving for Fustat.

Days of travel through the delta, heat and monotony, the swaying, lumbering gait of the camels, their unsettling, primordial noises, the smell of their droppings, sand in her every pore. A couple of days later, they reach the small oases of the north-west Nile Delta. They are sometimes menaced along the way by predators and snakes, and the diet is nothing like what she's accustomed to. After just a few days, she is sick to her stomach. She develops colic, diarrhoea, dehydration, fever, crusty eyes. The vomiting racks her body for days on end; she is laid in a large wicker basket on a camel's back. A plump woman with a perpetual smile nurses the child, who lies staring in silence at the eternal, unchanging sky.

Kafr El Dawwar, Sidi Ghazi. Desert wind, heat, blinding sand and sunlight; now the child, too, shows signs of dehydration. She is a woman alone, unable to speak Arabic, using the limited Hebrew that David taught her, trying to make herself clear with signs and gestures. Now and then she produces a coin, careful not to give the impression that she has any more money with her. Sometimes she finds protection, sometimes courtesy as a prelude to fraud, other times she is threatened, and once she comes close to being raped. Yet thanks to Obadiah's letter of recommendation, she is usually treated with respect and remains a privileged traveller, despite all her woes. At night she sleeps side by side with the other women, her child in her arms; fire keeps the jackals at bay.

About halfway through her journey – in the Gharbia region, close to where Kafr El Zayat is today – the caravan comes to a halt by the Nile. Fishing is good there, the riverbanks are fertile, there is fruit in the marketplaces, olive oil, goat's cheese, vegetables, spicy lamb and delicious flatbread; the travellers can recuperate. They sleep in one of the numerous stations along the river. The next day is a rest day; she bathes her baby and tends to his needs. Summer has reached its height. The heat seems like a permanent hallucination; the odour of camel shit permeates everything. She is tired, so disoriented and drained by the journey that she refuses to travel any further with the caravan. The heat makes her sluggish; sand and sweat sting her eyes and skin. The solitude of the desert landscape is behind them; the vendors at the bustling riverside market shout in a mixture of Arabic, Aramaic, Greek and Turkish. Levantines and Byzantines, Seljuks, Ethiopians and Maghribis mingle there.

She lies in a kind of stupor all day, in the shade of a canvas canopy, depleted by diarrhoea, with sand in her eyes and a hot wind sweeping over her face. She starts crying again, a heartbreaking sound; the merchants who had agreed to accompany her to Fustat stand around her, uneasy, urging her to pick up her child, stand up, and mount the camel that is kneeling for her. She shakes her head no; her weeping is raw, almost animal. She pulls her dark blue chador tight over her face, sobbing, and curls into a foetal position. The child begins to cry now too. The men confer, give her a little time to collect herself, and ask again half an hour later whether she will join them. Again, she shakes her head no, weeping noisily.

A larger crowd of men has now gathered around the canopy under which she lies. One of them comes closer; it is Embriachi, the merchant from Palermo who had his eye on her aboard ship. The rabbi who offered to escort her has already moved on. Embriachi kneels beside her and explains that a barge to Fustat will arrive the next day, a vessel called *Al-Iskander*, that he knows the captain, that she can travel with them if she shows her letter. That way, he continues, she can sleep and recover her strength during the trip. He will wait for her the next day.

She looks up in surprise, half understanding what the man is saying; then her head slumps back again and she seems to fall asleep. The caravan prepares for departure; the men pile up sacks and packets; the baggage is roped to the kneeling beasts of burden. With much ado, the procession sets off. The camels bellow; the men shout. The women's cries are shrill and seem unreal. Then the noise fades into the distance, leaving only wind and heat.

The exhausted woman can vaguely hear the rustling treetops by the banks of the Nile and the voices of boys at play in the shallow water by the fringe of reeds. She falls asleep and dreams of a quiet mountain village where she once picked thyme, her children playing in the cool spring breeze. But the memory is bloodstained, tinged with unfathomable darkness in which she sinks and almost suffocates. Gasping for air, she looks around.

Two women are squatting beside her; one is cradling Hamoutal's child in her arms. She shoots upright; the woman pushes her back down with a laugh, stands up, and walks off with the child to a small hut nearby. Hamoutal stumbles after her, but the woman won't give her the child; she smiles and shakes her head. Hamoutal yanks at the woman's arm, the baby cries, the women both tug at it, shrieking and shoving. Hamoutal sees the pain and panic in her child's eyes. She lets go and follows the women.

They reach the dark hut: the deafening buzz of horseflies, the smell of rotting meat. She wants her child back; the woman shakes her head in refusal. Then she sees the second woman place a bowl of cloudy water in the sand in the middle of the hut. They sprinkle the child and laugh again. Chattering away, they remove the tattered rags, perfume the boy's body, notice he's still uncircumcised, giggle and wrap him in light cotton. Then they return the child to her. Hamoutal's head tips back, and she drops like a stone. She lies unconscious in the sand with foam on her mouth. The women lay the child on a few palm leaves and fan the collapsed woman to cool her.

When she wakes, night has fallen. Her eyes are crusted shut, her lips split; her throat is burning and her breathing laboured. She has a high fever and is wasted with illness. Her heart races; she is drenched with sweat. It is pitch-dark. Through a small opening, she sees the twinkling heavens like a dream. By the muddy banks of a few pools by the river, frogs are croaking to raise the dead. She has the feeling she's let go of everything and now is nowhere, in a place between, without a body of her own, without weight; she lies in a soft, soothing glow, a pool of flame that scorches and soothes her mind, a state between sleeping and dying, in which sorrow and mild euphoria can no longer be separated. She's succumbing to typhus but doesn't know it.

She wakes again in the pale morning to the gravelly sound of a heron's cry. The women are already hard at work, pulling off her clothes, rubbing her with a bitter-smelling blend of wormwood, hemp and fish oil, and making her drink something that's hard for her to swallow. She is swaddled in sheets; she throws up the elixir; she falls asleep again. More than a week slips past that way; she remains unconscious of time or place, teetering on the brink of life and dream, gliding gently into a dark tunnel. Whenever she stops breathing, the women poke her, slap her cheeks, sprinkle water on her. She drifts over the bottomless pit of her tempting, comforting, enticing, irresistible death; she put everything behind her a long time ago; an unreal calm fills her; she sees David in an alley; he passes her, holding Yaakov's hand, but then he's a walking torso without a head; she wakes up and vomits again, goes back to sleep.

A full month passes before she can rise to her feet and take a few cautious steps. She's become so thin that she looks like a living skeleton. Her eyes are inflamed; a wound on her left arm is infested with maggots. The women wash her again, still chattering away and as incomprehensible as ever. She gives in to all of it, not even asking about her baby, who is crawling in the sun with skinned knees, following the other children along the riverbank. Her recovery is slow, because she struggles to keep food down, but in time she begins to ask herself some questions. Why are these women nursing her? Why isn't there a man around?

It takes her a few days to figure out that the two women work as prostitutes, serving the passing boats on the Nile; they are outcasts, pariahs, trying their luck together in their hut not far from the river, scraping by in their primitive way with whatever they can lay their hands on. They are left alone; they know the customs and the codes, there's no fooling them. Once Hamoutal is feeling a little better, they take her to the river to bathe. An hour later the next felucca arrives, and the women offer her to one of the boatmen. Hamoutal puts up a struggle, so he hits her on the head, knocking her unconscious. She drops like a stone. The women drag her back inside the hut and leave her there half dead, showering her with curses.

She wakes that evening in a panic. The sun is low, the hot, humid air is stifling, the insects swarming around her are maddening. Her child is not there; she hears the women's peals of laughter by the distant riverbank. Where is her letter of recommendation? The rest of her baggage? She sees none of her things in the hut. Where are the few silver pieces she concealed with such care? Where is *she*, for that matter, where in this maddening world is she, where is she to go? She jumps up. Her lip is split, there's dried blood on her chin, when she licks her lips the blood starts flowing again. She swallows blood, and her heart almost leaps out of her chest. She totters outside; a few goats mill around her legs. Where are the children?

She hears children's voices in the distance and, stumbling towards them, finds her baby sleeping amid rags and rubbish. A few greasy sheep are wandering by the reeds. She picks up the grubby, underfed child, which seems to feel nothing. Nearby is a vulture with a snake in its beak, whipping it back and forth, slamming its head against the sandy ground until it no longer moves but hangs limp as a rag from the bird's beak. Then the vulture rips into it, gagging down its repulsive meal. Where is my boy Yaakov now? The question tears through her like a scream.

She kisses the motionless boy on his hanging head, lays him gently on a few sheets in the hut, searches in a fever for her things, turning over everything she sees, but finds only the pouch with the rolled-up parchment, her letter of recommendation, and David's tefillin; her silver coins have disappeared. She stuffs the pouch underneath a scrap of fabric that she winds around her waist like a scarf. She grows dizzy and pitches forward, bangs her shoulder into the mud wall, picks up her child, wraps him up in the dirty rags she finds in the tent, and stumbles down to the river. Speechless, she displays the starved child, flies swarming around his head, to a few men sitting on the bank drinking. She stammers something in broken Hebrew; one of the men shouts in the direction of a flat-bottomed boat tied up nearby. A man comes out and asks her what she wants in Aramaic. She falls to her knees, sobs, pulls out the letter, and shows it to the man. He unrolls the parchment, scans the document, gives the woman a distrustful, probing look, and then nods his head towards the galley. She stands, picks up her groggy child with care, stumbles on board, and is shown to a bench, where she lies down, panting with exertion.

After darkness falls, one of the women comes out of the forecabin and, finding her there, lets out an angry, high-pitched stream of words and kicks her. Embriachi appears from nowhere, pushes the ranting woman off the boat, and beckons Hamoutal to stand up. How did Embriachi get here? She follows him meekly; he leads her to his small cabin; she lies down on the wooden, rag-lined berth and falls into oblivious sleep again. When she wakes up a few hours later, she feels him moving on top of her. He has lifted her skirts, he is already inside her, she is not even startled. A defeated warmth spreads through her body, a desolate glow, something she can't control. He reeks of hashish and fish; she doesn't move but feels her wetness and desire and lets him have his way. After a few minutes he comes with a grunt; she feels his calloused hand on her nipples, his unshaven cheek rasping along her throat. He rolls off her and falls straight to sleep. At the first glimmer of dawn, as the ship slowly starts to move, she clings to the man, silent, her eyes shut, and catches herself stroking his shoulder. The boatmen sink their poles deep into the mud by the banks; the old, low sail is unfurled. The felucca glides upstream with the wind at its back, to the middle of the brown and yellow river, seeking out the path of least resistance, the rowers toiling to the rhythm of the drum. She is on her way to Fustat, old Cairo, a hundred kilometres away. The sun is already beating down. The smell of mud and fish, wood and rope, fills the stale air of the cabin. Vapour burbles up out of the water; the world is in motion again. The merchant snores. The child, bundled up in cloths and rags, is no longer breathing.

VII

Cairo

1

Tunub, Alqam, Al Birijat, Jizayy, Al Khatatba, Abu Ghaleb, Al Qata, Al Qanatir Al Khayriyyah, the places in the delta where dirty white settlements rise today, names that come and go – which ones existed then?

Again I must sweep the map clean of almost everything I find there now, leaving only a few scattered names and things. But she and I share the elements. Brief squalls, sudden rain, clouds and haze, mist, burning sun, deep-purple morning skies with circling eagles, sickly-smelling nights on the water, darting fish, clear voices on the bank. Docking, provisioning, haggling, pushing off again, sailing against the current, sometimes barely inching forward, mooring in sandy bends. Scraped skin, a dead goat drifting by, swollen like a balloon. The rowers' rough hands, the strange singing at nightfall she does not begin to understand. The languid lowing of the water buffalo in the yellow mud of the banks. The herons and the frogs.

After two days, the anointed dead child is brought up from the hold, as Hamoutal is held back by three men; she screams like a woman possessed. The little mummy is thrown overboard while two men pound a fierce drumbeat and a third wails on a wind instrument. The women let out shrill cries that drive her into a panic. The bundle slips away in the brown eddies. Just below the surface, she can see the supple curve of a crocodile's back. For one terrifying moment, a vague red cloud rises in the brown water, then nothing more. Hamoutal gasps for air and pulls free. The boatmen urge each other on in a rhythmic chorus; the musicians go on drumming a little longer; then silence descends, and there's only the lapping of the current against the low prow. Hamoutal, seizing the opportunity, tries to jump overboard; one man leaps forward and holds her in an iron grip. He smacks her and pushes her down onto a bench. Her cheek is bleeding: snot, dust, blood and tears. For the rest of the day she no longer resembles one of the living. She has a stunned, inward look and rocks with the swell of the water. That evening the sight of the men eating raw fish makes her gag. She is all alone now, except for the lecherous merchant, who tries three times a day to draw her in with words that mean nothing to her and a gap-toothed smile, which sometimes distracts but more often repulses her. She eats little, sleeps most of the day, wakes in the evening, and goes to the foredeck to sit and listen to the flowing water, slow and majestic.

Beyond the last bend, a week and a half later, the buildings of Fustat lift from the horizon, shimmering in the sunlight from behind. The July heat is stifling; everything seems like a mirage. She feels almost untethered from the material world, drifting half conscious through her days, distant from everything and everyone. Silent and indifferent, she stares at the world floating past, a world she neither knows nor wants to know. The season is Shemu, when not a single drop of rain falls and everything turns dry and stony. The ship glides as far as the famous pontoon bridge that has connected Fustat to the island of Roda since the eighth century. From there, the small Nilometer building is visible. Beyond it, the great Mosque of Amr ibn al-As comes into sight, with its dreamlike minarets from the Umayyad period, an impressive skyline that bespeaks the power of the Fatimids over Egypt. On Roda, along this narrower stretch of the Nile, Muslim soldiers guard the entrance to the city; Hamoutal sees buildings, soldiers, swaying boats along the riverbanks, swarms of people.

Fustat-Misr gleams and glitters in dust clouds and afternoon sun. Hamoutal disembarks from her Nile boat without any baggage; Embriachi helps her off. He's been grumpy for the past few days, because she no longer responds to his advances. Before she can say a thing, he thrusts a primitive map of the city into her hands, with Al-Shamiyin Synagogue identified in big letters. He signs to her that she must go there and show her letter of recommendation from Obadiah. Then he nods, with a sour grin, and walks off, leaving her alone on the sandy quay.

She feels small and lost. She hopes the Egyptian Muslims will leave a Jewish woman alone, or help her if they can, even if their help is casual and impersonal. Long ago in Narbonne, David's father once told her that the Spanish Muslims left Jews in peace as long as they paid for the privilege. The *dhimmis*, as they called Jews, could even count on a degree of protection, since they were a source of income. She hopes the situation will not be too different here. But for the time being, Hamoutal, dirty and destitute, with northern features, has no claim to any help. Until she finds a place to stay and some form of protection, there is no telling what will become of her.

*

There she stands, the erstwhile Christian Viking girl from Rouen, born four years after the Battle of Hastings. It is July 1097. Cairo rustles, churns and quivers in the broiling sun. In her home city, almost all the Jews have been murdered. The yeshiva she knew so well has been burned down and all of its library's holdings are lost. She knows nothing about all that, nor about what her mother screamed as she watched the massacre, still embittered by her daughter's disappearance: That'll teach you, accursed Jews! Hamoutal is almost twenty-seven years old and has become nobody – a woman loose in a world not her own, roaming lost in a life story she scarcely understands, on her way to Yerushalayim, the city of three gods, where she hopes to be reunited with Yaakov and Justa. She turns her eyes to the sky, the hot, salty sky of Fustat; to the boatmen unloading their cargo on the riverbank; to the wild cats wandering among the discarded remains of fish, the dogs leaking pus from their eyes, pissing on wooden poles, or gnawing on smelly bones; to the little boys with perfect, gleaming calves, fast as the wind, carrying luggage for new arrivals in exchange for alms; veiled women coming out of dark doorways. Her blonde hair, once a wild mass of curls, lies drab and sweat-soaked on her head under her dark shawl; the skin of her cheeks is scaly and pale; her eyes are dulled by fatigue and deprivation. She watches in astonishment as Embriachi walks away, feeling the momentary urge to rush after him, fall to her knees, ask him to take her with him, take her under his protection, marry her, anything. Then he steps into a camel-drawn chaise, and she soon loses sight of him in the crowd. She wanders a while through the masses by the riverbank, unnoticed, inconspicuous, more a shadow than a person. She begs for a piece of bread and goat's cheese, asks for a slice of watermelon somewhere, drinks water from a fountain where stray yellow dogs press their dirty noses into her skirts. She wanders through the dust of an ancient district of broken-down dark shacks, reaches a square, and sits down stiffly under the branches of an old acacia, which snake out gnarled and crooked from underneath a white ruin. She is muddled from days of bobbing down the river, her legs weak. She cannot sit up straight. The world spins; she falls on her side and stays down, dazed. Her hands clutch at the sandy grass. Swarms of gold-blue flies buzz all around her; a dog licks her cheek with its stinking tongue. She scarcely reacts. It is growing dark by the time she comes to her senses. No one gives her a second glance. She walks down a few streets and then, with a questioning look in her eyes, shows her map to a well-dressed man, who looks her up and down and points her in the right direction. By nine in the evening she has reached the old Mar Girgis church and is stumbling towards the synagogue. It is already dark. The narrow streets are deserted; they smell like dust and piss. The district comes to a sudden end at the city wall, next to which she finds the synagogue. By a large well behind the building, she lies down and falls asleep, with no notion of the viper that slithers into the folds of her clothes, of the yellow scorpion next to her hand, of the stray dog that sniffs at her, of the fact that the dog saves her life, grabbing the viper's head in its jaws and tossing the writhing snake away; no idea of the dark path the scorpion follows between her hand and the little hollow among the stones of the Well of Moses. She has no idea whatsoever. She's still breathing, that's all.

That is what the rabbi observes the next morning after opening the synagogue gate, when beside the well in the back courtyard, he finds, to his surprise, the haggard form of a sleeping woman.

2

I plunge into the metro, leaving the hectic traffic in Tahrir Square behind. At Mar Girgis station, I step off into the crowd of women in niqabs and Nikes and men holding smartphones. I need a moment to get my bearings because, just like in Rouen, the entrance to the old city is a few metres below the modern world. The heat is starting to take its toll on me, this Saturday in February, when at last I descend the nondescript stairs to the medieval remains of Fustat, now known as Old Cairo. Fenced off like a ghetto, I can't help thinking when I see the ornamented gate to the district. As I cross the white, dusty street I notice, against the blue, the blinding stone of the Coptic church dedicated to St George – Mar Girgis – shining in the morning sun. But it's not the building Hamoutal saw – that one burned down a century after she passed this way. It's cool here in the narrow streets. An elderly Jewish man offers me a brochure for twenty Egyptian pounds, but I turn it down. I'm constantly beckoned into shops to buy a piece of junk, drink a cup of tea, pay baksheesh, hear a rambling story, see a dusty booklet. All I have to say is 'synagogue' and every finger points ahead, to the end of this small, intimate labyrinth. I keep going, and an instant later I see it: Ben Ezra Synagogue, known in the days of Fustat as Al-Shamiyin. I take a deep breath and approach the entrance; someone says Shabbat shalom. It's like coming home in a dream.

This place is legendary. According to tradition, the well behind the building is where the pharaoh's daughter found the newborn Moses in a basket, and he grew up here. Straight in front of the synagogue is the ancient church of Abu Serga, on the site to which Joseph and Mary are said to have fled during the mass infanticide ordered by Herod. As the story goes, they stayed there for three months. Ben Ezra Synagogue in Fustat was one of the world's oldest; Abraham ben Ezra – not to be confused with the eleventh-century Abraham ibn Ezra –bought the land for 20,000 dinars in the year 882. The previous building on the site was an old Coptic church dedicated to St Michael. For that reason, the synagogue is similar in design to a small Coptic basilica.

In 1169 Benjamin of Tudela found Ben Ezra's Torah here and described it in his writings; the fourteenth-century Egyptian author Al-Maqrizi also mentioned this Torah, in his book *Al-Muqaffa*. By the time Hamoutal arrived here, that priceless manuscript had been kept in the synagogue for more than two centuries.

I hesitate before entering the building, the destination of my private diaspora. After the yeshiva in Rouen, the crypt in Clermont and the ruins of medieval Monieux, this is the fourth place where I can touch Hamoutal's life. The interior is expertly restored and nothing short of magnificent. It is not the medieval sanctuary that met the eyes of that exhausted, wandering woman, but it is this spot, this house of worship. The restoration, which took fifteen years, was a result of the Egypt–Israel peace treaty of 1979.

From the right side, I look up at the women's gallery on the left and gasp: up there at the end, I can see the opening of the genizah, the black hole into which hundreds of thousands of manuscripts were thrown so that Yahweh would take them back into the obscurity of the ages.

The German scholar Simon von Geldern was probably the first Western traveller to see this storage space. That was in 1753. Von Geldern, also known as de Gueldre, was the great-uncle of Heinrich Heine, who describes him in his *Memoirs* as a kind of saint, an eccentric figure known as 'the Oriental'. Von Geldern may not have realised what he had in front of him. The documents were not stacked or archived but jumbled in messy heaps in the dark, confined space. Many such genizot were later emptied out, the masses of discarded documents removed and ritually buried. The Cairo Genizah was never meant to survive for centuries and become one of the greatest troves of cultural heritage ever discovered.

The scholar Solomon Schechter was the first to suspect what a world of knowledge it might hold. In 1888, he at last received permission to open the treasure chamber. What he found there was beyond his wildest dreams: fragments of Ben Sira's Hebrew *Ecclesiasticus* from before AD 1, previously thought to be lost forever; works by Maimonides; poems and letters by Judah Halevi; fragments of Aquila's Greek translation of the second-century Hebrew Bible; copies of Sadducee texts predating the destruction of the Temple; eyewitness accounts of the crusaders' attack on Jerusalem; papers and letters from Khazar Jews; countless documents from merchants and Jewish military officers; records from the Islamic administration and agreements between the two communities; tax assessments and receipts; geographical and medical writings; payment records; fines; communications with and ordinances from the Muslim authorities; legal statements relating to marriages and divorces; con- tested claims to land and property; applications for loans; bills for mari- time transport; letters appointing rabbis and administrators; documents in inheritance cases; love poems; and requests for clemency or for over- due salary payments – all tossed into the dark hole, century after century, because documents bearing the name of Yahweh may not be burned or otherwise destroyed; the Supreme Being Himself must reclaim them. Nowhere else are forgetting and remembering intertwined in such a paradoxical way as here in this oubliette with its unfailing memory. That is precisely why it has become the greatest treasury of Jewish heritage; its importance in Jewish culture outweighs that of the Dead Sea Scrolls.

I can scarcely imagine Solomon Schechter's amazement. He boxed up two hundred thousand documents – scraps and snippets of papyrus and parchment nibbled by rats and mice – and sent them to Cambridge. To this day, the university there holds most of this enormous shipment, known as the Cairo Genizah Collection. There's a photo of Schechter sitting and reading in an office in Cambridge with one hand on his head, surrounded by the mountain of manuscripts. The process of exegesis was explosive, sensational, a 'battlefield of books' still growing today. The collection is studied in universities around the world. The great scholar Shelomo Dov Goitein has filled four thick volumes with his reconstruction of life in medieval Fustat. One of the myriad documents is about a proselyte from the north and her tragic fate. It's number T-S 16.100; the letters refer to Schechter's name and that of Charles Taylor, the man who funded the research and later continued the work. Document T-S 16.100 was translated and annotated in 1968 by the American scholar Norman Golb, who concluded that the proselyte in question had lived in a village in Provence. He gave a lecture on the topic for the University of Chicago's Medieval Jewish Studies programme on 20 April 1968 and published his findings in the *Proceedings of the American Philosophical Society* in January 1969.

The Hebrew letters that form the place name in the manuscript have been partly torn but are legible as מניו – from right to left: mem, nun, yod, vav. In transcription: MNYW. Monieux.

*

An impressively sturdy remnant of Fustat's medieval walls rises from the ground just behind the synagogue, preserved more through neglect than out of any historical awareness. This fragment is a dusty monolith, a rough mass of uncompromising sandstone, a heap of hot rubble whose angular persistence says more about the indifference of history than any words I can find. Among the few scattered houses behind it, you can see the beginnings of the Arabic cemetery, a labyrinth dotted with piles of refuse where a woman in rags invites me into her home – a ruined mausoleum she has furnished with a few carpets and a small cooker, where she's trying to bring up her children. She offers me coffee and invites me into the tomb, but I notice her eyeing my bag and hear someone shuffling behind the tall tombstone. I politely decline and amble back through the dusty alleys.

I pass the church of Abu Serga. The building is being restored; large sheets of plastic, covered with dust, hang from the rickety scaffolding. Dozens of young men in slippers are standing on tall wooden ladders without any protection or dust masks, chipping away at the stone. Arabic music jangles from a small radio.

I spend more than an hour rambling around the nearby Coptic cemetery. Names from many regions, lizards and pill bugs, lush bougainvillea flourishing in a small, dilapidated Greek temple. In Hamoutal's time, this area must have been an international melting pot. The old man at the entrance to the historic district again offers me the brochure, which tells the history of the synagogue. Preoccupied, I ignore him once more as I pass, but then go back, take the brochure, and forget to pay him. I walk up the stairs, then retrace my steps, hand the man – who is still shaking his head in sorrow – twenty Egyptian pounds, and rest my hand on his arm by way of apology. He points to his swollen, ailing foot. I tell him the reason for my visit. His eyes widen in disbelief; he staggers to his feet, clasps me in a tearful embrace, and slaps me on the back. Shabbat shalom, Shabbat shalom, he calls after me, an endless, fading incantation that echoes in my mind for days.

*

Now I'm trying to reconstruct Hamoutal's route from her landing place along the Nile to the synagogue, although I'm walking in the opposite direction. I pass straight through the Mar Girgis metro station and find myself in a breathtaking slum. The run-down blocks of flats seem on the verge of collapse but are full of life and energy; the balconies are bathed in the intimate glow of the lamplight through the windows; here and there I see eyes glittering in the shadows. The streets are unpaved, covered in dust and improbably dirty; camels lie in the sand as they must have a thousand years ago. Chickens cross the streets, cackling; dark, open houses prove to be small shops; everything smells like burning charcoal, excitement, the allure of a dream. I know I have to pass straight through this district to reach the legendary Nilometer, so I stop now and then to ask the way. Many eyes are levelled at me from the dim interiors; it seems no tourists ever come here. The smell, the balmy air that barely moves, the intimacy of this unconcealed reality – it catches me unawares. In the smoke of the smouldering incinerators, I smell incense and myrrh, the primeval conflagration of the world. I feel a strange urge to linger here, enter a house, sit down and not get up again; then I realise I'm being indiscreet and should walk on. But the few hundred metres through this ancient district will remain branded into me, a short, intense trip through time, during which I smelled, sensed and experienced something that flung me straight into the heart of the story I've been pursuing for so long.

The transition is brusque, like everything else in this city; when I reach the end of the district, I am plunged back into Cairo's frenzied traffic, four lanes thick, a continuous, ear-splitting riot of honking in a haze of exhaust. The other side of the road – which you can reach only by slaloming, contemptuous of death, between cars that never brake – runs along a thinner arm of the Nile. The banks are covered with litter, chickens are scratching around the reeds, a pale yellow dog is chasing them.

A picturesque footbridge takes me to the island of Roda, home of the Nilometer. It's a well three floors deep with a floodgate where the ancient Egyptians could measure the level of the Nile. That enabled them to predict whether the flood waters would leave the riversides fertile, reduce them to mud, or stay too low to irrigate the fields. In that last case, they could expect a summer of drought and scarcity. All you can see of this underground structure from the outside is a small pointed tower. Now the deep cellar is dry, and swarming with self-declared tour guides begging for alms. By 1097 it had already been there for centuries. I take a long look at the slender column in the captivating depths, the floodgate at the bottom where the water could be let in, the marks in the sandstone, the inscriptions, the timeless ingenuity that went into measuring the water's rise and fall, the ancient theology that permeated the design. If Hamoutal did come here and even lived here, she may at some point have seen this. To reach the synagogue, she had to pass through the dusty streets I've just left behind me.

On a nearby embankment over the flickering water, my wife is waiting for me, her eyes filled with light and enchantment. As I take her in my arms, I feel we've completed one leg of this journey together. The play of the shimmering water entrances us for hours.

I have found Hamoutal.

3

The rabbi shakes Hamoutal awake, scoops a handful of water from the well bucket, and sprinkles it over her face. She opens her eyes and looks around, befuddled. He helps her up, noticing how light she is. Supporting her weight, he walks her over to a step where she can sit. There she rummages mindlessly under her clothes and hands him her leather pouch. As she sags to one side, dozing off again, the elderly scholar reads the imploring letter, written by his fellow rabbi Joshuah Obadiah in a mountain village far to the north. He reads the letter twice, his lips moving. He rolls up the parchment again and finds the small tefillin at the bottom of the pouch, rolled up and coated with dust: the phylacteries that David Todros used in prayer. He ties the pouch to his belt, helps the woman to her feet, and leads her to the synagogue entrance. There he fetches his wife and asks her to take the exhausted foreigner under her care. Once Hamoutal has been led away, he goes back inside the synagogue, says a prayer, sets aside the letter and David's tefillin, and returns to his daily routines. Later that morning he climbs the stairs to the upper level and, with a brief, murmured prayer and a measure of religious decorum, flings the two objects through the dark hole at the end of the women's gallery into the old genizah, relinquishing them to the dust and the centuries.

*

Misr al-Fustat means something like 'Egyptian city of the tents'. According to legend, a dove built its nest in the tent of Amr ibn al-As, the seventh-century Muslim leader who conquered Egypt. Amr was charmed to find the dove brooding there and saw it as a sign from God. Instead of packing up his tent before he went into the field, he left it behind to shelter the dove's nest. When he returned victorious, he saw that the tent was still standing, untouched. The doves had flown away. Amr decided to have a whole tent camp erected around it; Fustat was born from a dove's nest.

The Jews of Fustat may have had their best years under Fatimid rule. Their prestige and prosperity grew, and they could count on respect and a privileged status. The Ben Ezra Synagogue became the hub of the largest Jewish community to have formed since the fall of Alexandria. 'The Jews who live there are very rich,' wrote Benjamin of Tudela around 1170. Fustat became a centre of Jewish power that extended beyond Egypt to Palestine and Syria. It was, without a doubt, the best place Hamoutal could have washed up in those days.

She needed all conceivable forms of care and emotional support, and the congregants attached to the synagogue, after learning the identity of her distinguished father-in-law, must have been more than willing to offer that support. They would no doubt have dissuaded her from travelling onwards any time soon, and not only because of her weakened state. They received news almost daily of the atrocities committed by the crusaders in the East. After the so-called People's Crusade met with its first defeats, the Christian soldiers gathered near Constantinople – vast armies of French, Flemish and Norman warriors – and advanced on Jerusalem, slaughtering and looting as they went. The age-old balance of peoples was thrown into disarray. Cruelties and abominations were perpetrated left and right in the name of revenge and counter-revenge. The catastrophe of the crusades had descended on the Near East, making the world an unpredictable place. It would have been reckless for Hamoutal to follow in the crusaders' footsteps, seeing as they were now her worst enemies.

So Fustat is a turning point in her quest. She is well cared for and treated with great honour and respect – which she richly deserves, in the eyes of the community there. For her, it's like slowly waking from a nightmare. But something inside her has given way; her grief has become a kind of vacant staring into space. After a few months, she starts to get a grip on herself and her dealings with the considerate, chatty women around her. It begins to dawn on her that there is almost no chance she will ever see her children alive again; maybe they found themselves in a disorderly rearguard of the People's Crusade and were killed in one of the great defeats inflicted on those hordes. How could the crusaders, in the miserable conditions of their campaign to bring down the world order, possibly look after of a couple of children? Even in the best case – if they're still alive – they were sold as slaves at an Oriental market months ago. She begins to understand that Fustat is not just an oasis for her, but her journey's end. Here, around the Ben Ezra Synagogue, she is safe.

Each month, she must descend into the mikveh again. She grows accustomed to the lukewarm darkness, immersed in Nile water. One day it takes her mind back to the ice-cold waters of the Nesque in the mikveh in Moniou. For a moment she thinks, I don't want to come up again. But a person stays alive as long as she can't stop breathing. Panting, she rises to her feet, her hair dripping, and shivers in the heat of the day. She hears new psalms, Arabic in origin, old poetry and prayers, *piyyutim* and *hizana*, Talmudic texts mixed with Egyptian incantations. She is instructed by the rabbi and absorbed into the community's everyday life.

It takes her a long time to adjust, but step by step, day by day, she does. She is able to correspond with her husband's family, thanks to the excellent ferry services run by the Jewish merchants in Fustat; when the sea is calm, letters are delivered in three weeks at most. That's how she learns that, in any event, her children haven't returned to Narbonne.

*

Did Hamoutal ever see the pyramids in Giza, the head of the sphinx in the burning sun? Maybe not – the suburb of Giza is on the far side of the ruins of Fustat. She would have needed a very special reason for travelling to that desolate spot to see things that no one could fathom. Sightseeing was unheard of; the past was not yet a tourist attraction. By the time I arrive, the place is teeming with day trippers, and there's no chance of experiencing anything remotely historical. The whole site is spoiled by the shouting vendors, the jovial traders, the Arab students taking selfies. Tourists ride around the desert in camel-drawn carriages. Taking refuge nearby in the cool of stately Mena House, I try to imagine what Hamoutal's contemporaries made of these colossal vestiges of a then-unimaginable culture. What questions might they have asked themselves? These structures must have seemed unearthly, and in times when everything was seen in terms of Christian, Jewish and Muslim religion, they were utter enigmas. I have found no eleventh-century accounts that even mention this place. The Sphinx's head may have been buried deep in the hot sand.

*

One day she is an accidental witness to the public execution of an adulteress. The woman has been convicted by an Islamic court and is to be stoned. She kneels prostrate, her face in the sand, as the men around her engage in lively discussion. The gaon, the head of the yeshiva, is there too. He disapproves of the stoning and draws the Muslim law enforcers into a learned argument. The gaon speaks with calm authority, making a strong impression on the listening crowd. But then, from behind the backs of the arguing men, someone throws a large, sharp stone that hits the woman right in the temple. She falls to the sand like a rag doll. Pandemonium breaks out; the bystanders start pushing, pulling, cursing. The gaon's voice goes unheard in the racket. The woman's head is running with blood. The next stone hits her full in the stomach. Then the torrent begins.

The gaon backs away from the bloodbath and sees, in the outermost circle of the crowd, a blue-eyed woman in tears, biting her lip. He is startled; he knows this woman by now, he was involved in her introduction to the congregation, but it surprises him to see her here, crying with such abandon at one of these events – which, sad to say, happen all the time. Did she know the stoned woman? Does she have some personal stake in this matter? It always pains him to see how heavy-handed the Islamic court can be in such cases – the issue has been debated for generations.

Moved by the foreign woman's empathy, he goes to her and asks, Why are you crying, Hamoutal? His question elicits a stifled sob; Hamoutal turns to leave. He takes her by the arm. Don't go, Hamoutal. He walks beside her as she hurries home to the women's quarters. She knows the gaon; his name is Shmuel, an unusual name for a Romaniote Greek Jew from Alexandria. His presence intimidates her; no words have ever passed between them before. He grasps her by the arm again and says, What made you cry like that? What exactly happened to you?

Hamoutal shuts him out. She shakes her head, tugs herself loose, and flees into the house.

The gaon strokes his beard and walks on.

But it's a small community. A few days later, he sees her sitting alone by the river, watching the goings-on around the moored boats. She throws pebbles at alley cats. He sits down beside her and says nothing. The sun glides through the warm mist. Half an hour later, she starts to stand up, but he stops her and looks into her eyes. Only now does he notice that her blue eyes are slightly crossed; the sight fills him with affection. They say nothing. Minutes pass. Then he stands, laying his hand on her shoulder. *Galana*, he says, laughing: blue-eyed one. He wanders off to chat with some fishermen standing nearby. She sees him against the sunlight, and her thoughts are confused and dark.

In the weeks that follow, they run into each other often. Eye contact becomes more awkward. In the evenings, she likes to sit by the Well of Moses. One day, she finds Shmuel there beside her, gazing at her. *Galana*, he says again. He laughs, showing his teeth, and without further ado asks her to marry him.

She stands up, walks away, roams the streets. A few days later, the congregation is informed of Gaon Shmuel's proposal. The gossip begins. Women and giggling girls latch on to Hamoutal, eager for news. She shakes her head and hides in the women's quarters.

The gaon is a wealthy man who has earned the trust of the Muslim authorities and belongs to an elite profession, the mintmasters. He has a reputation as strict and fair, but she doesn't feel ready to share her life with a man, not ever again. For a long time, she repels his advances, which grow more formal and more insistent, until one day the rabbi's wife tells her that this principled man is just the husband to offer her a balanced, sheltered life, that she will live in a fine, peaceful house, and that he would do anything for her. She goes to the rabbi that evening, who gives her the same advice.

She has a message sent to Narbonne to ask her father-in-law's opinion. He responds that she has the right to remarry and therefore has his blessing. After a few weeks of sleepless nights, she decides to choose life over endless mourning. It becomes clear to her that the people here are her new home, that she cannot pass up this second chance.

One warm, wet evening she heads for the gaon's house. In the drizzle, the smells of damp fabric tingle in her nostrils. She knocks on his door; he opens, sees her look of dread, bows and invites her in. She agrees to marry him on one condition: she wants to travel on to Yerushalayim after all, with his help. Her request irks him. He sits opposite her in silence and says, Let's get married first. I'll take care of you. Hamoutal nods; he lays his hands in hers. The next day they go to the rabbi and set everything in motion for the marriage that will take place six weeks later.

4

The Jewish community in Fustat has a much more rigid hierarchy than the progressive, enlightened community in Narbonne. Their morals and social forms are more conservative; women are less liberated. Hamoutal has to adjust to her life's new pattern. She spends most of her time in the women's quarters, sometimes without seeing her betrothed for days. In any case, their relationship is a good deal less sentimental than her romance with the silver-tongued young man who stole her away to Provence. She often sees Shmuel at the evening meal, which tends to go by in silence. He treats her with perfect respect, but since their bond was formalised, he has grown reserved. Everything is so close and out of reach. The bell of the Coptic church comes clanging through the Jewish evening prayer; in the distance, they can hear the muaddhin's *Allahu akbar*.

She meets with a tailor in Fustat to discuss the ritual prayer shawl he will make for her future husband. They do not see each other at all the week before the ceremony, as tradition demands. Her hair is dyed dark with henna. The day before the wedding, Hamoutal plunges into the ritual bath. Underwater she sees a shapeless horror, a small bloody thing in a monster's maw. She surfaces, steps out of the bath, and accepts the towels the women offer her, as they laugh at her golden gooseflesh.

The making of the *ketubah*, or marriage contract, is a long process. It is planned and drafted by the rabbi and then presented to the leader of Cairo's Jewish community, the *rayyis*. After that it is submitted to the *muqaddam*, an Islamic official, and once he has consented, it must go to the supreme leader of Egypt's Jews, the *nagid*. Only then can it be returned to the Ben Ezra Synagogue. After all the formalities have been completed, they marry; once again, she becomes the wife of a prominent Jewish man. They sign the *ketubah*, which is then solemnly presented to Hamoutal for safekeeping. Shmuel covers her face with the veil. The ceremony is much more exotic and the guests more diverse than at her first wedding; Muslim leaders and a few Coptic Christians attend. After they step underneath the *chuppah*, strange music is played. Shmuel smashes the glass; this time there's no cloth wrapped around it. Shards glitter and crunch beneath his feet. The Muslim drummers at the banquet fill her with strange emotion. The guests bring gifts to the bride and groom, greeting and welcoming Hamoutal with distant courtesy. By the standards of the day, she is already an older woman, but everyone agrees she makes a good match for her solemn new husband.

The beautifully illuminated marriage contract, on papyrus of pounded sedge from the banks of the Nile, must have been cast among the countless documents in the dark genizah half a century later and consumed at some stage by mice or rats. Or maybe it's found its way into the hands of researchers in Cambridge, or somewhere else in the world, but the names are no longer legible.

*

Bit by bit she gets to know the Jewish community's elite, although she never leaves the house without an escort. But she can move more freely now with the other women. She receives instruction from her mother-in-law, who acts as her *muallima* or teacher. Side by side with that vigorous, fleshy woman, she elbows her way through the cacophony of the Arab souks, learns to cope with the traders' mannerisms and ways of speaking, grows used to haggling over price and quality, and gains insight into the household of a well-to-do Egyptian Jewish woman. In her own house, she has about ten servants: brisk, unspeaking people who remain leery of their new mistress. Over the weeks, she wins a degree of trust by rolling up her sleeves and setting to work. From her cook, she learns how to bake pieces of huge Nile perch in hot ashes, to dry figs and dates, and to cure olives and lemons in brine. She looks up at the birds and the sky, so bright it always stings her eyes. She enjoys the smell of smouldering fires in the alleys, of orange blossom when rain passes over the city, and of the swaying oleanders in the courtyard. She and the other women go to the olive oil mill, a tall, gloomy building where flat stones rotate and screech, turned by a blinded mule. The oil runs out of a spout into the old jugs; its fragrance is bitter-sweet; the shining skin of the half-naked boys has a green-gold lustre. She learns to make *ful*, mashing boiled fava beans in olive oil and adding cumin, lime and sesame. She stirs and stirs and still cries sometimes in secret, remembering her lost children. The hours blur during the slow siesta, a warm, unreal fold in time where memories come to life, a hot languor that makes her weak and dreamy till she flinches awake to the sing-song call of the muaddhin from near the old city wall. Many Egyptian Jews speak fluent Arabic; after a few months, she can understand most of the jokes in the souks. Her imperfect Aramaic, which showed traces of Sephardic Spanish, now has Judaeo-Arabic undertones. Only when she's caught by surprise, or in dreams, does something northern surface, a language from another life, something hard and grey and cold for which she sometimes feels homesick beyond bearing. By the time the Egyptian winter arrives, she is pregnant again.

One day she is standing with Shmuel by the Fustat harbour near the ancient Babylon Fortress. As they watch the activity around the pontoon bridge, she gives into a sudden urge to tell him about the port of

Rouen. She explains to him what a snekkja is, and admits that her father descends from one of the Vikings who overran northern Europe two centuries ago. With slight dismay, Shmuel realises that in fact his new wife is related to the cruel, despised Normans rampaging like demons through the cities of the Orient. All she had told him before was that she was of Flemish descent. She was the daughter-in-law of the chief rabbi of Narbonne; that had been his guarantee of an honourable marriage. Now he's confused and even feels somehow cheated. The revelation gnaws at him, a little more each day. That's when he starts to view her with suspicion.

A few weeks later she learns the story of the brutal pogrom in Rouen from Jewish refugees and tells him about it. It begins to dawn on him how hard it is to be involved with a proselyte – as he should have known when this unfamiliar woman first drew his attention. Yet their marriage holds firm, partly because it is supported by the family and very formal in character, unlike the unforgettable *amour fou* of her childhood.

She is tough; her body has adapted to the new climate, diet and culture. She does all she can to regain Shmuel's trust. She has opportunities to join him in conversations with the *nagid* and with Jewish scholars, and they even welcome Islamic theologians and dignitaries as guests in their home. She learns all about the tangled social and political networks in Fustat, and in the process finds out more about the chaos in the Orient, caused by her kinfolk. Jews debate with Muslims, and Christian pilgrims headed for Jerusalem are warned of the danger there; word has it the crusaders are quickly remobilising and seem determined to take Jerusalem. Troops are marching across Europe, traversing the Mediterranean, arriving by the shipload on the coast of Lebanon and attacking the coast-dwellers there. In one place after another, Muslims are taking up arms to defend themselves from the Christian aggressors. But there is often little they can do to stop the uncoordinated slaughter, the rape of their women, the destruction of their communities. Sometimes they win short-lived victories over the heavily armoured knights; they ride small, supple horses and learn to aim at the eyes in the helmet visors or the legs and eyes of the northerners' clumsier steeds. The violence reaches Egypt's eastern desert. Tensions are mounting everywhere. She hears tell of unrest in Spain; there are said to be crowds of refugees moving north to Narbonne, because the Reconquista shows the Jews no mercy. Many Christians see them as accomplices of the hated Saracens. The lively social circles of Fustat, where everyone has a story to tell, make her feel as if the threads of her life are winding together. At the same time, she is more aware than ever that she will never again be truly safe anywhere – as if she's living on a raft that is drifting towards a cataract.

She bears her fourth child at the height of summer, a fast delivery. It's a boy; she wants to call him Yaakov again. Her husband says no, the child's name will be Avram. The circumcision ritual takes place in the syna-gogue. Afterwards she hears that her son did not cry or even flinch, but appeared to be smiling.

That evening a venomous viper shoots inside through an open door and nestles in the basket where the newborn is sleeping. The nurse comes inside, notices the snake and shrieks. The snake slides into the baby's swaddling clothes. In a panic, the nurse snatches the child out of the basket; quick as lightning, the snake bites her in the wrist and holds fast, twisting in the air, eyes glittering and jaws wide open around the arm of the screaming woman. Its venomous fangs sink deep into her artery.

Other women rush in and take the child from the nurse's arms; one of them beats the snake with a stick till it lets go, and a few fleet-footed women crush the writhing reptile's head. The nurse collapses as the poi-son takes effect, and passes out a moment later. Not long afterwards she stiffens, her throat swollen and her tongue black. Her rolling eyes come to a stop, their light extinguished. The women surrounding the nurse see her final, choking spasm, the bloody foam that rises to her lips. By the time Hamoutal rushes in from her adjoining bedroom, roused by the noise, the women are already wailing and carrying the nurse's body out the door. She takes her baby from the woman holding him and thinks, God, whichever god you are, why do you keep coming after me?

She falls to her knees, rocks the baby, and clasps him to her chest in desperation. The child gives a soft whimper and searches for her breast. She feels the warmth and breath flow back into her; she lets a servant lead her back to bed. As the child drinks, she is soothed by the scent of her own milk and the intense sensation of his mouth at work, his small tongue massaging her nipple. She strokes his head; the fontanelle is still open.

Half a year of relative calm follows. Her cultured, prosperous surroundings do her good. She orders attractive new clothes and furnishes her quarters in luxurious style for herself and her child. She rarely sees her new husband; one day in late August he departs for Alexandria on family business she doesn't learn much about.

A few weeks later, he's back. He comes up to her with a strange look in his eyes, takes her in his arms and says, Sit down, Hamoutal. I have something to tell you.

Her heart pounds in her ears; she falters, doesn't know what to expect, but feels she's losing her mind.

Hamoutal, the man says, Yaakov and Justa are alive. They are with your parents in Rouen.

She stares at him, wild-eyed, unable to utter a word, opens her mouth and shakes her head as she grips his arm.

5

From that moment she knows no peace.

She lies awake at night, her mind racing: how on earth did her parents find the children? Somewhere along the route to the East, divisions of the southern and northern armies must have met. Evidently, the many Norman knights accompanying the foot soldiers included a few from Rouen. And after that fateful night in Moniou when the children were taken by knights who had never heard of them, her eldest must have told them who his father and mother were. It's even possible that one of her older brothers heard news of the children, came looking for them, and had them taken home. The thought obsesses and disturbs her; at the same time, she worries about her brothers, who may be laying down their lives in some siege in Antioch or God knows where. In any case, it's more than likely that a number of Norman knights have heard her scandalous story. It couldn't have taken long for one of them to figure out that these are the grandchildren of Gudbrandr, Vigdis Adelaïs's father, and to send them off with the next set of messengers from Zadar to Rouen. Her Jewish children with her Christian parents – the idea is so strange that it hardly bears thinking about. Do David's parents know?

She sends word to Narbonne. Although her new husband is opposed, he cannot possibly stop her from contacting the chief rabbi of France; propriety forbids it. After a few weeks, she receives a reply; her former parents-in-law were unaware of the situation and ask her to come back to France and confer with them on how best to obtain custody of the children. She tells her husband, who flies into a rage and curses the day he told her that her children were still alive. At the same time, he knows her request is reasonable; he can't expect her to pass up any opportunity to be reunited with her older children. But it would be impossible for him to leave the community for such a long time; she will have to travel alone. He permits her to go, on two conditions: their child Avram will remain in Fustat, and she must leave at once, while the Mediterranean is still open to navigation. She will have to stay in Narbonne for the winter, when maritime transport comes to a halt, and return on one of the first spring ferries.

*

On a warm night in early September, she stands in front of the bronze mirror in her large bedroom, and as she changes for bed, she finds herself saying, My name is not Vigdis. My name is not Hamoutal. My name is. My name is. She can't get any further, goes to the window and looks out over the city, sees the stars there in the distance where she knows the Nile is flowing in silence. Everything in her is spinning. I am not Avram's mother. I am the mother of. Again she gets no further; something in her mind has cracked.

Knowing her children from Monieux are with her parents in Rouen, while she is here, married to an Egyptian Jew from Fustat and the mother of his child, she cannot be reasonable. She is reeling. For the past few days, she's been lashing out at the women around her, no longer capable of patience, irritated by her baby's cries. She has too little milk to breastfeed and lets other women nurse her child. She avoids speaking to her husband. After meals, she goes back to her rooms early. She realises it will be impossible to stay here. As Shmuel becomes more and more concerned for his wife's welfare, she secretly sends a letter to her former father-in-law in Narbonne with a convoy from Fustat, asking him to pass on the news about her children to Rabbi Joshuah Obadiah in Moniou and to request his assistance. Assistance with what? She doesn't know. She announces her plan to arrive in Narbonne in late October and travel on to Rouen – a disastrous idea that is sure to distress David's father.

One nightmare keeps returning: she sees Yaakov and Justa caught in the coils of a huge snake in the Nile, which pulls them into the depths. Each time, she sees the cloud of blood in the brown water. She wakes up shivering and coated with sweat, her eyes scanning the room as if she recognises nothing. She feels she will lose her mind if she does not leave now. The night is cool and enchanting; her room with its breeze-blown curtains is suddenly a hell. She looks out over the district below; by the city wall, the thieves and whores are in whispering motion. Her heart pounding, she dresses in silence, takes a few silver pieces from the box in the large wardrobe and wraps herself in a light djellaba belonging to one of the Ethiopian wet nurses. Passing the room where little Avram is breathing quietly, she looks at the child, touches his motionless face, and murmurs an apology. Just as she's about to leave the room, she turns and goes back to the sleeping infant. On impulse, she takes him in her arms and wraps him in a silk shawl. She steps outside, into the light of the waning moon. It's a quiet night; a few trees rustle peacefully. She can hear a jackal in the distance. Above her head, an owl breathes its call. She thinks of the story of the man who killed another man over the soft cry that obsessed him. Is that the voice of God, then? A sound you make yourself, which you hope is from the other side and will show you the meaning of life? She no longer knows what time, what year she's living in; everything rotates and revolves in overlapping circles. She says, Be quiet, Yaakov, to her sleeping baby Avram; she hurries through the Mar Girgis district, heedless of the danger, and onto the jetty by the pontoon bridge.

There, in the mild dawn, she waits for the morning ships, boarding the first one bound for Alexandria. She offers no explanation. The boatman gives her an appraising look, feels two silver coins pressed into his hand, notices the delicate collar under the white djellaba and says nothing. She has to try to breastfeed her baby again now, with no wet nurses to help her, and she must find food for herself. The ship speeds down the Nile at a startling pace, snaking with the current along shoals and riverbanks, past the morning's first fishermen and last beasts of prey. Before she knows it, they have passed the large bend and Fustat is sinking beneath the horizon behind them. That's when it hits her what she's done; again, she has simply fled. As if fleeing has become her only response. Without a letter of recommendation or any proof of her origins, she is completely vulnerable, with no claim to anyone's protection. Once again, she left a family behind who will come after her, because she'd promised to leave Avram in Fustat. Again, she rushed to leave as fast as she could without being spotted. Again, she has left a caring household in utter distress; she tries not to think of Shmuel waking up, standing in desperation at the door to her room, crying first her name, and then Avram's – the same anger and sorrow that she can no longer bear. She tries not to think of her act of betrayal, of her mother-in-law, of the troubles she's left in her wake. She may not be alive, but she has survived her own death once again. She's breathing, she's moving, that's all. Until that evening a thought strikes her: If I don't move then death won't see me. So she lies frozen in a corner as her child sucks, pointlessly, painfully, on her cracked left nipple.

After only three days, the cedar-wood felucca has already passed through the foam-crested waves of the Rosetta estuary. The next day, it safely reaches the Pharos of Alexandria. A day and a half later, she is sitting, veiled, on a merchant ship to Palermo. By the time that graceful vessel reaches its destination, to the groans of the exhausted rowers, a heavy autumn storm has transformed it into a wreck with a broken mast. She too is broken, by nausea and confusion, her child worn out by his mother's hardships. She staggers on shore and goes to the house of a money-changer she remembers from her previous stay in the city. She lies to him about the reason for her voyage and spends two days there before taking a boat to Marseilles. There, on the coast of southern France, she pays another visit to the wealthy shipowner's house. Again she lies about her journey, about the child. The shipowner's wife understands that some kind of disaster is in the making but asks no questions.

The courtyard with the blue bird, the orange tree, the white sheet floating above. Back in the room where she stayed before, she confuses Avram with the child who vanished into the crocodile's jaws. They can hear her talking in a loud voice, pacing, rummaging around, deep into the night. Not until dawn does exhaustion calm her down. She puts the child to bed and lies on the floor beside it, talking in her sleep. The lady's maid finds her there around noon, still sleeping with the whining child in the bed beside her. Hamoutal wakes with a start: Leave me alone, leave me alone, I won't, leave me alone. She swears and rages and only then is wide awake, her eyes darting back and forth, foam on her lips. The child is cared for; later, she too is dressed; soothing words are spoken. The shipowner's wife sends her off with a package of food, a bundle of clothing, and a small dark slave girl who speaks nothing but Greek. The girl accompanies her to the docks and helps her board a coaster bound for Cap d'Agde.

The child is severely underweight, and his mother looks like a savage nomad. In Agde she goes begging, because she's forgotten she brought money with her. She sleeps in the shade of a fortress where beggars, dogs and whores menace each other until the moon sinks behind the archways. The next morning, she is woken by a girl who has taken the crying Avram onto her lap. Hamoutal pulls the child out of her arms and walks off, followed by the girl's curses. To her surprise, she hears Norman being spoken nearby. She runs away, heading towards the harbour, and hides behind a few bales of hay. Rifling through her bag, she finds her last few precious coins. She gives one of the silver pieces she grabbed as she left Fustat to an old man with a primitive covered wagon who says he'll take her to Narbonne. Throughout that bumpy, drowsy ride she mutters old prayers – she's forgotten where she learned them. She mixes up languages, sees children she never had. She thinks she's riding back to Fustat and laughs.

6

Her reunion with her parents-in-law is thrown into confusion by the new child in her arms; that was not the arrangement. Seeing those admirable people, she bursts into tears and struggles for words. David's parents, too, can scarcely contain their emotion. Over the past few years, her father-in-law has grown old. His hair is white and his skin mottled with brown patches. Her mother-in-law is slower and heavier; her hair, which once gleamed jet black with olive oil, is now dull and grey. Hamoutal, she says with feeling, Sarah Hamoutal, and does not seem capable of saying more. She takes the child and calls out to one of the women in the back of the house, who recognises Hamoutal and claps her hands to her face. To her surprise, the family has a house guest: Joshuah Obadiah from Moniou, older and stiffer than ever. She flings her arms around him. The conversation turns to stories of the pogrom. Little cries of lament escape the rabbi as they revisit the massacre in the mountain village. Narbonne, too, has had attempts at pogroms, so far no more than scuffles.

Later that day, ten men say Kaddish in the synagogue. The sounds are unfamiliar – part Aramaic, which means almost nothing to her. In any case, her mind wanders.

That night, Hamoutal stays with the women of the household, who tend to her needs and soothe her. She is in almost constant tears. A painful joy, a misery full of warmth. Tragic and happy memories. An uprooted feeling, a momentary sense of coming home, the sorrow of David's death welling up again, and the fear of what's ahead. Shmuel becomes David, David becomes Yaakov, Avram becomes Gudbrandr, Gudbrandr becomes David, and where is Justa, maybe with her mother in Rouen. Was Justa bitten by a crocodile? Oh, that poor child, stolen by a whore in Agde as she slept, a whore with the jaws of a snake. One vast confusing whirlpool. The world is abandoning me. I can't do anything about it, I'm scared. My brother is a crusader, may God help him fight the Saracens in Fustat. She bites her cuticles till her fingers bleed. She feels like she's possessed by the Devil, she says with a grin to the women, who cover their mouths and tell her not to say such things.

*

Over the next few days, it becomes obvious how troubled Hamoutal's mind is. She sees her late husband's cousin, Yom Tov, and calls him David. She laughs and says her name is Vigdis, Vigdis the Viking, and bursts into loud, devilish laughter. Her parents-in-law are worried; they ask her not to travel on to Rouen and put her life at risk to no good end. Instead, they propose, Richard Todros will ask his contacts at the Rouen yeshiva to mediate with her parents in the matter of the children. But two weeks later, the rabbi learns that all his contacts there died in the great pogrom of 1096. No one would dare to approach a Norman knight as things stand now, and certainly not to request the return of children to Jews.

Old Rabbi Todros realises that Hamoutal cannot be brought to her senses. With each passing day, she seems more confused and obsessed. And every day, she is more insistent: she wants to go to Rouen. The rabbi tries to make her see reason; he tells her the land route is no longer possible and she'll have to go from Narbonne to the Atlantic, taking the road to Santiago de Compostela. Along the way, she must be very careful and pose as a Christian woman, because that road is crawling with Norman knights. From Santiago she can go on to the Bay of Santander and take a ship up the coast to Rouen. Hamoutal bursts into carefree laughter, her eyes blank. Yes, Papa, she says, yes, and she moves to embrace her former father-in-law, who dodges her arms. She seems to have seized on the feverish hope of finding her children alive and being reconciled with her parents. Rabbi Todros strokes his beard in thought as she speaks of her plans. One thing is clear: she must no longer travel alone. Yom Tov and Joshuah Obadiah will escort her, for company and protection.

VIII

Nájera

1

They cannot put off the journey for long; autumn has begun. The ships will soon stop plying the coastal routes for the winter. A few days later, they set off in a small covered wagon. Hamoutal does what she'd promised she wouldn't do again, snatching little Avram out of his bed at the last moment, taking him in her arms, and hiding him in a basket between the bags and sacks in the little wagon. The two men don't discover her deceit until a couple of hours later, when the child starts crying. The road is dangerous; now she sees why her father-in-law didn't have them take the southern Compostela route when she fled Narbonne with David, but instead sent them north-east by sea. Wherever they go, they run into packs of excited young men off to join the campaign in the East, wandering farmers whose huts have been burned down, and homeless children. Fleeing Muslims warn them of murderous fanatics who are just as merciless to Jews. Sometimes bands of robbers turn up, who profit from the confusion and take cruel advantage of careless travellers. The small Jewish communities they pass are wary and fearful. No one knows what the next day will bring. Now and then they are stopped and interrogated by suspicious soldiers at checkpoints.

Having a baby with them makes the journey much harder. When Yom Tov first found out about the boy, he threatened to take them straight back, but old Obadiah's cooler head prevailed: You can't take a child away from his mother, they'll understand back in Narbonne. Besides, they have no time to lose. So they travel on, over bumpy roads in dust and driving rain, with Hamoutal and Avram inside the juddering wagon.

After three wearying weeks on the road, they decide to rest for a couple of days in the small town of Nájera, a little less than a hundred kilometres from Burgos, before going on to the northern coast. The two men search for an inn, ask for accommodation for two nights, and take Hamoutal and her child to one of the rooms. There she tends to Avram, cuddling him and rocking him, but she calls him a Norman name, the name of one of her brothers. Arvid, she says, Arvid. The child laughs; she tickles him, making him squeal with delight. Arvid, how good it feels to say the name, Arvid, I'm your mother Vigdis. As they are eating together that evening in the gathering darkness, Yom Tov of the Todros family and Joshuah Obadiah hear her call the child by that name. Confused and a little nervous, they smile at her. I am Vigdis, she shouts, the mother of Arvid the Norman, and she screeches with laughter. A man at a nearby table nudges his comrade and points at her.

Did you hear that? the knight mutters. He takes a closer look at the woman. You won't believe this, he says, but the Devil take me if that's not the runaway daughter of old man Gudbrandr in Rouen. You heard her too, right? I am Vigdis, she said.

The other man stares in astonishment. Could a woman who's been missing for years be sitting here at the table, simple as that? His eyes betray his scepticism.

The first man says, It must be her, I'm certain. She looks like that brother of hers we ran into last month on his way to Sicily. Those same pale eyes, that thin nose and that high forehead. Arvid. She's saying his name, did you hear that?

He rises to his feet, goes to the commander of his garrison, which is stationed in the town, and reports what he has heard. The commander recalls the substantial reward for the capture of the wealthy dignitary's daughter. The instructions were to send a messenger as soon as she was found and deliver her to her father in Rouen. If he means to claim the bounty, he must bring her to her father alive and well.

As Hamoutal falls asleep with her child, laughing and cooing, humming Arvid, son of Vigdis, you are Arvid, son of Vigdis, two sentries are placed at the door to the inn and a courier is sent to Rouen by way of Bordeaux. Another one leaves at dawn for the port of San Sebastián; when he arrives there, two days later, he will instruct the next ship to Rouen to wait for two envoys with a special and unexpected guest, Gudbrandr's daughter, Vigdis Adelaïs by name.

That morning, Hamoutal feels well rested but extremely tense. She is glad to be on her way to Rouen at last, where she can see her parents and explain everything – after all, she has Arvid with her, the Viking child, no idea who the father is, the thought sends her into helpless giggles. Arvid, son of Nobody! she cries, and doubles up with laughter. The sentries are given the sign to enter the inn. Two of them grab the woman in the dining hall by the arms; another wrests the child from her. Yom Tov and Joshuah Obadiah rush over to stop them but are shoved away. The old rabbi falls over and hurts his back.

Jewish dogs, hisses one of the knights as he draws his sword, try anything else and you're dead. Hamoutal cries out, I am Vigdis Hamoutal, I am Vigdis Hamoutal Adelaïs Gudbrandr, leave me alone, give me my boy back, he is Arvid Todros, he is my child, the child of my father, he made it. She spits and rants and screeches and tries to pull herself loose. The dining hall fills with commotion; men stand up as they see the woman lash out in all directions, swiping and kicking and spitting.

My father sired him! she shouts, with a haggard grimace.

She is dragged outside by her legs, thrashing and writhing from the waist up like a cat in a bag.

My child, she cries, Arvid, son of Gudbrandr, he fucked me, slept, ha ha, fucked by the Devil!

The men tighten their grip.

Shit sacks, all fucked by the Devil!

She swings her head, her eyes wheel, there's foam at her mouth. A priest runs in, aghast at what he's just heard this woman shouting. He makes the sign of the cross, three times, and mutters with staring eyes, *Vade retro Satana.*

The woman shrieks, Ha ha ha, fucked by Satan!

She swings her head back and forth fiercely, her dingy curls coming loose and flopping around her head.

The priest steps up to one of the men and asks them to tie her up.

They do so, with brute force.

My child! Arvid, son of Shmuel, Hamoutal cries, watch out for the demonic crocodile! He'll bite you, oh, oh, oh, no, don't sink, my baby!

She twists and tugs and bites like a mad dog. One of the knights punches her in the face, and she drops to the ground with a bloody nose.

There you go, witch, he says, we'll drive the Devil out of you, sure enough.

The priest crosses himself; Yom Tov shouts that they must let her go, that she's a Jewish woman and not to be tried by Christians.

She's no Jewess, the garrison commander growls, that's a Christian woman, damn it, named Vigdis Adelaïs. Her father Gudbrandr is a personal acquaintance of mine. You filthy dogs have no business here, run off or you'll pay with your lives. May the Devil take you!

Meanwhile, Hamoutal, still stunned by the blow, is trying to scramble to her feet. She falls flat, and one of the knights kicks her. Devil's whore, he cries. The pointed toe of his armoured foot stabs into the small of her back, and she passes out. Blood gushes from her nose. The scene has drawn a crowd of excited onlookers. As the soldiers discuss how to load the woman onto a wagon as fast as possible and take her to the coast, the priest cries out that she is possessed by the Devil and will be impossible to transport because the Devil will sink the ship.

A wave of horror sweeps through the growing crowd.

Burn her at the stake! comes the cry.

At once, others echo it.

Burn the witch at the stake!

Hamoutal returns to vague consciousness; the commander struts over to her.

Are you Vigdis Adelaïs, the daughter of Gudbrandr the Norman? Can you confirm that?

She spits at him.

I am Hamoutal, daughter of the Devil, she hisses, stay away from me with your dirty Christian paws.

Possessed, the priest crows, possessed by the Subtle Serpent! *In nomine patris et filii et spiritus sancti!* She must be burned as soon as possible, before the Devil plays more tricks on her and on us.

Burn her at the stake, the crowd roars, burn her, burn her!

The garrison commander can just picture his reward going up in smoke if this high-born woman is lynched here and now. He hesitates, tries to change the priest's mind, but it's too late. The swelling crowd tows the woman along with it, tearing the clothes from her body. Half naked and covered with blood, she is dragged through the sand to the red cliffs, where men start to gather dried brushwood. Hamoutal, now bound hand and foot and half unconscious, is propped up against the cliff face in the fast-rising sun. The blood on her face is black and stringy now, mixed with dust. It trails down her neck as far as her partly bared breasts.

Sign of the Devil, one man shouts, her nose is running with pitch! The Devil is in her, sending pitch out of her devilish body! Don't touch her!

Hamoutal rolls her eyes; the pain in her back makes her grunt.

The crowd grows nervous; someone throws a stone at her, hitting her smack in the forehead. Her head slams into the rock face behind her. She slumps to one side.

Men bring bundles of wood, and the pyre grows rapidly. One thicker log is sharpened into a stake, driven into the ground, and lashed into place. The stacks of brushwood are now almost a metre high. The priest strides up to Hamoutal and asks one last time, Are you Vigdis Adelaïs from Rouen, the daughter of Gudbrandr the Norman?

I am Hamoutal Todros, she cries, Hamoutal Todros of Fustat! I am a Jew, a Jew, to the Devil with you!

The onlookers draw back with a gasp. Jewish and possessed by the Devil, a Jewish she-devil, the words go from mouth to mouth and their eyes widen. Some cross themselves and pray; soon, the whole crowd is praying as one. They fall to their knees and beg God for assistance as the woman rambles on under the sun.

Someone begins a sacred song. From one moment to the next, the mood has turned solemn.

A man approaches with a lit torch. A second man winds a shawl around Hamoutal's neck and tucks twigs inside it, so that she'll catch fire faster. They pull and yank at her. She dangles, half unconscious, between the two men, who drag her towards the pyre. Bruised and bloodied, with that wreath of twigs in front of her face, she looks like a witch, a demon, a monster from the underworld.

All at once, she lifts her head and starts squirming, trying to resist.

Where is Arvid, son of Hamoutal? she screams. Where is Arvid the Jew's son from Fustat?

The terrified onlookers cannot stop crossing themselves. Hamoutal lets out harsh cries; they shrink back. The Devil is tormenting her, the priest says. Don't dawdle, or he'll show himself.

The thought drives the crowd into a panic.

Hamoutal is pushed onto the pyre, her arms wrapped around the stake and tied in place. The man with the torch steps forward.

At that moment, Yom Tov dashes out of the crowd.

Stop, he cries, no more, this is a mistake! I am known as Yom Tov of Narbonne, and I take this woman under my protection on the authority of the venerable Rabbi Todros.

He is shoved aside.

Then old Joshuah Obadiah comes forward, trembling. He raises his hands in an imploring gesture.

Good people, he says, listen for a moment before you burn this woman. I have a story to tell you.

Noise from the mob, but the garrison commander tells them to settle down.

The old rabbi tells the story of Vigdis the proselyte and the man she loved, who died in a pogrom.

Good riddance! shouts a man in the crowd. Burn all the Jew-dogs!

But seeing shaky old Obadiah's fragile form, people are moved to let him go on speaking. He seizes this shred of opportunity. As the fire rises in the kindling, he says, I will give thirty-five denarii to redeem this woman from the pyre, and for the right to accompany her to Rouen. It's a modest sum, I admit: thirty-five denarii for your community. But it's all we have. This woman's mind is sick with grief and suffering. She doesn't know what she's saying. She's not possessed, believe me. Give me charge of her, and I will take her home. He looks around the circle of faces.

The fear of this woman possessed by the Devil runs deep among the onlookers, including even the garrison commander. But fear hasn't robbed him of his wits.

What's this, you sly old Jew? he asks. So you've set your sights on my reward?

He draws his sword again.

I will sign a statement, Obadiah says, that you may deliver the woman to her father in Rouen. Since I am a Jew, your devil has no hold on me. Entrust this woman to my care. I will board the ship with her and take her to her father. I'm familiar with Rouen; I spent time at the old Jewish school there in my youth. If you've been to Rouen, you know where that was. I even know the way to the street where her father lives. You can trust me.

The commander understands this is his last chance to claim his reward. He calls to the soldiers to put out the fire and untie the woman from the stake. Hamoutal, hanging limp as a doll from the pole, doesn't understand what's happening to her. Yom Tov and Obadiah carefully drag her away from the pyre. She hacks and coughs and blinks her eyes. Her head lolls back. Obadiah asks for water for the redeemed woman and sprinkles it on her face. Holding her upright, the two men take her back to the inn. There, the garrison commander sees to it that her child is returned to her. She still seems not to realise what has happened; she's in a kind of trance. She mumbles to herself, babbles nonsense at her child, coughs and wheezes. Her hand, of its own accord, strokes the baby's head.

She says to Yom Tov, Dearest David, kiss me.

She puckers her lips, an unbearable sight with her soot-streaked face, swollen mouth and caked blood. Obadiah lays a cape over her bare, soiled shoulders. The two men bring her up to the room and ask for water so that she can wash herself.

Obadiah plans to set off with her for the coast the next morning – another few days' journey, in Yom Tov's company. They'll have an escort of a few soldiers and the garrison commander, who in his absence will relinquish command of his men in Nájera to a deputy.

2

Now that Hamoutal is alone in the room, she seems to have calmed down a little. Obadiah comes to see her and tells her it's really Yom Tov who will advance most of the money for her redemption. He only has five denarii to contribute. The sum must be paid by sunrise tomorrow. Obadiah asks her how many silver pieces she has with her.

Hamoutal waves him off and slowly shakes her head no.

What's got into this woman? Obadiah demands that she tell him where she's hidden the wallet. He knows old Todros gave her money. Hamoutal curls up like a sick animal, shakes her head no again, seems to fall asleep.

I will deal with this matter tomorrow, the old man thinks. She is too shaken to talk now.

And although he is right – Hamoutal has been shaken to the core by what happened to her – she comes to her senses as the night goes on. She no longer wants to be delivered to her father in Rouen. It's madness to think he'll forgive her; her heresy, becoming a Jewess, is punishable by death. The Rouen to which she would return is no longer the peaceful place where she grew up; her head echoes with the stories of the great pogrom at the yeshiva and in the city streets. What would become of her child there? Won't they just lash her to the stake again? She found out today what that's like. No, going back to Rouen would mean certain death. She has to flee. What else can she do but flee, as she always has? How could she ever repay Yom Tov, anyway? She has no more than a handful of coins, which she wants to save for when she'll need them most. She sits up, the silent darkness all around her. The waning moon hangs low and yellow over distant hills. She can hear the child breathing.

She groans with the pain she feels throughout her body. She dresses slowly and carefully and wraps her child in a shawl again, as she did in Moniou, Narbonne and Fustat. She creeps down the stairs, pausing a moment after the creak of each step, and finds herself outside in the cool night air. A warm wind is blowing; she hears wild animals far away in the darkness; stars twinkle over the hills. She takes a deep breath and something in her seems to return to life. She knows what she wants. Her first steps down the road are painful and hesitant, but she soon settles into a smoother pace; the movement eases the pain a little; her child's asleep in the shawl on her back, she is on her way. She knows where she's going.

*

By sunrise, she has already walked a few kilometres. She hides among a few sheep in a fold to wait for nightfall before moving on.

In Nájera, the garrison commander knocks on the door of the inn. Yom Tov comes out, and they sit down at the table. Yom Tov pays the thirty denarii he brought with him and then counts out Obadiah's five.

Meanwhile, Obadiah is knocking on the door of Hamoutal's room. No answer. He calls her name, waits a few moments, knocks again. Still no sound.

He sits and waits. A while later, the garrison commander comes to fetch Obadiah and Hamoutal.

When there is still no response from the room, they open the door. The old rabbi realises at once what has happened. The commander seizes him by the throat and shouts, You let her escape on purpose! You cheated me! Your head will roll for this, old Jew!

Obadiah groans with pain and asks the soldier to let go. Yom Tov comes upstairs and tries to placate the commander: She can't be far, she must be trying to get to Rouen on her own for fear of being condemned to death again. She's lost her mind, it's not their fault she ran away. It will be all right: if they start out for San Sebastián as soon as possible, they're sure to run into her.

Again, the commander comes round to their point of view, thinking of the reward that awaits him in Rouen. Yom Tov offers to go with him. The two men depart on horseback, leaving Obadiah behind, panting and exhausted.

The old rabbi spends a few more days in the inn, recovering his strength. Then he begins his journey back to Narbonne to report on the events in Nájera.

Along the way, he begins to suspect that Hamoutal has fled to Narbonne. The thought gives him courage and the hope that all will end well. He talks to a wagoner who agrees to transport him, along with a few Muslim refugees from the south. They too are headed for Narbonne.

When he arrives at the home of the Todros family, he learns to his dismay that Hamoutal is not there. After waiting a few more days for her to turn up, they lose hope. The old rabbis sit down together to assess Hamoutal's chances of survival. Maybe her father will forgive her after all. Maybe they should send a message to the few surviving Jews in the community there, who don't know she's coming. They can imagine what has happened: Hamoutal was found by the garrison commander and Yom Tov, the dutiful cousin. She was escorted onto the ship and must be at sea by now, well on her way to Rouen.

But after a few weeks Yom Tov returns home and tells them they couldn't find Hamoutal anywhere; he narrowly escaped a lynching himself. With no remaining prospect of good news, Obadiah passes the entire winter in Narbonne. He is too old and fragile to travel home to the mountainous area where Moniou lies; the wind is cold and treacherous there in the heights. In Narbonne, near the sea, the climate is milder, and the company of his distinguished old friend does him good. But the news they hear from passing travellers is distressing. No place is safe from pogroms any more; a hundred years after the Christians' millennial fears, the great beast seems to have descended to earth after all, plunging everything in its path into blind hatred and fanaticism. Cheerless song still rises from the churches every day; bells toll in the morning twilight; incense spirals in the sunbeams that press through the stained-glass windows. In the dim synagogues, the Shema Yisrael is heard, as dark and ageless as the unfathomable horrors now visited on the Jews. Spanish mosques are burned down; the Reconquista ignites a blaze of everyday cruelty and vengefulness against Muslims; chaos is rife. The old rabbis bend over their Torah scrolls and murmur. The hands of their silver pointers glide over the ancient parchment.

*

It is late March 1099 when Obadiah begins his journey home, which he guesses will take him at least a week and a half. He travels by horse over the Via Domitia, first to Arles and then north-east to Apt, where he spends a few days. The weather has changed; a sudden cold snap has brought late flurries of snow, making noon seem like night, and mist wafts from the dark woods of the Luberon massif. He waits until one morning the sun bursts through the clouds. Wisps of haze rise over the hillsides. The first, fresh warmth of spring is in the air; the old rabbi takes heart. He will first cross the plain to Roussillon and then take the road over the heights of Saint-Saturnin, along the clefts and fissures of the waking countryside. The blackthorn is already in bloom; hares leap over the dark rocks, the first irises are budding in the valleys, and the last berries still hang, inky, from bare branches. At some point he ducks into a cave to wait out a shower. His horse is nervous and skittish; he ties it to a tree some distance away. The rain patters across the landscape like a curtain swept aside. Too late, he notices he's sitting near a she-wolf's litter. The cubs whimper with hunger and pad towards him on shaky legs. The wolf comes closer, growling and showing her teeth, prepared to defend her young; the old man slowly, carefully lies down and holds still. The wolf waits for a long time before relaxing and coming over to sniff at him. Then she lies down beside her whelps. The old man falls asleep next to the nursing she-wolf. When he wakes, she is gone. A weak sun shines over the hills, the branches are dripping, wherever he looks water glistens. He stands, cautiously, and goes to his horse. As he rounds the corner, he sees the eyes of the she-wolf, tracking him.

His heart is with the proselyte; all day long he thinks about her. In fact, he mourns her, certain she'll be put to death. He feels he hasn't done enough for her. By evening he has reached the heights of Saint-Saturnin. His back is in agony from the long ride; he is stiff and exhausted.

Yet he yearns to be home as soon as possible. He catches a few hours' sleep in a thatched lean-to, far from any house, by a fire he stokes now and then to keep away the wolves. Several times that night, the horse snorts in fear.

The next morning he feels the warmth of the dew.

As soon as the sun is up, he mounts the horse, rides past Lioux and the place called Le Château de Javon in our day – which was then nothing more than a low farmhouse with a few sheep and goats and a nervous sheepdog barking. Finally, he descends from Saint-Jean and passes close to the dry riverbed at La Croc, where the Roman arches curve over the valley, on the north-east side of the high plateau of Moniou.

Seeing his solitary old village again in the distance stings him with pain; holding back tears, he presses his heel into the horse's side. He rides across the valley and up the slope towards the village, beginning to hear the faint everyday movements around the walls, the clucking chickens, a yapping dog. The sun shines on the tower and the chapel above it. Men are at work expanding and reinforcing the ramparts.

He is moved by the smells and colours of his old village. His heart is spent. The first bees buzz in the vines, the first spring blossoms overwhelm him with fragrance, the small, rain-wet wild roses on the village's outskirts smell like spring water. Obadiah hitches his horse at the gate. The villagers are surprised to see him back; tears in his eyes, he stumbles home; the climb is harder than he remembered.

He's been away for more than six months; here, time seems to have stood still.

He rests for a few hours and then, in the late afternoon, makes the rounds of the village, shaking hands.

And then sees, next to the half-rebuilt Portail Meunier, a woman sitting on a stone.

It is Hamoutal.

He hurries over to throw his arms around her in joy.

She gives him a blank look.

Hamoutal, he says, how did you get here?

The woman shakes her head no and stares at her feet.

Hamoutal ... ?

The woman tips her head, as if to shift something in her mind, but nothing comes.

She looks up, no recognition in her gaze. Her pale blue eyes are terribly crossed.

Her hands are covered with scratches and dirt.

Her swollen left foot has a bite mark and is badly out of joint.

Her left hand is missing the little finger; pus runs from the crusted wound.

A man comes up and takes the dumbstruck rabbi by the shoulder.

Forget her, she won't talk to anyone these days.

The man tells him she arrived on foot, before the winter, ailing and broken, and that she likes to sit among the remains of the synagogue, at the edge of the mikveh. Sometimes she climbs down into the empty bath. She is thought to live in that old hole, covering it at night with leaves and branches. She begs a little; some villagers bring her food now and then. She accepts it all, gobbles it up, but won't say a word.

And where is her child?

The man shrugs.

A child? We never saw it here. There was no child with her when she arrived.

Obadiah tries again: Hamoutal.

He lays his hand on her shoulder.

Sarah Hamoutal?

The woman doesn't seem to hear him. She wrings her hands in her lap and stares into space.

Obadiah stumbles back into his house.

The next day, he writes a letter to the Jewish community in Fustat, to explain her disappearance and report that the Egyptian child, Shmuel's son Avram, has been lost.

3

The night is so unfathomably black and silent on the far side of the valley that she sometimes thinks this must be the end of the world. That whoever leaves the village will fall into an endless black pit, the unknown that surrounds the world and starts here, within walking distance. She hears the owls cry and some shard of her youth flashes through her addled brain. Another time, on an evening of wind and downpours, she watches the snails crawl over the paving stones to mate, a translucent, entwining tangle. She feels queasy. There are no stars any more, only countless pinholes in the blackness, too tiny for light to shine through. She descends into the dry mikveh, sometimes spending half the night there babbling nonsense. In the morning she shivers like a trapped animal, lying on dry ferns. She says names and mutters inaudible prayers. She gathers herbs and fruit in the first light. She caresses shrubs and bursts into tirades against the clouds. A wild boar slams into her right knee, and for a few weeks she walks with a limp. She drags her left foot like a clog. This pitiless landscape is her delirium; she stays clear of people and their ways. Through the long hot summer she sleeps by the banks of the Nesque, in the gorge, where it's cool and safe. In the autumn she gathers nuts, picks apples, wanders. She's doesn't see how time is slipping past. She is thin as a lath, tough as a wild animal. She has almost forgotten how to talk. The onset of winter menaces her with the silence of icy death. She creeps into stalls to lie beside the animals. No one pays any attention to her, except the old rabbi, who these days can hardly walk. He begs her to come inside, at least at night. She can't understand his words, or pretends not to. She doesn't want to live and cannot die. Names, echoes of names in her head, she no longer knows which. In her imagination, she sometimes spends day after day in Rouen, in the courtyard, playing with her brothers. Arvid, she says with a toothless smile, Arvid my love. At other times, a glow spreads through her hips, a man is on top of her, his weight bearing down on her, making her laugh and gasp till she falls asleep. She knows the rats and snakes; sometimes they creep into the warmth of her dirty skirts, but they leave her be. Frost comes, then snow, then thaw in swift succession one late afternoon under low-hanging clouds; meltwater runs all around, the steep paths turn to streamlets. She sleeps in the dry mikveh, under branches and old fox skins. There she's heard shouting, laughing, shrieking and praying. She digs up truffles with her dirty nails, the Devil's hooves. She laughs hoarsely and talks to herself.

In the heights, where the ruins of the village of Flaoussiers now lie, a few houses without memory in a sheltered side valley, she settles into an old *borie* for the snowy season. In the morning she walks to the ravines of the Nesque to watch the birds fly back and forth in the depths below. She dreams she's floating high above the world. She hears the rush of the river; she watches the swift white clouds. In the morning she sees the sun rising fast against the great cliff, the Rocher du Cire, its orange glow reflected onto the cold blue stones where she lies shivering. The hard frost sends chunks of rock bursting out of the cliff face and rolling down into the valley; she can hear them clattering and tumbling down deep. She longs for death.

She will have what she longs for. It comes unexpectedly, one day in December. She has eaten poisonous toadstools; she vomits herself through the horror in her thrashing, dying body. Gagging, she stumbles to the edge of the ravine, somewhere more or less opposite the stony mass of the Rocher du Cire. The ice-cold sun breaks through and does not warm the rocks. The plants are eternal and soulless; the heights rustle with snakes where the wind tugs at the crooked elms. She looks around for one last moment at the world, a thing she no longer understands. Vigdis, bright sweet sister, she says, I am black Hamoutal. The sour laugh shoots like a knife through her body. Then she stiffens, her heart thumping like mad. Her pale eyes bulge. Her tongue swells out of her mouth, dripping black saliva. She feels the chill rising in her body like a great wave from her feet, slow and gradual, as if she herself is as large as this cold, impervious world. For an instant, her eyes open wide and stare straight ahead. She feels herself filling slowly with this new feeling, this cooling and sailing away into an endless dark depth in her own body.

*

A few days later, the year 1100 begins.

The inhospitable place where she lies is hidden from passers-by.

The wolves sniff at her body. The snakes slither past it. The toads hop up against it. Fluids soak into black soil. The world. The earth. The crows and jays circle above her. In the depths of the ravine, under the place where she lies decomposing, a young monk has arrived at St Michael's Chapel in the cliff. The hermit prays to God and is moved by his own devotion. The bears sleep in the caves. The fish leap against the current in the rising, ice-cold water that courses from the heights of the Plateau d'Albion to the depths of the gorge. The last butterflies die under winter oaks, in dry leaves that rustle in the morning breeze. The cocooning insects bide their time in the shadows. The sun is weak, something like a faded dream. In the distance, a snow devil spins its way over the rocks. In the thorn bushes, juniper berries glitter like drops of darkness. No one comes to pick them.

In time, her soiled clothes disintegrate.

Her hair grows in the grass.

After a year and a half, small scavengers have eaten away everything; the well-known worms of song and story do the rest. Her bones whiten; not a soul discovers her remains.

The crusaders have captured Jerusalem at last.

Soon it is February 1106. An enormous comet, like an apparition shooting through the membrane of a dream, rips through the night sky, terrifying the whole Western world. Preachers with rattles return to the streets; wolves and dogs howl to wake the dead. It streaks over the valley of Moniou, like a divine visitation, something defying all reason. Rabbi Obadiah looks up and asks God what is to become of humanity. The silence up there, where that apparition races, is overpowering. In the weeks that follow, several ewes have stillbirths; the faces look human, but twisted like devils. Their throats are slit there and then, and they're tossed in a well. A mass is said for forgiveness of unconfessed sins. A few kilometres away, at the lower end of the village, the body of David Todros has already rotted in the Jewish graveyard. Hamoutal's bones are likewise turning to dust, which looks like a handful of yellowish soil and can no longer be separated from the timeless motion. She lies untouched and is absorbed into the earth.

No grave, no trace of the fact that she ever existed.

All that remains is to tell the story of her life – described in the moth-eaten documents from Cairo. After a while, the rabbi also threw the second letter from Obadiah, passed on to him by Shmuel, into the genizah. He had to climb the small staircase to the gallery before he could reach the back wall. There, a metre and a half up from the floor, was the opening to the storage space, glimmering with darkness. The second document, too, contained the name of Yahweh. So Yahweh had to take it back; no human may destroy God's word. The letter flutters down onto the others, somewhere between rubbish and dust.

Years passed; the tempestuous history of Fustat, the once-proud city founded by Amr ibn al-As near the ancient gate of Babylon, came to an unexpected and tragic end. Less than seventy years after Hamoutal's death, the Kurds, led by the legendary Shirkuh, mounted an unstoppable advance on the city and brought the golden age of the Fatimids to an end. In 1168 the grand vizier of Egypt, unable to stand the thought of his city being sacked, decided to put it to the torch himself. He hoped this would prevent the crusaders, who were taking advantage of the Kurdish invasion to snatch territory from the Arabs, from using the city as a base of operations. This act of self-destruction was one of the many disasters that befell the cultures and societies of the Near East around that time. The city burned for more than two months. The fire devoured a whole world; every trace of the colourful multicultural society it had been was reduced to ashes and scorched earth. Scholars wailed; panicking masses fled the inferno; rats and snakes, cats and dogs tried to escape the sea of flames; children were buried under falling debris; hardly a stone was left atop another. For twenty kilometres around, the black smoke clouds were visible week after week, drifting over the waters of the Nile like a sign of doom and downfall. At night, millions of sparks leapt and whirled over the orange glow; the elders wept and beat their chests, watching from tents on the banks of the Nile, certain the end of the world was approaching. The fall of Fustat was a catastrophe on the same scale as the destruction of the Library of Alexandria: the end of an age, the ruthless gates of oblivion slamming shut. There is no telling how much knowledge was lost to us then. Astonishingly, the district containing the Ben Ezra Synagogue was spared. The genizah reposed in its dark depths, cherishing its secrets, only tens of metres away from the last, undefeated remnant of the great city wall, right next to the Well of Moses.

IX

Cambridge

One journey still awaits me, a journey Hamoutal, the eternal fugitive, never made and could not even have imagined: in pursuit of her letter of recommendation, the letter that Rabbi Obadiah wrote for her in Monieux. My destination is Cambridge, England, home to the manuscript collection that Solomon Schechter brought back from Cairo. There I hope to see for myself the document she carried with her – maybe even touch it.

When I arrive in the university town, the heat is intense. The inviting quads of the old colleges are heavy with the scent of blossoms. Students perch on window ledges, absorbed in Maynard Keynes, Thomas Aquinas, Milton or Wittgenstein. On the edges of the ponds, Pre-Raphaelite beauties are highlighting their anthropology readers in fluorescent colours. Guides drift past in punts through the shallow waters of the River Cam, playing their energetic part in the town's little Venice. This is the life of the centuries-old elites, charming and a bit unworldly, the centre of the old civilised classes who stubbornly pretend half the world is not burning down. Girls, the same age as Hamoutal when she fled Rouen, tuck elegant white earphones into their blonde hair, listening to ambient loops of Hildegard of Bingen supplied to them by torrents without name.

I stroll down the avenues through the scent of mown grass to the old tower of the University Library, climb the wide steps to the entrance, pick up my library card at the desk, step through the electronic gate, take the broad staircase up to the first floor, cross through the grand reading rooms, mount the narrow steps to the tower's third storey, pass the endless bookcases that line the entire North Wing, and find, at the far end, a modest door. I push it open, traverse another narrow corridor, and at last reach the Manuscript Room, maintained and guarded by people every bit as courteous as the guides who must be waiting for us at the pearly gates. I leave behind all the things the folder says I can't take with me, like ballpoint pens, fountain pens and ring binders; bags, hats, scarves and mittens; pencil sharpeners, pocket knives and paper cutters.

Once I've been relieved of these modern-day burdens, my card is scanned, the small glass security gate opens with a soft click, and I step into the reading room. At the end of the service desk, a trolley is waiting for me with two large black boxes from the Cairo Genizah Collection, bearing the numbers 12 and 16. They are about 100 by 50 centimetres in size and 10 centimetres high. I sign the declaration, take a seat at the assigned table, open my small laptop, and remove my magnifying glass from its old case. I start by opening box 12 and finding document T-S 12.532. This colourful scrap of paper looks more like an old map than a letter, or maybe a primitive cut-out of a half-imaginary continent. It never ceases to amaze me that these ancient fragments have reached our hectic age, or that their discovery had such an impact.

In 1964, two years before Norman Golb reported his findings on Monieux, the historian and textual researcher Eliyahu Ashtor discussed this document. It describes the near-execution, in the vicinity of Nájera, of a proselyte who had lost her husband in a pogrom. Three long decades later, in 1999, the researcher Edna Engel in Tel Aviv suggested a possible link between this manuscript and T-S 16.100, the letter about the Proselyte of Monieux. She presented strong evidence that the two were written by the same author: the handwriting, the distinctly Sephardic turns of phrase and the materials used. Her article, first published in the Hebrew-language journal *Sefunot*, includes a summary of the document's contents. Joshuah Obadiah of MNYW, the named author of the first letter, may therefore have written this manuscript as well. If he did, it may be about the same woman from MNYW – an unexpected new chapter in the proselyte's life. But because the woman was led to the stake in the northern Spanish town of Nájera, Edna Engel decided that the place where she fled after her release was not Monieux, but Muño, a long-vanished medieval village near Burgos in Spain. The Hebrew writing system, which leaves out the vowels, allows for this possibility. Her thesis received additional support from Joseph Yahalom, who quoted her in his article on old Spanish documents and stated without reservation that the place in question was Muño.

But what were the exact words of T-S 12.532? I wanted a literal translation. So I asked Cambridge University to send me an electronic reproduction of this manuscript, just as I had obtained a copy of T-S 16.100 earlier. Then I forwarded the copy to Norman Golb's son, Dr Raphael Golb, who gave it to his father to read. The scholar from Chicago was perplexed; the philologists who had challenged his theory with such confidence in 1999 had never contacted him. Golb, a very elderly man by now, became intrigued once again by this story from the early days of his illustrious career. A colleague of his prepared a word-for-word translation of the tattered manuscript. I was surprised to read Golb's conclusion: T-S 12.532 provides little new information about the places or circumstances. It is clear, however, that the woman was tied to the stake in Nájera until, at the last minute, her freedom was unexpectedly purchased. Her generous rescuer's somewhat unusual name is given in the document: Yom Tov Narboni. Vivid details are thrown out in passing: after her redemption, the woman was sent away at midnight. The document ends with a fragmentary list of names: Samuel bar Jacob, David bar […] and Iusta. Jacob and Iusta were the names of Hamoutal's children; the other two names almost match those of her husbands.

Each name is followed by the words 'the departed'. Does T-S 12.532 show us that Hamoutal's children had died? In that case, why did she turn up in northern Spain? Did Obadiah really write this letter? Is it really about Hamoutal? I peer at the strange letters but keep running up against those frustrating edges where the text breaks off. I am stuck with my questions.

*

I return box 12 to the desk and am given box 16. I open it and see an even thicker stack of documents in plastic sleeves. The binder starts with number 1. I carefully slide each large sheet over the metal rings until I reach the hundredth and final document: T-S 16.100. It's one of the best-preserved manuscripts, and very beautiful too. Through the plastic sleeve, it's hard to tell whether it is parchment, as Norman Golb suggests, or handmade paper – though that was a rarity in the eleventh century. The letters are the colour of oxblood; the manuscript is pale yellow to greyish-white, with darker tones here and there. I look for the smallest opening in the sleeve, which is sewn shut, and place my fingertip there for a moment, on the edge of the document Hamoutal carried against her body. The room is so quiet I can hear myself breathe.

With my magnifying glass, I pore over every detail of the surface, each tiny wrinkle, concentrating on the worn spots, which bear the traces of events that can no longer be reconstructed. The ragged document has four holes of different sizes, three caused by visible wear and tear, humidity, and the gradual weakening of the material. But towards the top, near line 9, is a monster of a hole, in a spot where the material is firm and shows no wear. It looks more like a piece was torn out. Through the glass, parts of the Hebrew letters mem, nun, yod, vav are visible along the upper edge of this large hole: מניו. MNYW. Where and when was that hole made? Did someone rip something out on purpose? Did Hamoutal brush against something sharp and tear the letter by accident? Was it damaged by David's tefillin in her bag? Was the hole made in the depths of the genizah, during those nine centuries in the dark? When Jacob Saphir visited the synagogue in 1864 and asked to see the genizah, the guard assured him there was nothing in that lightless hole but snakes and demons. The moisture that ate away at the document could have been sweat, blood, seawater, or even mould. For the first time I think to turn over the letter, carefully, in its transparent sleeve. To my surprise, I see two large creases on the back; the parchment was not rolled up, as I had always assumed, but folded lengthwise into thirds. The creases are sharp; it stayed folded for a long time. So Hamoutal could have hidden it under her clothes. Strange that those creases are invisible on the front of the document. The patch of moisture damage is brownish on the back. This letter was soaked through, and not just with Nile water. I take another long look at the document through my magnifying glass. If the letter was folded into three parts, as it seems, then the large hole was on the inside. A mystery. What could have happened? T-S 16.100 will always remain a riddle. I take photographs of this light-sensitive hide covered with letters. Make a few notes. Sit and stare a while longer. I know so little.

*

The puzzle exerted such a pull on Norman Golb that he visited Monieux twice, in December 1966 and 1967. His articles were accompanied by his own photographs. After publishing his landmark essay in 1969, he contributed an article to the French-Jewish news magazine *L'Arche* in 1978 in which he mounted another, succinct and persuasive, defence of the Monieux thesis. In 1979, the same magazine published a brief response from a reader, noting the existence of a so-called Jewish cemetery in Monieux, well known to the locals. I have a copy of an old photograph showing the Golb family seated on a bench in front of the house where I've written this book.

In April 2016, Golb published a new article on the website of the University of Chicago's Oriental Institute, entitled 'Monieux or Muño?', based on the information I'd sent him about Yahalom and Engel's articles and my own research in Monieux. He too concluded that nothing could be said with certainty about either the interpretation of MNYW or the relationship between the two manuscripts. Yet for topographical reasons, he had doubts about the Muño scenario and still had faith in the viability of the Monieux thesis. It seems improbable, I might add, that the chief rabbi of Narbonne would have sent the two fugitives to Muño, down the road to Santiago de Compostela, heavily trafficked by Norman knights. Monieux was a much more sensible route, especially considering that Provence was then still part of the Holy Roman Empire. The fact that Joshuah Obadiah's Hebrew shows Spanish influences is easy to understand, considering he may have studied in Narbonne, which was then mostly Spanish-speaking, and must have had a personal connection to Rabbi Todros. Although Edna Engel's philological observations were correct, I believe she draws the wrong conclusion.

In any case, T-S 16.100 is well known as the story of the Proselyte of Monieux. In his magnum opus *The Story of the Jews*, Simon Schama uses that title without reservation, and devotes a short paragraph to her. Even the Jewish Virtual Library, based on the *Encyclopaedia Judaica*, refers to 'a Cambridge manuscript, evidently from the town of Monieux, Provence'.

*

This is where my search ends. It's hard for me to leave the quiet reading room. Later, I walk the streets of this peaceful, old-fashioned town. The Fitzwilliam Museum has an exhibition about Egyptian burial rituals. I wind my way through the dim galleries of sarcophagi and canopic jars, distracted by thoughts of Cairo and my evenings on the banks of the Nile. It's like coming full circle. As I leave the building I notice that, out of the warm, bright sky, an almost invisible rain has begun to fall.

X

The Treasure of Monieux

1

On All Souls' Day 1968, an article in the Provence newspaper *Le Méridional* was devoted to what the two journalists called the secrets of the plateau. They went in search of the last remaining locals with stories about the famed treasure of Monieux, said to be hidden somewhere under the rocks or in a secret cavern. They evoked the atmosphere of these Alpine foothills in the language of travel brochures: the farandole is not danced here, no cicadas sing, this is a place of *'équilibre et austérité*. Here you find yourself not in picture-postcard Provence, but in the old and nameless landscape of the mountains all around the Mediterranean. No plane trees, but horse chestnuts and old lime trees along the road. Small Alpine cattle roam some meadows, and sheep bells ring from morning to night. A shepherd snoozes in the grass by the wayside. Little has changed since time immemorial. It's like stepping into one of Virgil's *Eclogues*.

In their dealings with the dour villagers the journalists put on a naive, cheerful air, and this stratagem paid off. Mrs Calamel, a woman of a respectable age even then, told them her grandfather had spoken of the hidden treasure. The baker recalled that Mrs Jussiand, at the age of nearly a hundred, had known a thing or two about the treasure, but she'd died without ever giving away her secret. Ferdinand Bres, a local with a divining rod who was persuaded to accompany the journalists, travelled back and forth several times that day along the steep, dangerous road between the medieval tower at the top of the cliff and the village at the bottom, clambering over the rocks and stones. Next to a ruined section of the old ramparts, his twig started to tremble and shake ominously. Gold, there must be gold here somewhere! The rod leapt about so frantically that it fell out of Mr Bres's hands, onto the path that runs through the wild palms. Just a few metres away, that's where you should dig. The villagers observing the proceedings shook their heads in disbelief. Nonsense! How could it be here? Hasn't the story always been that the treasure was left in the entrance to a collapsed cave somewhere over there, high up in the rocks?

So what? Isn't that just a legend?

The journalists returned to the town hall to consult with the elderly mayor. Are there any archives of old public records? No, that sort of thing has all been lost – even the exact year when they completed the medieval tower, an impressive thirty-metre-tall structure in a state of serious decay. You see, some time in the nineteenth or eighteenth century – who can say? – there was a huge fire and the old archives went up in flames. Whatever's left may be in Carpentras, who knows. Would you care for a glass of wine?

In slight desperation, the journalists turned to a couple of villagers looking on in silence.

Do you believe the story?

Of course I do, Mr Ughetto said primly, at least until someone proves otherwise.

And yes, there are tales of fruitless quests, of treasure hunts, digs and disputes, of clues leading this way and that, past the bend in the road, down some ravine or other, third cave to the left or right, not quite sure any more, ancient weapons were found there once, an old Roman stone, Neolithic axeheads, all kinds of rubbish turns up around here. There's a well near the Augier farm, no purer water to be found, who knows what you might discover there, and no, say the old folks who've just laid their lamb chops in the hot ashes to cook, we don't believe a word of it. Someone else suggests there may have been an underground passageway from the tower up there to the Tour de Durefort on the other side of the valley, a ruin about five kilometres away. If they could find the entrance, maybe they'd find the treasure.

A glum voice asks, How could they have dug a five-kilometre tunnel a thousand years ago? We can barely sink our picks into this rocky ground today!

People tell so many stories.

The last interviewee was a Belgian, a police commissioner from Antwerp who spent his summer holidays in an old house there, with the front cracked from top to bottom. His name was Albert Schilders, he looked friendly and flamboyant, and the surprised journalists reported that he spoke French 'sans accent'. Well, sure, he told them, I've dug a hole or two, thirty centimetres at most, I'm too lazy for real work. He shrugged, posed for his picture, flashed an amiable smile, and settled back down to his book on his small terrace overlooking the valley. In Albert Schilders's detailed diaries, I find no written record of his exceptional interest in the matter. I stare out through the window of the house where for decades he likewise sat and looked out over the valley.

2

It is the summer of 2015. Hot August days slip by like threaded beads; for weeks the sky remains a spotless blue. The blue is especially deep to the west of town in the early morning, so deep it dizzies you to see it over the ruins of the old tower. These days I take a lot of walks, tracing all the possible routes by which the Jewish proselyte could have reached the valley. I follow the path deep into the gorge, to the old cliffside chapel of St Michael. It's a mystical place; the ancient building is inside a natural cave. The old walls were carved with low reliefs and scratched with now-illegible words by reclusive monks. Just in front of the cave, nearly lost in the thick undergrowth, the Nesque is not much more this summer than a trickling line of water. The smell of damp rock and stone.

Sitting down by the stream, I remember that in Andy Cosyn's book *Le trésor de Monieux*, a couple of eighteenth-century characters naively imagine that the famous treasure is hidden here. Cosyn takes pleasure in toying with the reader's curiosity, including photos in the book of a cave he discovered somewhere in the area, with skulls inside. They may have been so well preserved because no air could enter the cave till he hacked it open. Were they the skulls of the men who buried the treasure, trapped under the rubble of a collapsing tunnel? Everyone knows it's just idle speculation, but before you know it, you're walking down hard, rocky paths to solitary places and trying to guess where the treasure might be.

For what it's worth, I'm now convinced that the centuries-old legend is really about the meagre possessions of the synagogue of Monieux, which Joshuah Obadiah and two other men tried to hide in a safe place: in other words, several brass candleholders, maybe a few gold coins, and above all their Torah scrolls, a few sets of tefillin, and their own collection of documents, like the one in the Cairo Genizah – manuscripts that could not be destroyed because they bore the name of Yahweh. In other words, the greatest treasure of Monieux, which might strike us dumb with astonishment if it were discovered, could only be a genizah. The Hebrew word *genizah*, I might add, can be found in the Hebrew Book of Esther in the meaning of 'treasure chamber'.

If anything is left of the manuscripts from the genizah, the *shemot* of Monieux, I suspect they cannot be found here in the depths of the gorge but in a place called the Combe Saint-André, a small, steep ravine impossible to enter without professional climbing equipment. A rope ladder may have hung there in those days. Two holes are visible in the rock face, one above the other – ideal places for hiding things, and not far from the synagogue if the fleeing men passed through the Petit Portalet, the highest watchtower on the Jewish side of the village.

It is not unthinkable that old Joshuah Obadiah wrote about the catastrophe. But written documents could not survive in this unpredictable climate as they did in Fustat. Nor can it be ruled out that he later recovered the synagogue's ritual objects from their hiding place and they were all lost some other time, centuries later. It's equally possible he no longer knew quite where he'd buried the objects that hellish night; he'd had to run for his life when the bear came out of the cave. Yet it *is* as good as unthinkable that any trace of them will ever be found.

I decide to walk down to the overgrown slope outside the village, which some call the old Jewish cemetery. Under the ground ivy, arum lilies and cleavers lie some old stones. I strain to turn a couple of them over. Can I see any ancient scratches or faded marks? As much as I wish I could, no clues remain here. If there are any old Jewish graves on this site, then after ten centuries they must be at least a metre and a half below the ever-shifting humus of this slope. The cemetery itself lies buried.

The only vague hint is the straight line of a little wall and three stone steps, sunk in the withered leaves.

Selah. The end of the psalm.

*

But that was not the end.

There's a small place in the ruins above the village where, summer after summer, I have known exceptional happiness. It's a field of dry grass; flakes of bark from dead cherry branches swirl down in the hot summer wind like black snow, some landing in my hair and on the pages of my book. I've spent whole afternoons there, unsuspecting, watching the shifting light on the plateau, hearing the caw of the crows echo from the rocky slope above me, and listening to the sublime music of Sébastien de Brossard: 'Ego sum pastor bonus' – God comforting the dying man and assuring him that He is the good shepherd.

The field is high on the south side of the medieval village, where the Jewish quarter must once have been, just below and to one side of the Petit Portalet. To reach it you climb a few age-old steps, stones shifted by centuries of persistent weeds. Next to those steps, you can see a partly buried Romanesque cellar arch. The house that stood here must have been large and stately; the foundations are thick and strong. A deep well was dug from the upper level, accessible only from above the cellar; it was this that made me realise what an unusual structure it must have been. Looking at the outline of the foundations, it's obvious the building was larger than a private home.

A sheet of corrugated metal covers the dark well. Through a narrow opening, I can see a pool of darkness in the depths, cool water gleaming. I pull away the metal sheet. To my surprise, I find beneath it not only the well, but also a primitive seat in the old stone. The well has the vague shape of a figure of eight; down below I see a space that must have been enlarged at some stage, but even before then could certainly contain about five hundred litres of water. That's when I realise this is a Jewish bath, a mikveh for the cleansing ritual. I sit down to collect my racing thoughts. Could this really be … ? A mikveh of this kind, on an upper floor, could only have been part of a synagogue, or perhaps the rabbi's house. There are even a few steps leading up to a still higher aisle, perhaps the women's gallery. In other words, the spot where I've whiled away so many happy days reading over the years is the very place where Joshuah Obadiah and David Todros bent over their Torah scrolls. It is where Hamoutal descended into the ritual bath. It is where the gruesome massacre took place. In an instant, this calm, grassy field has become a space full of voices screaming, wailing, cursing, with murder and man-slaughter, desperation and blood. Here I stand, literally in the place of their past. Shema Yisrael. Here, the day after the pogrom, Hamoutal fell to her knees in despair beside her husband's mutilated body. In her last days of madness and misery, it is the place where she spent whole nights hiding and crying like an animal.

I cannot stop staring at my discovery, in disbelief and wonderment.

I touch the edge of the old well. I touch Hamoutal.

*

It's drizzling over the dusky valley. The snails creep across the old stones of the upper streets, immersed in their dreamlike lovemaking. Watching out where I put my sprain-prone feet, I head downhill to Andy Cosyn's house, where I find him happily sipping his aperitif. I tell him what I've found; physical evidence of the Jewish community in the days of the southern crusades, the final piece of evidence that Norman Golb needed to demonstrate his Monieux thesis. Andy goes straight to his archives and finds the old maps from before the Napoleonic period. We search for the plot of land and see that the building with the mikveh was the only one in the village with a rear exit. The synagogue's back gate. It opened onto a narrow street, now long gone, which made a half-circle around that side of the village and ended at the southern Portail Meunier. Our eyes meet; this was the route the men must have used when they fled with the synagogue's ritual objects.

3

The villages in the south are emptying out as the social fabric of the old communities wears thin. A whole generation is disappearing, and hardly any young people have replaced them. Sometimes a couple of newly-weds move to Monieux, but after the first year, the solitude of the harsh landscape begins to weigh on them, and they go in search of less desolate climes. Even the buxom old woman at the bakery counter has retired and moved a few villages away, along with her husband Jean Jacques, the baker whose laugh rang through the village from morning till night for decades, like the sound of a gigantic, quacking duck. Each Sunday we hear Alex, the white-haired plumber, grumbling about his ruined knees as he passes by on his way to the home of the good-natured Hélène, where the two of them will drink themselves into a pleasant fog. He dreams of his fatherland, Croatia, but won't leave the village now. Renée and Henri Chanu, a childless couple, were the noblest souls I've ever met; he spent his days listening to opera, and when he felt like making himself useful, he repaired the broken finger of St Rochus in the village church with a delicate twig or fixed up some other old statue of a saint with infinite patience. Their romantic house with the large rose bushes has been vacant for years now; the cracks in the front grow wider every year. Inside, a centuries-old baker's oven is slowly crumbling away; I'm told the baker drew his water from the cellars under my house. The ageing Irish rocker down by the village square lives with his wife in a shop like a doll's house, set up for selling her colourful paintings. His hair, once a long, ferocious mane, has now turned a pale grey. This spring he discovered the field of grass by the synagogue and innocently turned over the soil and planted potatoes. He draws water from the old mikveh, which must have been deepened in later times. I tell him what I've discovered; he looks a bit sceptical.

The village's cheeky charmer, the former postmaster, is now well into his eighties and brags of his latest conquest – a girl barely sixty, what do you think of that? He smiles his wide, irresistible smile and eats his modest supper alone with half a bottle of rosé. Next to his house, the junk piles up, a museum of discarded bric-a-brac. The mayor and restaurateur, bestowing an affable smile on the guests who converse under the plane trees of his welcoming outdoor restaurant, has gone grey as well and walks with a slight stoop.

In the village square stands the girlish figure of La Nesque, as serene as ever, holding a jug in her graceful hand from which she symbolically pours the river's water into a basin where small bream swim. She is made of bronze, yet sensual, with a youthful, erotic glow in her light dress, which curves around her attractive form and clings to her shapely thighs – the statue was commissioned by Mayor Léon Doux in 1905. During the Second World War, it was hidden in a cave because the Germans were taking all the bronze they could find for their cannons. As soon as the war was over, La Nesque was triumphantly restored to her pedestal. This lovely river goddess could be a girl like Hamoutal. I take a long look at her and then at the head of the griffon at her feet, spouting water into the basin. Generations of women came here to fill buckets for laundry and house cleaning. I turn back. The church clock strikes four. Life here seems to roll along timelessly.

Soon more than three-quarters of the world population will live in megacities and agglomerations. This old, poetic way of life will expire without a sound. Maybe we're living through the end of an age – the age of the villages, which began in days beyond remembering and is now coming to an end.

The colossal lump of stone is still suspended over the rooftops, a millennium after it split from the rocky slope. It is barely held up by the crumbling remains of the medieval ramparts. By this stage, no one seems to believe it will ever fall. But when one day after a steep climb I lean in for a closer look, I can just make out that it's shifting, in silence, millimetre by millimetre. Or in any case, I can see the difference from when I first came here, twenty-two years ago. Maybe it's waiting patiently until the last villagers have left.

*

I've heard the mistral will die, like an ancient beast. Climate change will snuff it out slowly, year by year, as the glacier on top of Mont Blanc, which chills the west wind and sends it blowing back, trickles away. The ice-blue skies that have arched overhead since time out of mind, for which the Romans praised Provincia, may some day be a thing of the past. But the process is so gradual that I can grow old in melancholy anticipation.

Again I walk to the ruined village of Flaoussiers, a few kilometres away. There is something mysterious about this small valley, which has always appealed to me. You're sheltered from the wind, except for the few days each season when it blows straight through the cleft. Then you practically cling to the ground to escape the stinging cold. Now it's deserted and peaceful here. A pair of falcons circle over the sparse fields of grass. Somewhere a chained dog barks; the few lavender fields just above the valley look drab after the harvest. Mont Ventoux looms, large and bare, in the distance. Everything is desolate and ancient. From somewhere nearby comes the bleating of a lost lamb.

I leave the small valley, heading for the ravines of the Nesque, and sit down in the spot where Hamoutal's bones lay whitening in the sun. You can feel the emptiness of history here. A kind of peace washes over me, so vast and silent that I too lie down in that spot by the edge of the cliff.

They still exist here, those dreamy afternoons when the slow, white clouds resemble huge, dormant Greek gods drifting through Elysium, promising us a glimpse of paradise. More and more I too want to be buried here in this hard ground when my time comes. As I imagine it, that will give me a few years' grace – I can lie back and listen to time slipping past, to the murmuring of the cypresses, the peal of the church bells, the cry of the owl, and the chirping of the bee-eaters which glide, ecstatic, over my grave, with that untouchable blue high above my unseeing eyes.

The world spins, but if you hold your breath for a moment, it stands still.

Monieux, September 1994–July 2016

Acknowledgements

My thanks are due to Dr Ben Outhwaite, head of the Taylor-Schechter Genizah Research Unit at Cambridge University Library, and to Dr Melonie Schmierer-Lee, Research Associate in the Genizah Research Unit, who supplied me with digital versions of the relevant manuscripts, as well as to the management of the library and the Manuscript Room.

I am grateful to Professor Norman Golb and his son Dr Raphael Golb, who not only arranged for a translation of document T-S 12.532 but also provided a great deal of additional support in documenting the Monieux thesis.

I would like to thank Steve Krief, secretary to the editorial board of *L'Arche* in Paris, for tracking down Norman Golb's elusive articles from that magazine.

Thanks to the Egyptian author Alaa Al Aswany for the enlightening conversation about present-day Cairo, which took place in a very special spot in the city.

Thanks to Dr Raoul Bauer for the support and information and for reading my narrative with an eye to historical accuracy; he was the first to draw my attention to the Muño thesis.

Many thanks also to Andy Cosyn and Kurt Stegmaier, residents of Monieux, who first alerted me to the existence of Norman Golb's scholarly article. I would also like to thank Andy for giving me support and information, for our conversations and rambles among the rocks and shrubbery, for his pointers, and for his book *Le trésor de Monieux*. His description of the pogrom in Monieux set my imagination to work. He was the first I told about the discovery of the mikveh.

Thanks to Dr Ruth Kinet for the good conversation in Berlin and for her help in mustering arguments for the Monieux thesis, and to Reuven Namdar in New York for his critical reading of manuscript T-S 16.100.

Thanks to Esther Voet for her corrections regarding Jewish customs and practices and to Leonard Ornstein of the VPRO public broadcasting company, who put me in touch with her.

Thanks to my editors, Suzanne Holtzer and Mariska Kleinhoonte van Os, for their faith in this book and intensive support; thanks also to my former editor Wil Hansen for his advice.

Thanks to Jan Vanriet for his comments and fine suggestions.

Above all, my thanks are due to my wife Sigrid, who went through the whole diaspora with me and helped me, with love and devotion, to see this story through to a good end – a story about the place where we still experience our happiest moments.

Last, I would like to thank the ageing Jewish street vendor in Old Cairo who told me about the synagogue, gave me a faded leaflet, listened to my story with tears in his eyes and kept calling out to me as I walked away – since it was Saturday – *Shabbat shalom.*